Praise for
A Very NA...

"Cleverly written with ...
humor, a heartwarming ...
all make this a perfect Valentine's Day winner."
—*RT Book Reviews*
on *Under the Influence* by Nancy Warren

"Romance with a solid mystery and a cast of
intriguing characters...a pleasure to read...
A charmer to be sure, and an RRT Perfect 10."
—*Romance Reviews Today*
on *French Kissing* by Nancy Warren

"[A] thrilling, character-driven entry
in the Colby Agency series."
—*RT Book Reviews*
on *Colby Rebuilt* by Debra Webb

"Debra Webb's carefully laid plot and multilayered
characters add depth and texture to her latest tale
of greed, power and deception."
—*RT Book Reviews*
on *Identity Unknown* by Debra Webb

"Gina Wilkins does a grand job
of allowing these characters slowly to uncover
and discover emotions and feeling layer by layer.
Everything is achieved with a subtle, fine touch."
—*The Romance Reader*
on *Valentine Baby* by Gina Wilkins

"Gina Wilkins' holiday keeper is like a
Christmas stocking—brimming with an endearing cast
of characters and stuffed with warm moments."
—*RT Book Reviews*
on *Make-Believe Mistletoe* by Gina Wilkins

NANCY WARREN
DEBRA WEBB
GINA WILKINS

A very
NASCAR
Holiday

HQN™

If you purchased this book without a cover you should be aware that this book is stolen property. It was reported as "unsold and destroyed" to the publisher, and neither the author nor the publisher has received any payment for this "stripped book."

ISBN-13: 978-0-373-77411-1

A VERY NASCAR HOLIDAY

Copyright © 2009 by Harlequin Books S.A.

The publisher acknowledges the copyright holders of the individual works as follows:

ALL I WANT FOR CHRISTMAS
Copyright © 2009 by Nancy Warren

CHRISTMAS PAST
Copyright © 2009 by Debra Webb

SECRET SANTA
Copyright © 2009 by Gina Wilkins

PLEASE RECYCLE
THIS PRODUCT IS RECYCLABLE

Recycling programs for this product may not exist in your area.

NASCAR® and the NASCAR Library Collection® are registered trademarks of the NATIONAL ASSOCIATION FOR STOCK CAR AUTO RACING INC.

All rights reserved. Except for use in any review, the reproduction or utilization of this work in whole or in part in any form by any electronic, mechanical or other means, now known or hereafter invented, including xerography, photocopying and recording, or in any information storage or retrieval system, is forbidden without the written permission of the publisher, Harlequin Enterprises Limited, 225 Duncan Mill Road, Don Mills, Ontario M3B 3K9, Canada.

This is a work of fiction. Names, characters, places and incidents are either the product of the author's imagination or are used fictitiously, and any resemblance to actual persons, living or dead, business establishments, events or locales is entirely coincidental.

This edition published by arrangement with Harlequin Books S.A.

® and TM are trademarks of the publisher. Trademarks indicated with ® are registered in the United States Patent and Trademark Office, the Canadian Trade Marks Office and in other countries.

www.HQNBooks.com

Printed in U.S.A.

CONTENTS

ALL I WANT
FOR CHRISTMAS

Nancy Warren

For all the women out there who love NASCAR and romance, especially those of you who have shared your experiences with me on fan boards, by e-mail and best of all, at the races.

Happy holidays.

CHAPTER ONE

THE WILD CRY SPLITTING the silence caused Emily Littlejohn to drop the papier-mâché elephant currently making a sloppy mess of her kitchen table and cock her head. In the range of ten-year-old boy yells—of which she considered herself an expert—the current holler was closer to the ecstatic cry of a kid who'd whipped some computer foe than the dreaded cry that indicated *Hospital. Now!*

Still, she waited and sure enough soon heard, "Mom, come quick." Excitement bubbled through the words like oil from a gusher.

Since she and Darren were a family of two, Emily played the roles of mother, father and often best friend to her ten-year-old son. She knew that wouldn't last, so she did her best to treasure this time when Darren still wanted to be with her.

"Coming." She wiped her hands on the damp

cloth. The elephant in progress tipped onto its trunk, hovered there for a second then keeled over. Looked as though she'd have to default to the pig the students in her second-grade art class had been making for ten years. That elephant was clearly too complicated.

She tended to forget to move when she was working and as she rose, her back reminded her that she'd been trying to turn a couple of balloons, some shredded newspapers and wallpaper glue into an elephant since she and Darren had eaten their after-school snack, two hours ago.

Jogging up the stairs got her blood moving again, but even at her top speed, she was still met on the upstairs landing by a bouncing dynamo. "Come on, Mom. You gotta see this. You'll never guess."

His face was lit with excitement, his eyes blazing blue with happiness. Something much more thrilling than reaching a new level in one of his computer games had to be the cause.

"You got an A in Math?"

"Funny, Mom."

Darn. He was too young for girls, and it had been a while since the infrequent visits or calls from his dad had lit him up. Stumped, she followed him into his room.

He raced to his computer and displayed the screen proudly. Even from the doorway she could see the NASCAR logo. Of course.

Darren's greatest enthusiasm in life was stock car racing, and his hero was Jason Bane, the local boy from their own small town in Minnesota who had taken the racing world by storm over the past five years.

Bane was prominently featured in her son's room. He grinned down from glossy posters at a replica of his ride that held pride of place on Darren's bedside table. Emily had personally painted the racing border on Darren's bedroom wall, repeating the motif on the bedspread she'd also created. Maybe they didn't have much in the way of money, but Emily used every one of her arts and crafts skills to raise their lives above the mundane.

"What is it?" She drew closer to Jason Bane's handsome face grinning out at her from the computer screen and wondered if he might be coming home for a visit. Something he hadn't done in twelve years. That would account for Darren's excitement. If the prodigal driver returned, would she have the courage to remind Jason Bane that they'd gone to school together?

Even if fate, or more likely Darren, threw Jason in her path, she knew she wouldn't. She'd had a major crush on the guy back in high school and he hadn't noticed her then. Now that he was a rich, famous driver, he'd never remember a girl he'd shared a couple of classes with back in Hammersfield High.

"It's a contest," Darren yelled in her ear. "And I'm going to win." He was so excited he couldn't stand still, hopping on one foot, then both. "We get to see a race, and you get a shopping spree. How cool is that? Jason Bane's sponsor is Bailey's Department Stores."

"What kind of contest is it?" Emily asked, finding it impossible to read the details on the screen with Darren jumping, squirming and yelling all at the same time.

"An essay contest. I have to tell what NASCAR means to me in five hundred words." He made a *pffffft* noise through pursed lips. "Easy."

He shook her shoulder. "We are going to Hollywood!"

It wasn't Hollywood, of course. The prize was an all-expenses-paid trip to the race in Homestead, Florida, in November, for the final race of the season. The prize included a thousand-dollar shopping spree at Bailey's.

"A thousand bucks, Mom. You could buy yourself a nice Christmas present. And I get to spend time with Jason Bane and go to a race, and hang out with the pit crew. Everything!" His emotions so overtook him that he tossed himself backward onto his bed and bounced to his feet again.

Emily almost hated to hear the excitement in his young voice. She'd never been able to afford to take him to a live race. And now he thought he was going to win his way there?

"Honey," she said, in that tone she hated hearing come out of her own mouth, "There are going to be a lot of kids who enter this contest. I don't want you getting your hopes up too high."

He looked dumbstruck. "But who writes the greatest essays in the world? Mr. Donaldson said I'm real creative." He patted her on the back. "Mom, I can ace this."

"I know you can, Dar. You just have to remember that life isn't always fair."

No one knew that better than Emily. Who'd once had her head filled with the same kind of naive belief in life that she recognized in her son. Amazing how a bad marriage and nasty divorce could cure a person of believing in happy outcomes.

Well, she'd let him write his essay, encourage him as much as she could and then be there when his young world fell apart. Again.

CHAPTER TWO

JASON BANE WAS SUFFERING writer's cramp from signing his name so many times, but at last the two-hour publicity event was almost over. The main level of Bailey's flagship department store was bustling, and lots of folks were hanging around to watch him and the very pretty young starlet beside him, also signing pictures of herself.

He still hadn't quite gotten over the fact that because he could drive fast, people wanted him to do other things he had no natural talent for.

Like acting.

The cameo appearance in a family comedy movie had been fun, but Jason had never been so bored in his life. All that sitting around waiting for someone to call "Action" wasn't his style. He preferred remaining in action until someone yelled at him to stop.

Even now, after sitting at a table for two hours, his feet were tapping and twitching. He needed to go for a run or shoot some baskets or something, just to get rid of the excess energy. The workout would have to wait, however. He had another appearance right after this one.

At last he'd signed the final photo, grinned his last grin, and could thankfully shake out the stiffness from his signing hand.

He rose, then remembering his manners, turned to his signing partner.

"Thanks. It was great meeting you."

His "winning grin" as the press people liked to call it, was threatening to crack from overuse, but he pulled it out one more time.

"Her name's Sydney," his assistant, Paige, whispered in his ear.

The starlet also rose from her seat and stretched. It was the kind of stretch you couldn't help watching if you wanted to call yourself a red-blooded man.

"I'm parched," she said, running the tip of her tongue over luscious pink lips. "Going to slip off for a quiet drink. Care to join me?"

"Thanks, *Sydney*," he said with a regret he was far from feeling, "but I've got to run to another event right after this one."

She shrugged. "Maybe next time."

"You got it." Where he would have shaken hands goodbye, Sydney was more a kiss-on-the-mouth type. She pulled away slowly and slipped a card into his breast pocket. "Call me."

The young woman left with her own handlers and he turned to Paige Summer, his personal assistant and Randy Oldham, Bailey's marketing guy. "I cannot believe you turned down heaven." Randy sighed.

"Not my type," he said. Paige handed him a tissue and he wiped away the sticky lip gunk Sydney had left on his mouth.

"I don't envy you the money, and I sure as heck don't want to be driving a track at one-eighty miles an hour," Randy said as they walked away from the signing area, "but I envy you those women who throw themselves at you."

"It gets old," he promised.

The three of them took the elevator up to the executive level of the store. Back when his greatest ambition was to drive faster than anyone else on the planet, Jason hadn't thought a lot about the rest of life as a NASCAR driver, but now that he was in the club, he'd discovered that there was a lot of activity that had nothing to do with driving. Sponsors were vital. And the sport wouldn't exist without the fans, so he cheerfully did his part to make both sponsors and fans happy. First by winning as many races as he could, second by being accessible.

It wasn't tough. He remembered all too clearly being a young boy in a no-account town, a kid with dreams that were so big it sometimes hurt to dream them.

Those dreams had brought him here, along with a lot of hard work, and some talent. Whenever his hand tired during an autograph session, or a fan got a little too enthusiastic, he tried to remember that boy from Hammersfield, Minnesota, and he tried to treat every fan as if they were him twenty years ago.

"The contest's had great response," Paige informed him as they rode up. "More than ten thousand entries, didn't you say, Randy?"

"Yep. Close to eleven thou. You're one popular dude with the kids."

"We've got media waiting up top," Randy explained. "Local and national and the press conference is going on the Web live. We've already chosen the winner, but—"

"You read all those entries?"

"Heck, no. Interns. Crystal Bailey and I reviewed the top ten. Frankly, it was a tough call. There's some great kids out there. Wish they could all win."

Jason nodded, thinking once again of his young self. "Let's make sure and send them all something, okay? A signed photograph, and we should include a letter from me telling them—I don't know—to me they're all winners. Something like that."

"Great idea, 'course the postage—"

"Don't cheap out on me, Randy."

The department store PR man sighed. "We'll include a coupon for Bailey's, too, and maybe a perfume sample for the moms."

He nodded. "Can't have ten thousand, nine hundred and ninety-nine little NASCAR fans and future Bailey's shoppers disappointed, right?"

"Right." The elevator sighed to a halt, but Randy took an extra minute to brief Jason and handed him a page of printed speaking notes.

Before heading to the next smilefest, Jason opened his mouth wide, as though about to chow down on the biggest burger in history, and then did a few facial limbering exercises an actress had shown him. They'd dated for a little while, but the thing he remembered her most fondly for was the exercises that helped him get through a long day of holding his smile in place.

When he was done, he checked to make sure his shirt with his sponsor's logo was still clean. He nodded and they headed out of the elevator.

The boardroom contained maybe twenty people. Paige murmured in his ear as they entered, reminding him of everybody he should know by name, so that when he got into the middle of things, he was ready.

Crystal Bailey came up first and they kissed in that European style he'd never quite gotten used to. One cheek and then the other. Crystal was the granddaughter of the original Bailey who'd founded the store and, though she was older than his mother, she was a fine-looking woman. She also had a sharp eye for business, making Bailey's one of the leading department store chains in the nation.

He shook hands with the other execs and said "Hey" to the media people, all of whom he knew.

"Well, if we're ready," Crystal said, and led him to a table where a huge glass tank was filled with envelopes containing essays by kids all wanting to come hang out with him and send their parents shopping at Bailey's while they did it.

Camera lights were adjusted, he heard the whirr of a TV camera, Crystal said a few words about the contest then turned things over to him. He'd read the notes, and then put them aside. Now, as he looked at the camera, he imagined he was speaking to the kids themselves. "I can't believe how many of you kids took the time to write and tell us what NASCAR means to you.

"There are some great writers out there and I'm proud of you all for taking the time and effort to write an essay. I want to tell you right here and now that I think every one of you is a winner and even if you didn't win the big prize, you'll be getting a little something in the mail from me and the good people at Bailey's." Beside him he felt Crystal stiffen, but he figured it was good PR for all of them and if he said on TV that they'd send stuff out, then Randy was less likely to try and wiggle out of the obligation.

"Now," he continued, "it was a real hard decision to make, but in the end, we chose an entry." He picked up the paper in question. "The lucky person who will be coming to Miami in November to hang out with me and my team is Lizbeth Monterey. Lizbeth, you did a great job in your essay, which we'll be putting up on the Web site for everybody to read. I'm looking forward to hanging out with you and your folks when you come to the race in November. Thanks again, kids, for taking the time to write these wonderful essays." He grinned at the camera. "See you at the track."

Crystal took over again and he sat down to read Lizbeth's entry. She sounded pretty smart for a twelve-year-old, saying she hoped to be a driver herself one day, which he was sure Crystal had liked. 'Course, little Lizbeth had kind of ruined the feminist effect by including a hand-drawn picture of him standing by his car. She'd drawn little hearts all around them both.

He shook his head. The rest of the finalists' entries were stacked neatly beside the winner and idly he flicked through the envelopes. They'd come from all over. Seattle, Washington. Nome, Alaska. Missouri, North Carolina and Hammersfield, Minnesota. He almost laughed when he saw that last postmark. His own hometown.

Curious, he opened the envelope. Back in his day nobody had cared too much for auto racing up in Hammersfield. They were more into ice fishing and dirt biking. Maybe times had changed.

Dear Jason,

My name is Darren Littlejohn and watching NASCAR is the best thing about Sundays. At first I started watching because there's nothing else to do...

Oh, yeah, he remembered the feeling. Seemed as though nothing much had changed in good old Hammersfield.

He opened the folded page to read the rest of the essay and a photograph fell out of a young kid with glasses proudly wearing one of Jason's T-shirts. Beside him was an attractive woman who—wait a minute—Jason looked closer. As the woman's face came into focus, he fell back through time, to high school, to his younger, shyer self, and the girl he worshipped from afar. Emily Calder.

Eagerly, he flipped back to the envelope and was rewarded. The return address label was one of those preprinted affairs. Emily and Darren Littlejohn, and the address. It had to be the same Emily.

And there didn't seem to be a Mr. Littlejohn. Not that it mattered of course. High school crushes were long in the past.

He finished reading the entry and he felt as if he knew Darren Littlejohn. He'd been that kid.

Things were winding down at their little press conference. Randy was now saying a few words, then Crystal would finish and they'd all go on their way.

Darren Littlejohn's essay felt like a live thing, hot in his hand.

Jason's gift as a driver, he'd come to believe, was in acting before he let conscious thought set in. Most of the time following his instincts paid off, letting him take the right chances, navigate tough spots on the track when visibility was limited, win races. That same instinct caused him to lean over to Crystal and whisper, "What would I have to do to get you to add a second winner?"

Cool gray eyes met his. She hadn't become one of the top CEOs in the state without being as good under pressure as any driver. She flicked a glance at the cameras, then back at Jason. Put her hand over her mic.

"The Santa Claus parade," she said.

He groaned inwardly, having already negotiated his way out of being Santa's celebrity driver during the store's annual pre-Christmas parade.

He looked down at the photo in his hand. If he let common sense dictate, he'd drop the entry back on the table with the others.

But common sense had never been his strong suit.

He looked back up at Crystal.

"Deal."

CHAPTER THREE

EMILY AND DARREN SAT side by side in front of his computer screen for the live press conference announcing the essay contest winner. She'd tried to keep Darren's hopes reasonable, but she might as well have saved her breath.

"Here it comes, Mom. That's my entry right there. I know it."

"Honey…"

"Shh."

So she shut up and watched on the computer as a guy she went to high school with and an extraordinarily elegant woman took their seats at a table set up beside an enormous tank of envelopes. Her heart sank. Not that her hopes had been high, but even she hadn't imagined there would be so many entries.

Her stomach was in knots. *Please,* she begged

silently, please choose Darren's entry. He needed a miracle in his life. Maybe they both did.

Jason was speaking but she could barely concentrate, until she heard the words *little girl*. Her stomach twisted, making her feel physically sick. Lizbeth something. It didn't matter. Some young girl named Lizbeth had won the contest. Not Darren.

He didn't say a word, her son, he just stared at the computer screen, all color drained from his face.

For a moment they both sat there, miserable. "Oh, Darren, I'm so, so sorry."

He didn't answer, just kept staring at that screen. The woman was talking again now, but Emily couldn't stand to watch.

"I'm going downstairs right now and I'm ordering us a pizza," she said. Delivery pizza was such a rare treat it usually had him hollering with joy, but he only shrugged his small, bony shoulders.

"And soda," she added, knowing that junk food couldn't relieve his disappointment, but right now she couldn't think of anything else that might lessen the sting.

Leaving the NASCAR screen in the background,

Darren was already pulling up a computer game he'd gotten from a free site. The object was to help Santa get from the North Pole and deliver gifts while bypassing hazards and overcoming obstacles. She wasn't very savvy about computer games, but watching for a minute, she got the distinct feeling that her son, instead of guiding Santa to safety, was trying to annihilate the jolly red elf.

Even though she'd known he probably wouldn't win, Emily felt as if somebody had kicked her, hard. One of the things she'd never known about motherhood, until she had a child, was that bad things that happened to Darren were a thousand times more painful than anything bad that happened to her.

She wished she had a Bailey's credit card, just so she could cancel it. That would show them.

But then Lizbeth, whoever she was, probably wanted the treat as much as Darren, and for all Emily knew, deserved it, too.

Digging through the take-out menus, she decided to add a nice rich dessert to the order.

She was picking up the phone when she heard a strangled yell from upstairs. "Mooooom."

Dropping the phone, she bolted for the stairs, racing up them. She rushed into his room. "What? What is it?"

Her son pointed to the screen where he had the press conference back up. She leaned forward and squinted. Read the words, "Surprise second winner."

"You don't mean—"

The elegant woman was talking again, but on the screen she clearly read Lizbeth's name and then, as though they were being typed then and there, appeared the words, Darren Littlejohn, Hammersfield, Minnesota.

"I don't believe it," she said softly.

"You missed it. They said that there were so many great entries that they'd decided at the last minute to choose two winners." He looked at her, still unnaturally quiet, and said, "I'm the second winner."

"Nobody deserves it more," she said, giving him a high five.

The shock was wearing off now and Darren leaped to his feet and ran out of the room doing his best imitation of a race car. In between roaring engine sounds, he'd yell, "I won, I won!" Then his personal imitation of a NASCAR race would continue around her house.

Once he'd roared out of the room, she did the oddest thing. She pressed her fingers to her lips and touched them to the screen where Jason Bane sat grinning at the camera.

"Thank you," she whispered. Not that Jason would have had anything to do with picking the winner, she reminded herself, but she didn't care. Looking at him made her feel warm and fuzzy.

CHAPTER FOUR

"SWEET!" DARREN YELLED, piling out of the mini-van almost before it had rolled to a stop.

Emily struggled out of the other side of the van to grab hold of her son before he got sucked into the streams of fans making their way toward the track. Paige, the nice young woman who had met them at the hotel this morning and who was giving them the VIP treatment, was fortunately fast-moving. Her freckled face broke into a grin as Darren urged them forward. He was so anxious to get inside the gates that he looked as though the top part of his body was running while his feet were walking.

"You might want one of these, Darren," Paige called out to him, letting passes swing from her hands.

"Are those the tickets?" He swung around and the sun glinted off his glasses.

"Better," she promised.

He came closer, looking like a puppy called to heel that was dying to run and play.

"Hot passes," she said.

Darren stopped dead. "Does that mean…?"

"You can go pretty much anywhere with these. Hang out with the pit crew, check out what happens behind the scenes." She glanced around then dropped her voice. "We had to pull some strings to get you these, since you're too young for a hot pass. This is really special."

He came closer and Paige slipped the lanyard over his head. The pass featured a picture of Jason Bane, Emily noted, and even the cord was printed with his name. She'd known he was a big shot— she'd seen his picture in sports and celebrity magazines—but somehow seeing his name and likeness here at the track made it so much more real.

"Wow," she said softly as she slipped her own lanyard around her neck.

The hot pass meant they could go through a special entrance. To Darren it was like entering a magical world. Pulling out her digital camera, she snapped a few photos as he darted from here to there, happiness coming off him in waves.

"Do you want to meet Jason?" Paige asked.

"Duh," Darren replied.

Duh, Emily silently echoed.

She wouldn't be nervous, she reminded herself. He would never in a million years remember her.

"Come on, he's in the hauler. This way."

They followed the young woman into an area where lots was going on. Crews, in assorted team uniforms, were busy doing mechanical-looking things she mostly didn't understand, and the haulers were lined up like so many blocks in colorful rows.

Paige led them to Jason's area. His hauler, basically a huge trailer, had a larger-than-life photo of him and his car on the side. As they approached, Paige introduced Darren and his mom to the guys out front, all of whom had an easy word for him and a nod in her direction. The three of them climbed a couple of steps into the hauler, which was pretty much the neatest and largest storage cabinet Emily had ever seen. At the back was a door. Paige rapped on it and they entered a surprisingly cozy living area with built-in leather couches, a plasma TV and a food prep area.

There were three men in the room, all watching race footage on the screen, but her eyes were drawn to only one.

Jason Bane.

He'd changed. Well, it made sense that he would have in twelve years. They'd both changed, of course, but where she felt that the years had beaten her up a little, they'd only improved her high school crush.

No doubt about it, the skinny cute guy from high school was all grown-up, filled out and gorgeous. Unlike the men outside, Jason's glance flicked first to her before dropping to her son.

"Hi," he said, rising from the couch and holding out a hand to the boy. "You must be Darren."

Unlike her, her son didn't seem a bit fazed. He grinned up at the tall guy, shook the offered hand and said, "What's the fastest you've ever gone?"

Jason laughed, the big smile taking over his face and making him seem a lot less intimidating. "Let me say hi to your mom and then we'll talk."

He stepped past her son and moved to where Emily hovered in the background. He nodded to her politely, the way he must have nodded to a thousand fans. Friendly and impersonal. Held out his hand. "I'm Jason."

Of course he hadn't remembered her. But somewhere in her pea brain, she supposed she'd imagined a double take and a, "Did we go to high school together?" remark said in a kind of gasp. But, if he'd ever noticed her all those years ago, which she doubted, he'd long forgotten her in his meteoric rise to one of the hottest young drivers in NASCAR.

Still, she thought, whatever had happened to her in her life, she'd have remembered him.

He had clear gray eyes that seemed intent. He'd always appeared to be listening during class, for instance, but there was a twinkle in the depths of his gaze that suggested he didn't take anything too seriously.

His hair was dark with a hint of curl that was ruthlessly kept in check by a short crop, tweaked weekly by some fancy stylist, no doubt. His jaw was square and his cheekbones sharp, which gave him something of a dangerous look.

She clasped his hand in return, felt the warm strength of his palm and muttered something totally incoherent. She realized he was smiling at her and there was an expression in his eyes that confused her, almost as though they were sharing a private joke. Then he let her go and the moment was gone.

Paige consulted her clipboard. "We got some bad news, by the way. Lizbeth Monterey, the girl who also won the contest, had an attack of appendicitis last night. She had to have emergency surgery. She won't be able to travel for a while."

"Oh, that is too bad," Emily said. "I hope she'll feel better soon." She hoped it wasn't totally obvious to everyone that her son was all but doing cartwheels now he knew he'd have Jason Bane to himself.

Jason said, "Make sure to send her a get-well card from me, would you? And let her know we'll reschedule her visit for when she's feeling better."

"Will do," Paige said, scribbling a note. "I'll take Darren and his mom on a tour and then—"

"I'll take them," Jason said.

"You? But—"

"Sure. We're finished here and I don't have anything to do for a couple hours." He glanced at Darren. "And you look like you've got a stack of questions."

Paige and Emily exchanged a glance of equal surprise. As a teacher, Emily lived her life by schedules, and she completely understood Paige's surprise that the driver was departing from the clipboard timetable. Not that Emily was complaining, and as for Darren, he looked as if he'd just swallowed the brilliant Florida sun.

They went back outside and Jason held the door for her. As she brushed past him to follow her son into the colorful chaos outside, her glance flicked up to Jason's. As their gazes met he said softly, "It's great to see you again."

Her eyes widened in surprise. He remembered her? He gave her half a wink and then they were outside.

"Can we go see your ride?" Darren was wasting no time in ticking off every item on his own mental clipboard, she noted. But Jason didn't seem to mind. If anything she thought he liked her son's enthusiasm.

"I'm all yours until four," he said. "Come on, it's this way."

"Sweet."

Emily followed the two of them at a slower pace, her brain whirling. So he had remembered her. But then why hadn't he said anything earlier?

Probably vaguely recognizing some girl from high school wasn't important enough to make a big deal about, but she had to admit to being deeply…well, she supposed flattered was the only word that fit—that he had recognized her.

She pushed her hair behind her ears and dug out her sunglasses. Maybe she hadn't changed so very much after all.

CHAPTER FIVE

SHE HADN'T CHANGED AT ALL, Jason thought in amazement, careful not to let his gaze stray her way too often. Her hair was the first thing he'd ever noticed about her, swinging free around her shoulders, blond, but with darker shades beneath the surface when it danced and settled around her shoulders. It had been a lot longer back when he used to dream about her during history class. Way down her back. Now it was just past her shoulders, but it still swung, and when the light hit it, he was still reminded of a wheat field with the wind rippling through it.

Her eyes were the clear blue of the lakes up north. She looked like a true Minnesota Swede. Maybe it had been five generations since some burly Scandinavian had made the trek to the new world, but the gene pool was pretty unpolluted as far as Jason could tell. With her fair skin, blue eyes and blond hair, she could walk down the street in Stockholm and fit right in.

He, on the other hand, had a gene pool as murky as a swamp. Irish, Finn, some Hungarian and, his favorite part, an eighth share of Ojibway. He was as dark as she was fair.

She still moved like a girl, too, he noted. Not that she was exactly old at thirty, but she had a child and somehow he'd expected her to look more like a mom than the stuff of his boyhood fantasies.

If anything, she looked better. Her curves had filled out and she'd grown into herself. She radiated quiet confidence and whenever she looked at her son, an expression of pride crossed her face.

Then Darren grabbed his attention, and Jason found he had to concentrate to keep up with the rapid-fire barrage of questions. "What's it like when you crash? Is it awesome?"

Jason shook his head. "First, a crash really messes up your chances of winning a race, obviously. Plus, if you're out there wrecking cars all the time, your owner's not going to be too happy. You want your owner happy. Believe me."

"I guess."

He pointed at the vehicle they were circling

around. "I always like to have a good-looking race car at the end of the day."

"Do you get nervous?" Darren asked, touching the car the way he'd touch a good-luck charm.

"No. Keyed up, sure, but the most important thing is to relax and have fun. Every week I go out there and put everything else in the season out of my mind. Every week is an opportunity to gain points."

"I bet you wish you could race every day. Don't you get bored?"

He laughed. "Not hardly. When I get the time I like to golf."

"My mom golfs," Darren put in excitedly. "She organizes a fundraising tournament, too, to raise money for education." He glanced back at his mom and then to Jason. "You should come. You could be the celebrity guest."

"Darren—" his mom warned.

"What?" Innocent blue eyes opened wide behind the kid's glasses. "He'd be better than the celebrity we got last year. Some guy who got voted off *American Idol*. Like anybody cares. You'd be totally cool. You do charity appearances, right?"

"I do. Sure." Paige was making a noise behind

him, as if he'd better shut up before he committed himself to one more event in an already-crowded calendar.

"And you're from Hammersfield, so you'd be a true hometown celebrity."

"I tell you what. Get your mom to send the details to Paige, okay? She looks after my schedule."

"You mean, you'll come?"

"No, you little hustler. I mean I'll think about it."

"Cool. So, what do you like about the Homestead track?" The kid's questions ranged from topic to topic so fast that Jason had to concentrate.

"I love driving down the back straight, palm trees all down the side. And I think, right, I'm in South Florida, racing. How cool is that? I like the way the turns are banked. This is a good track for me. One of my favorites."

"What about how hot it gets?" The boy had already removed his sweatshirt. He was obviously still acclimating from a Minnesota winter to a Florida one.

"You get hot being in a stock car. I'm sitting right over the engine, so it gets toasty in there. I take a bag of ice water in with me."

"What if you get hungry?"

"I carry granola bars. Eat them during pit stops."

"Do you want to see the engine, son?" Will, one of the mechanics asked.

"Yeah."

Darren was as enthralled by the engine as he had been by the driving.

Luckily, Will had a son around Darren's age, and he took over answering some of Darren's more technical questions.

Jason stepped back a couple of steps to where Emily stood, looking torn between pride in her son's obviously intelligent questions and boredom.

"I take it you aren't a racing fan?"

"It's more that I'm not too interested in what's under the hood of a stock car, or how many liters of fuel it can take and how fast the lug nuts go on and off the wheels during a pit stop. I hope he's not exhausting you."

"Not at all. It's good to have someone around who's so knowledgeable."

"Look, I'm sorry he put you on the spot like that about our piddly little golf tournament. I'll explain to him—"

"No. Really. Send Paige the information and if I can fit it in my schedule, I'll come. It would be cool to go back and see the old place. I haven't been home for a long time."

There was a slight pause. She said, "I know. I didn't think you had recognized me."

"Are you kidding? We went to high school together. I'd have recognized you anywhere. I didn't want to make a big deal about it publicly is all. Don't want anyone thinking the contest was rigged."

She looked at him suddenly, kind of strangely, and he realized that she might well have been watching the live feed when they chose the contest winner. When they'd suddenly added a second winner. Please let her not figure out he'd been driven by forces he didn't understand at the time, but now thought might have been the truly humiliating vestiges of a high school longing.

CHAPTER SIX

"TODAY YOU GET TO GO shopping," Darren said, reading the schedule the ever-efficient Paige had provided.

"Aren't you coming with me?" she asked. There was nothing else on the schedule for that time, and she really didn't want to leave a ten-year-old alone in a hotel room.

"Yeah!" He tapped the printed schedule. "Photo op, remember? With Santa and the good people at Bailey's Department Store. Photo op. Jeez. At least Jason'll be there."

His face set suddenly in mutinous lines. "If they make me sit on Santa's knee, I'm not doing it, Mom. I don't care if it is rude and Bailey's gave us this nice prize. The guys at school might see."

"I'm sure you won't have to sit on Santa's knee. They know you aren't a little kid."

"Maybe you can sit on Santa's knee." He shot her a crafty look. "It's different for girls."

She ruffled his hair, which she knew for him was a pretty severe punishment. "Go brush your teeth and put on a clean shirt. And don't think I'm spending all my shopping spree in the sports and electronics departments."

"Nah," he said with affected casualness. "I'm not shopping with you. Jason said I could hang out with him while you get your retail therapy. He has to go to some meeting anyway. He's driving the store Santa for the annual Santa Parade next weekend."

"But it's not on the schedule for you two to hang out. I'm not sure— He's awfully busy."

Darren gave her a look that told her he had read her mind. His words proved it. "He won't forget. He's not like that."

Emily wished she could be so sure. It was easy to make plans, but a driver must have a million demands on his time that would take precedence over a ten-year-old boy.

"I'm not—" The phone rang. Her son grabbed it before she had a chance.

"Hey. I'm good." His whole face lit up, so she knew immediately who was on the other end. "Yep.

We were just talking about you. Mom said you were too busy for me today, but I told her we were hanging out." He glanced up at Emily. "Yeah. Sure."

He passed the phone to her. "He wants to talk to you."

Before taking the phone, Emily checked her hair with her hands to make sure it was straight. Darren looked at her like she was crazy. He whispered, "He can't see you."

Knowing her cheeks were heating, she grabbed the phone. "Hello?"

"Emily. Hi. Jason here." Without the noise of the track all around them, his voice sounded lower. More intimate.

"Hi."

There was a pause. She couldn't think of a single thing to say. He didn't speak for a moment, either.

Finally he said, "So, if it's okay with you, Darren's going to stay with me while you go shopping."

"Yes, but I don't want him to impose—"

"He won't. He's a great kid. Reminds me of myself at that age." There was a pause. "That is, I didn't mean—"

She laughed, almost convinced that he was a

little nervous when talking to her, just as she was when trying to make conversation with him. "You were a great kid. I remember."

"Do you?" He sounded almost wistful.

Her high school crush came roaring back. "Yes. I do."

"Well, here's the thing. I have to go to a charity dinner tonight. I was wondering if you'd like to come. Paige wants to hang out with Darren and order pizza and play video games, so…it would be the two of us. What do you say?"

The two of them. What did that mean exactly? Was it a date? Was her high school crush—now famous race car driver—asking her out?

"Um, yes. Sure. I'd love to," she finally managed to spit out.

"Great. That's cool." He sounded almost as excited at the prospect of the two of them going out together as she felt.

Which was ridiculous.

When she got off the phone, Darren regarded her in an entirely inappropriate I-told-you-so manner. "Okay, you're right. He didn't forget and he has time for you."

"Have fun shopping, Mom." Her little boy gave her a surprisingly grown-up look. "And don't buy me anything. I'm serious. I won the contest so you could get some nice stuff. The spending spree is my present to you."

"But, honey, you need—"

"Promise me, Mom."

She couldn't do it. A thousand dollars was a lot of money and meant she could buy him a decent winter coat and—and then she saw his face. If he hadn't won the essay contest, there wouldn't be a thousand-dollar shopping spree.

Foolish tears threatened as she looked down into his sweet, serious face.

"You have to let me buy you one thing," she insisted.

He cocked his head to the side. "Only one thing, Mom. The rest is for you. I'm already getting the best Christmas present ever. Did you hear where we're watching the race from?"

"Yep." She thought they'd probably heard it in Beijing when Darren first bellowed the news to her. From inside the pit stall. On top of some box where Jason's crew chief would be sitting. Darren would get his own headset so he could listen in on the back-and-forth chatter between Jason, his spotter and his crew chief.

She wasn't sure she'd be able to watch. The cars

drove so fast, and she was pretty sure she'd worry and no doubt do something completely foolish like leap over the wall during a pit stop, rush up to Jason and beg him to slow down!

She might still have argued a little more with Darren, but then she thought about this "charity thing" she was attending with Jason and that she had nothing remotely appropriate to wear. "I'm buying you one practical thing. Deal?"

"And the rest is for you. Deal."

They were in the lobby waiting when their town car pulled up. To her surprise, she found Jason in the back along with Paige. He wore jeans and a Bailey's shirt. A ball cap with the company's logo sat beside him on the seat. "Hey, guys. How's it going?"

"Great," she said, sliding in, wishing she'd had some warning she'd have Mr. Sexy Driver as a traveling companion.

She wished she knew how to ask for a few more details on this do tonight, but had no idea how to casually find out if she was a date or a convenient escort.

Not that she got much chance to talk to Jason. Her son monopolized the driver. Though she figured Jason had no one to blame but himself when he asked to see the portable gaming device Darren had brought along.

"I got a new Christmas game," Darren told him, and then explained how it worked.

"So you have to avoid meteors and rabid reindeer and alien warships to get Santa from the North Pole to deliver presents, huh? That's cool."

"Yeah, and check out the renegade elves. Look there's a rocket-launching elf. See what happens if you turn him 360." An ominous noise rose from the device. "Santa explodes," Darren said with barely contained glee.

"You can't kill Santa!" Emily protested.

Her son rolled his eyes. "News flash. Santa's not real, Mom."

CHAPTER SEVEN

When the town car pulled up in front of Bailey's, she felt like a celebrity. A photographer commemorated her meeting with the owner and CEO of the store, Crystal Bailey, the woman she recognized from the online press conference. Randy something or other, who seemed to be in charge of marketing also greeted her and finally she was turned over to a woman named Sally, who was a personal shopper.

"Wow," she said, "I've never had a personal shopper before." She'd never had a thousand bucks to spend in a morning, either, but she kept that knowledge to herself.

Darren went off more than happily with Jason, Paige, Crystal and Randy, which left her in the hands of Sally, a gorgeous young woman who looked as though she split her time between tanning on the beach, working out and shopping. She wore a simple white dress with black-and-white heels and chunky black beads, and Emily immediately felt pale, dowdy and as if she seriously needed to up her workouts.

"So," Sally said brightly, "I'm all yours. I won't bore you with my résumé, but I used to work at *Vogue* and before that I was an assistant at Marc Jacobs. I love fashion, and I'm pretty good at knowing what looks good on a person."

"I'm a teacher," Emily blurted, as though to explain why she looked like a teacher from the Midwest and not a featured character on *Sex and the City.*

As they talked, Sally led Emily to an escalator.

"You're a size six?"

"Right." Wow, she was good.

"Anything special you have in mind?"

"Well, I'm going to a charity event tonight." She forced herself to sound casual. "With Jason Bane."

"Not the Make-a-Miracle Foundation Ball?" The young woman sounded truly impressed.

"Yes. That's the one."

"Nice. Swanky."

"It is?"

"Sure. Last year they raised over a million dollars for homeless kids. Celebrities will be there, a few athletes and the usual rich and beautiful crowd."

"What do people wear to this thing?"

"Anything in this room would do," Sally said, ushering Emily into a hushed space with more mirrors than clothes. The place screamed *expensive*. There was no sale rack in sight.

"These aren't me at all," she said, looking at the long dresses nearly all adorned with sparkles or jewels. "I need something I can wear in Hammersfield, Minnesota."

"I agree. They're not you. Come this way."

In the end, with Sally's help, she chose a devastatingly simple little black dress. And heels. Even though Sally insisted there was a store discount, Emily still bit a huge chunk out of her shopping spree money, leaving not much more than enough to buy Darren's jacket.

"Thanks so much, Sally," Emily said when they were done, hugging the woman who felt like a friend, since they'd spent so much time in changing rooms together.

"Not so fast. Crystal told me to send you to the third-floor salon to get your makeup and hair done for the photo shoot. And you'll look gorgeous for tonight."

While she was pampered in the salon, she reflected that buying the dress and heels was frivolous. Unnecessary. Not the action of a sensible teacher and mom.

Yet she'd loved every decadent minute of it. Trying on the dress. Feeling the way it conformed to her body, the way the skirt hem flirted above her knees, the way the heels added height and a certain elegance to her form.

She looked, Sally insisted, hot. Then Sally had forced Emily to purchase the kind of underwear that wouldn't undermine the dress.

By the time they were finished with her in the salon, Emily looked a lot more glamorous than usual. Her eyes had been made up so they dominated her face, her hair hung in loose, sexy curls. She was definitely more Miami than Minnesota.

When she emerged, a butterfly from a cocoon, Sally and Crystal Bailey were waiting for her.

"Thank you so much for this," she said to Crystal. "Darren and I are having a fabulous time."

"I'm so glad." Crystal stepped back and looked Emily up and down as though sizing her up. Then she nodded briskly. "You were right, Sally. As always."

She turned back to Emily. "Sally suggested we might like to lend you something for the photo shoot. Something particularly festive for the holidays. Would you object to modeling one of the outfits from our winter collection?"

"Of course not."

So she found herself going to meet Santa in a gorgeous green silk dress. She'd peeked at the price tag in the dressing room and discovered this one dress would have cost more than her whole shopping spree.

Fortunately, Crystal and Sally hadn't attempted to get her son to model anything. Instead they'd given him one of their promotional shirts to wear, and since his was a match to the one worn by Jason, Darren was thrilled to pull it over his head.

"Santa's waiting for us in Toyland," Crystal said, leading the way to a discreet elevator. If she heard Darren's slight gagging noise, she chose to ignore it. "Jason will meet us there. He's going to be Santa's driver for our Christmas parade next week. We're very excited."

Bailey's Toyland was as much a retail fantasy as she'd imagined. Massive silver and red and green icicles, a forest of elves and reindeer surrounded by snow so fake it reminded her that the temperature was seventy-six degrees outside. The real snow was back home in Hammersfield.

Santa had his own throne, surrounded by

wrapped presents larger than her kitchen appliances, and in the midst of it all a large, jolly, bespectacled, bearded Santa complete with a belly that shook like a bowl full of jelly.

Beside him was Jason, staring at her as though he'd never seen her before. It was a measure of how surreal the surroundings were, she thought, that Jason seemed so real and down-to-earth. Somehow part of her world.

Crazy thought.

A professional photographer was setting up a fancy-looking tripod and his assistant was fiddling with enormous silver umbrella-looking things as though they were shooting for a fashion magazine.

Jason came forward and said, "Wow. You look gorgeous."

"Thanks. The dress is on loan, but I love wearing it."

Toyland wasn't officially open, but the shopping center was, and a few curious passersby stopped to watch the photo shoot.

"Will our picture be in the paper?" Darren asked, seeming excited at the idea. She'd signed photo releases, but somehow she'd been given the impression that she and her son would be featured briefly on the Web site and that would be it.

"Yes," Crystal said. "I think we might use these photos to publicize Santa's driver and let the folks know that Santa is open for business."

"That's right," Santa boomed. "Santa's ready to hear your wishes. The elves and I work hard all year for this, my favorite time of the year. And what do you want for Christmas, young man?"

CHAPTER EIGHT

OH, PUH-LEASE, THOUGHT Darren. He was ten. Who believed in Santa Claus at ten years old?

He'd almost been relieved when he found out in first grade that Santa was a myth. That's why the guy in the red suit hadn't given him the family he'd asked for. Because Santa was as fake as those pink and green icicles.

Darren was older now and a lot smarter. He looked at the old guy. What a sucky job it must be to be a mall Santa. Especially when you were that old. He was probably living in a seniors' residence and they let him out a few hours a week to fake out little kids.

The guy was looking at him with his lips already rounded as if he was ready to launch into *ho, ho, ho* the second Darren spoke. He answered. "World peace."

The old Santa dude laughed, a big rumbling sound that was way better than the acoustics on Darren's Santa game. "We all want that, son. But what kind of a gift would you like me to bring just for you?"

He seemed like a nice old guy, and besides, Darren's mom was only over by the lights talking to Crystal and Jason, and she had supernatural hearing powers when rudeness was involved.

So he settled for, "I'm ten. I don't believe in Santa anymore."

The fake Santa didn't look too upset. If anything, his eyes started to twinkle, or maybe that was the little round glasses reflecting the camera lights.

"I've always made it my policy never to disbelieve anything that makes people happy and hurts no one."

But he was wrong. Believing in magic did hurt. "You can't give me what I want. You're just an old guy with a fake beard and a bad velvet suit." He eyed the belly. "Bet there's a pillow under there. If I asked you for something I'd only be disappointed."

Santa looked at him almost sadly. "So young and so cynical. Why don't you try telling me what you want anyway? Lots of books are being written now about the power of speaking your wishes aloud. Putting it out to the universe, I believe they call it."

Darren looked at him with suspicion.

The gentle smile never wavered. "The photographer and his people are busy setting up the shoot and you and I have nothing to do for a few minutes." Santa settled his hands over his belly the way Darren's grandpa Dave did. "It would kill the time."

"Okay. I want a million dollars."

The chuckle came again. Darren didn't think a pillow could ripple like that. Maybe the old guy really was fat. "I think you'll get your million dollars. You seem like a person who will succeed in life. You question things and you're very intelligent. But I'm going to let you earn that money for yourself. It's much more satisfying. Come on, now. What do you really want Christmas morning? A train set?"

"Lame."

"Baseball bat?"

"Already have one."

"A new gaming station?"

Okay, the old guy had some clue. "My mom can't afford that. We don't have much money since she's a single mom and all."

"Ah."

Darren looked at his mom and Jason standing together. They really seemed to like each other. She'd told him that they'd gone to the same school, but the way they were talking it was as if they'd hung out together. It gave him a good feeling to see them laughing together.

Maybe the old guy was right. He should say what he wanted. Out loud. Not that an escapee from the old folks home could make it happen, but maybe if he spoke a wish aloud… He took a breath.

"I want my mom to find a new husband. Someone I like. I want to be a family again." He almost cringed at how stupid he sounded, but at least the words were out there.

"That's a good wish, Darren. It's honest."

"Yeah, but you can't make it happen."

"There are forces in this world that none of us really understand." Santa sounded like one of those preprogrammed mystics from a computer game. Darren was unimpressed.

However, the photographer finally seemed to have enough lights and silver umbrellas to take a picture.

"OKAY, LET'S HAVE JASON stand beside Santa's chair," the photographer directed them. "Let's see.

How about Mom on Santa's knee and the young man on her other side." They obediently took their places. Jason had been photographed so many times he felt like a professional actor some days. Emily giggled a little and exchanged a comical glance with Darren as she settled herself gingerly on Santa's knee. The green silk caught the light and Jason thought he'd never seen anyone so pretty. "Smile."

After some fussing with a light meter, they changed positions. All four of them standing. "Now, put your arm around Emily and a hand on Darren's shoulder." He did as directed and felt the soft silk of Emily's dress beneath his hand, the warmth of her skin seeping through. Under his other hand Darren's shoulder was as bony as a chicken wing. He was fidgeting, too. Obviously ready to be done with this nonsense.

"Good. And Santa just here." The photographer moved the store's Santa so he was looking on at the grouping.

A small crowd had gathered by this time. He had no idea if they were race fans or shoppers with nothing better to do than watch a photo shoot. He overheard two older ladies near the front talking about the sale in bedding. Then one turned to the other and said, "I didn't know Jason Bane had such a nice family. Don't they make a lovely picture?"

Beneath his hands two shoulders jerked, and he could swear the temperature rose in Emily's shoulder, as though her whole body was blushing.

He was surprised at the feeling that fleetingly passed through him. Pride, he thought, the way he'd feel if he had a real family, a nice woman like Emily by his side. Darren with all his questions, his too-smart brain and his definite need of a man in his life. All they'd need to round things out would be a little girl.

The picture in his mind was so real for a moment that he could see his little girl's face. She had Emily's pretty blue eyes and his dark hair. In the picture gallery in his head, Emily was holding the child and Darren was flopped on the floor nearby with a racing magazine.

In that second he glanced up and caught the mall Santa's eyes on him. For a spooky moment he felt as though the old man was reading his mind. Then the photographer called his attention back to the shoot and he blinked away the strange daydream.

CHAPTER NINE

THE HOTEL BALLROOM was awash in color, dresses in every hue wrapping figures that couldn't possibly have all come from nature. The flash of jewels was almost blinding. Right away Emily spotted a gorgeous young TV actress surrounded by eager admirers. *So this is where the beautiful people hang out.*

She felt like a small, black bird in the middle of an exotic parrot colony.

As though he could feel her intimidation, Jason took her hand in a warm clasp, making her feel connected, at least a little, for he was part of this world, she saw. He'd complained about the tux he was wearing, but she thought he looked amazing.

The decor was incredible. A winter wonderland with snow machines in the corners shooting out showers of sparkly white "snow" and drifts of the stuff everywhere. Champagne and cocktails flowed and the appetizers looked much too pretty to eat.

"What is it with South Florida and fake snow?" she asked, thinking this was the second time she'd found herself in a make-believe winter wonderland today. "I thought people came here to get away from the snow?"

He laughed. "Nostalgia? And you don't have to shovel this stuff."

"So, how come you didn't have a date to this thing?"

"It's not really my scene. I come because the gala raises money for a good cause. I pledge a few bucks, and then I leave." He glanced at her. "Usually."

Once she got over herself, the ball was fun. Crystal Bailey was at their table, stunning in some sparkly silver concoction that had designer written all over it. From years of parent-teacher interviews she'd become pretty good at conversing with strangers. Jason introduced her as "an old friend from Minnesota," instead of somebody who was here as part of a prize her son won. She caught the way people looked at the two of them, speculating about a possible romance.

She could feel Jason start to fidget after about

four courses of the most amazing meal she'd ever eaten. By the time dessert arrived, he was vibrating with suppressed energy. She wasn't a bit surprised when he asked her to dance the second the floor opened.

Of course, athlete that he was, he danced like a man who knew how to lead a woman in circles. Something she'd have to remember before she got too dizzy.

But it was impossible not to fall a little into the fairy tale. Here she was in a dress she had no business affording, in a winter wonderland in a city that was eighty degrees outside, with a man who reminded her that she was a woman. He was strong, and warm, and his chest so inviting she had to restrain herself from resting her head there.

They fit, too, she thought dreamily as the toes peeking out of her high-heeled shoes hit a drift of snow and sent a shower of sparkles in the air. Too much magic couldn't possibly be good for a person. But she didn't want the night to end.

"I have to tell you something," he said in her ear, his breath stirring her hair.

"Mmm?"

"It's been a really long time since I was on a date."

Her heart skipped foolishly. She glanced up into

his eyes set in that dangerously attractive face. "Is this a date?"

He looked so crestfallen she almost laughed. "Isn't it a date? Man asks woman to spend the evening with him? Suit and tie are involved? Sounds like a date to me."

She laughed. "And don't forget my new dress, shoes, hair—oh, heck, everything about me is new."

"No. You're still the same. When I look at you I feel like I'm in high school again. Young and unsure of myself." She felt her eyes widen. Jason Bane unsure of himself? "Anyhow, I would like this to be a date. You okay with that?"

"Yes. Of course." She'd only waited ten years for her high school crush to ask her out. How could she not be okay with this being a real date?

"Would you like to get out of here?"

"Mmm-hmm."

They slipped out of the ballroom and into the lush lobby. She glanced out and saw the beach at night. Palm trees, white sand, blue water. "Could we walk on the beach for a little bit?"

"Sure. Great idea."

She clipped her way along a winding path to the beach then slipped off her sandals and stepped into the sand. "Ah, heaven."

Jason had his shoes and socks off in a heartbeat and rolled up the cuffs of his dress pants. They walked along the oceanfront, listening to the lap of the ocean, the beat of salsa music coming from somewhere nearby.

He took her hand.

"You have to be careful with first dates, you know," he said, apparently continuing the conversation they'd started in the ballroom.

"You do? Why?"

"Well, my dad always told me to plan my first dates carefully because one day I'd be playing with my grandkids and one of 'em would ask about how I met Grandma and I wouldn't want to have to tell them it was the time we went to get fast food. Dutch treat."

"Wise words. My first date with my ex-husband, he took me to some party, where he got drunk and threw up in his friend's parents' kiddie pool." She shuddered at the memory.

"After a first date like that how come you married him?"

She sighed. "You know, I honestly don't remember. Maybe I thought he needed me and I could straighten him out." She shrugged. "Now I know better."

Had she ever felt the connection between herself and her ex that she felt between herself and Jason? The contact of their clasped hands swinging back and forth as they walked was like a slow, intimate conversation.

"Regrets?"

"No. I wouldn't have Darren if I hadn't married Larry. And I learned that I'm tougher than I thought I was." She hit a puddle of ocean water and splashed through it. "I don't think there's any point in going back and wishing you'd done things differently."

"I wish I'd done one thing differently."

"What's that?"

"I wish I'd asked you out in high school."

Surprise zapped her like a shot of electricity. "I beg your pardon?"

A wry grin lit his face. "I tried for most of junior year to work up the courage, but you were always surrounded by friends and I never could find the words. You were so pretty and popular. I was the weird guy, spending too much time in shop messing around with engines."

"You wanted to ask me out?"

"Yeah." He said it the way her son did when he thought she was being incredibly dense about something.

"But I thought you didn't even know who I was. I had a crush on you for…years I think."

He appeared stunned by this information. "You're kidding, right?"

"No. I remember you sat two rows over from me in history class." And three seats up, but she wasn't going to let him know she still remembered.

He nodded. "And three seats up."

"I didn't even think you knew my name."

"Emily Calder. Girl most likely to break a lot of hearts." He fingered his bow tie as though making sure it was still around his neck. "I probably would have asked you out in senior year. It's not like I had anything to lose, but when we came back from summer vacation you'd hooked up with Little-john."

Shock held her speechless as the film of her early life played in her head. When she substituted Jason for her ex-husband as the costar in the film of her life, the film seemed to stick.

"Imagine if you had. Maybe our lives would have been different."

"Maybe you wouldn't have had Darren."

"Maybe you wouldn't have left town and started driving professionally."

"Funny how things work out."

"Yeah."

"You were smart. I remember how you would always listen in class. Especially science."

"Not smart enough to talk to the prettiest girl in school."

She felt herself blushing, as off balance and bubbly with shyness as though she were still a teenager. "I was not the prettiest—"

"You couldn't possibly be in a position to judge. Trust me, as a guy who spent a lot of time researching the question, you were the prettiest girl in Hamm High."

She imagined all the beautiful women he'd met since those far-off days. "That was a long time ago."

"Sure seems like it."

Maybe because she didn't want the night to end, maybe because it had been so long since anyone she wanted had shown any romantic interest in her, however fleeting, maybe because she'd never entirely gotten over her crush, she asked, "So, where would we have gone?"

"Gone?"

"On our date. In senior year when you worked up the courage. Where would we have gone?"

"For a woman like you? I'd have pulled out all

the stops. Treated you to the finest dining in Hammersfield."

She started to laugh. "Uncle Olaf's Diner," they said at the same time.

"Is it still there?"

"Of course. It was there before we were born, and I'm sure it will be there long after we're gone."

"I miss the deep-fried walleye."

"It's still on the menu, along with Finnish pancakes and lutefisk, but they've added pizza to the menu since you left."

He shook his head in mock shock. "Everything changes."

The air was so balmy her skin seemed to drink it in. The sand was scratchy against her winter-tender soles, stroking her toes as she walked. He halted and turned her to face him. She felt a little shy suddenly when she saw the expression in his eyes. "I know how I would have wanted our first date to end," he said.

"How?"

"Like this." He leaned in and kissed her. Not like a seventeen-year-old, she thought vaguely, but like a man all grown-up, who knows who he is and what he wants.

She made a tiny sound like a sigh in the back of

her throat and melted against him. His arms came around her and he held her tight, kissing her until she thought her skin would explode into fireworks.

At last he pulled away. She licked her lips as though she couldn't quite believe what had just happened to them.

"Wow," he said.

If she could have spoken, she'd have agreed.

Wow, indeed.

CHAPTER TEN

THE NEXT DAY WAS qualifying races and she and Jason had little time together, but the times they did exchange a few words, or even a glance, she relived that kiss.

Darren was in his element, loving everything about the track, the fans, the pit crew and the noise.

By race day, she was almost as keyed up as her son. The stands were filled. They knew going in that Jason didn't have a hope of winning the NASCAR Cup Sprint Series championship, but he was definitely a contender for the Homestead race. He and his team had been working well together, his car had been trouble-free. His goal, as he'd told the television cameras during pre-race coverage, was to finish the season in the top five.

The day seemed to please everybody. The temperature had dropped slightly to seventy-three degrees; there were a few scattered clouds, but pretty obviously there wasn't going to be a chance of rain to spoil this last race of the season.

When she saw him in his firesuit, he looked like a stranger, more like the athlete she and Darren were accustomed to watching on TV on Sundays than the man who had kissed her—and then he caught her eye and winked at her, and he was her Jason again.

The race was among the most stressful hours of her life. It was so much faster in real life than she'd imagined. The thunderous noise as the cars roared past, the excited yells of the crowd, the mad scramble of the pit stops, each one timed to precision. They tried to keep the change to twelve seconds, Darren informed her and it seemed as though Jason's car was barely stopped for a second before it roared out again.

She was having trouble following his car as she watched the big screen. "Come on, Jason," she kept repeating.

The light was changing to dusk and she was exhausted. She wondered how Jason could drive intensely for four hundred miles when just sitting and watching left her limp.

As the race headed to its final laps, Darren, who

was hoarse from yelling, grabbed her arm. "He could win, Mom. He could totally do it."

In an amazing finish, as four cars swapped out the lead, so tight together that at times they appeared welded, Jason ended third.

She was so proud she thought she might burst.

As a third-place finisher he had to go to the media center and take part in a press conference, which she watched from the TV in the hauler. He looked sweaty and tired, but he still managed to joke around a little with the other two drivers, talk about the race and compliment his team.

Then he was there, among them, high-fiving and back-patting.

Paige had already informed them that Jason would be flying out right after the race, and they were flying back to Minnesota in the morning, so Emily knew this was goodbye.

But Paige appeared by her side, clipboard in hand. In a low voice she said, "Jason's decided to stay over tonight and head out in the morning instead. He wants to take you and Darren out for pizza before you go."

"I—" She wanted to throw her fist in the air and yell "sweet" the way Darren would. But she managed to restrain herself. "Yes, of course."

THE PLACE HE CHOSE was a tiny hole-in-the-wall, which offered not only great pizza but, she suspected, was the kind of place where racing fans were unlikely to hang out. She and Darren could have the driver all to themselves for a couple of hours.

Darren peppered him with questions, pretty smart ones, she thought, about the race. And Jason answered, obviously still keyed up by the whole experience. His standing at the end of the season was seventh. Very respectable.

Now that he was back in jeans and a shirt that didn't advertise anything at all, he seemed much more like a normal guy. They laughed and joked their way through dinner and she thought, looking at the two guys across the table from her, that she wasn't the only one who was going to miss Jason. Darren was going to miss him terribly.

There was a video game machine in one corner of the restaurant, and after he'd put away half a pizza, two glasses of soda and a gelato, Darren asked if he could go play it.

"Sure," she agreed.

"Wanna play?" he asked Jason.

"Nah. I'll keep your mom company."

As soon as Darren was happily engaged in play, Jason leaned across the table and took her hand.

"I want to see you again."

A thrill coursed through her at his words. She looked at him and realized he wasn't just saying this to make her feel better. He really wanted to see her again. And, if she had only herself to worry about, she thought she'd say yes and let the future lead where it would.

But she didn't have only herself to worry about. There was and always would be Darren. She'd let her son down once, saddling him with a dad who was only a step away from a deadbeat. She couldn't take another chance on a man who could hardly be relied upon. She had to face facts.

So she put a brave smile on her face and said, "This has been fun. So much fun. I can't even tell you. I'll always treasure this time we spent together."

The smile faded from his eyes. "Why do I feel there's a big *but* coming?"

She bit her lower lip, nibbling the edge as though she could chew off a chunk of courage. Because it really took courage to walk away from the possibility of seeing Jason again. However infrequently, however great the risk of heartbreak, she knew that she'd go for it. But for Darren.

"You have to understand. Darren's the most important thing in the world to me. I could never do anything that would hurt him."

If anything, Jason simply looked more puzzled. A small frown pulled his eyebrows together as though she had spoken in a language he wasn't familiar with. "But I like Darren. He's a great kid. And, not that I want to come across all high on myself or anything, but I think he likes me, too."

A bubble of laughter burst from her. "Like you? He worships you." The bubble burst and sagged like a spent balloon. "Which is the problem. Don't you see? His father's already let him down more than any boy should be let down. I have to be so careful." She shrugged helplessly. "We'd see you once in a while, watch you on TV on Sundays and then when you got—" she shrugged, looking for the appropriate way to say he'd dump her when something shinier came along "—distracted…"

"Distracted? What are you talking about?"

"You're a celebrity. You go to parties, like the ball the other night, with the rich and famous. You date swimsuit models."

"Only once, and she was a very nice woman. Went on to get her bachelor's degree. You'd like her." If he realized she could only know about his dating a swimsuit model by following his career rather more closely than she might have led him to believe, he didn't call her on it.

"But, don't you see? I could never compete with that."

He reached out with his other hand until both of hers were captured within his grasp. Warm and sure, those hands that could steer a car at ridiculous speeds, and then sign autographs for thousands of adoring fans. "You feeling a little insecure or something?"

"Let's just say I'm not a swimsuit model."

"I don't care about that. I don't care what your body looks like—" His eyes crinkled and shut as though he knew he'd just landed in it. "That's not what I meant at all. Of course I care, I mean, I'm sure you're gorgeous, naked, and even if you're not perfect, I don't care."

He opened his eyes slowly since she hadn't said anything and sagged in relief at her obvious amusement. "You see what I mean? I'm not some smooth guy. I'm me. The same guy who fumbled all over himself in high school."

"But you're not that guy anymore. You're Jason Bane, the NASCAR race car driver and if you break my heart I could survive. But I couldn't survive if you broke Darren's."

The twinkle appeared, deep in his eyes. "I could break your heart?"

Lie or not lie? Protect herself or go for the truth? She felt at least she owed him the truth. "Yes. I think you could."

"Well, you're breaking mine right now. How do we know unless we give this thing a try? I can't promise things will work out. I know I like you more than I've liked a woman in a long time, and Darren—well, I wouldn't want to hurt him. Not for the world. So, do we kiss and say goodbye in case somebody gets hurt? Is that how you want to live your life?"

"I don't think you—"

"You can't tell me there hasn't been another man in your life since your husband left."

"Well, not exactly. I've had some men…friends. But nothing serious. And obviously I keep some parts of my life private from Darren."

"So, then, theoretically, I could come to town from time to time and hang out with him and you, and if there was a part of that that was between you and me, we could keep it to ourselves."

"But what if he got hurt? What if you stopped coming and we—I—"

He got up, stepped around to her side of the

table, pulled her to him and kissed her. Which was truly unfair because it knocked every sensible argument out of her head. His lips were so warm, so sure, so absolutely right on hers. The connection between them was so instant and powerful that she wanted to collapse against his strong chest and let the kiss lead wherever it would. After a long time, he broke away slowly.

"I'm not sure Darren's the one you're worried about. I think maybe you're scared for yourself."

"Of what?"

"I don't know. Why don't you tell me?"

She smiled wryly. In the corner Darren let out a cry of triumph, which meant he'd beaten some foe or other. "Maybe it's the big fancy boyfriend jetting into the little town and sweeping me off my feet. Then dumping me on my butt. Maybe that's what I'm afraid of."

"You know, driving is a job. It's what I do. The rest is—I don't know—window dressing. I wouldn't care if I was racing some old dirt track with a rusty car and an engine I built myself, like I used to. Oh, don't get me wrong, being in the big show is great. The money's nice, the fans are cool, but none of that matters. Inside I'm the same guy I've always been. You need to believe that."

Darren came running up. "Can I have another five bucks?"

Jason pulled out a ten and handed it to him.

"Thanks." The boy took one look at his mother's face and stopped. "You okay, Mom?"

"Yes, of course."

"You look kind of funny. Sort of sad."

"I'm only sorry we have to go tomorrow."

"You know what you need?" he asked in a tone of authority.

"What?"

"You need a Christmas miracle. Then we could stay here forever!" And with that he was gone.

A Christmas miracle sounded like an excellent idea. Or a crystal ball that could reassure her about the future. Or maybe a fairy godmother who could give her a handsome jet-setting prince and promise them happily ever after.

"At least give me your phone number."

What could she do? She was only human.

CHAPTER ELEVEN

DARREN TURNED ON his Santa game and found he didn't really feel like hurling rabid reindeer and mutant elves at the poor guy with the sack of presents. He was only trying to do his job. Besides, every time he looked at the Santa on his screen, the face reminded him of the old dude at Bailey's.

And the wish he'd made aloud.

He stared out the window, feeling as if he was inside a snow globe. Florida and their time with Jason Bane seemed a long time ago in a land faraway.

Fairy-tale stuff.

With no happy ending.

How could he have allowed himself to believe, even for five seconds that a retired fatso in a red suit could make his wishes come true?

He hadn't. Duh. But saying what he wanted out loud, watching his mom and Jason hangout together, laugh, and even kiss—yeah, he'd seen them when they didn't know he'd been watching—had given him ideas.

He knew his mom talked to Jason on the phone, and he was pretty sure she was e-mailing the driver, but he wanted a dad not a pen pal.

The phone rang.

He wasn't planning to answer it, but he heard the shower running upstairs and knew he'd never hear the end of it if he ignored the ringing.

"Hello?"

"Darren? Hey. It's Jason."

"Hi." Knowing it was long distance, he said, "Mom's in the shower. Want me to get her to call you back?"

"No. I wanted to talk to you. Too bad you don't have your own cell phone."

"I know. I'm practically the last person on the planet who doesn't have one. But Mom said 'No' about fifty times."

He heard Jason's low chuckle. "How many times you gonna keep asking?"

"At least fifty more."

"That's the spirit. So, listen, I want to talk to you. Man-to-man."

Nobody had ever called him a man before without sticking the word *young* in front of it, which usually meant he was in big trouble. "Okay."

"I'm thinking of coming to visit you guys for Christmas. But I know it's a family time, and if you want to spend the holiday with your mom and whoever, I totally understand."

For a second Darren felt the way he had that time he got laryngitis. As if he couldn't get a sound to come out of his throat that wasn't a weird squeak. Finally he managed to croak, "You want to come here for Christmas?"

"Yeah. If you're cool with it."

"Oh, yeah. I'm cool with it." Cool? He was so pumped he jumped in the air, almost touching the ceiling with his free hand.

"Good. That's great. Then I'll talk to your mom and see what she thinks."

Darren stopped jumping, his brain working almost as fast as his heart was hammering. "No, wait, don't do that."

"What? You've changed your mind? I promise you, dude, I'm not trying to take anything away from you, it's—"

"No, no. I want you to come and my mom will totally want you to come. But I think you should surprise her."

"Surprise her?"

He could not believe that he was giving advice to a NASCAR driver who'd ended his season in the top ten, but then Darren had lived with his mom for ten years, so he figured he knew her pretty well. "Yeah. She loves surprises and she hardly ever gets any." He thought of the baseball he'd blasted through the kitchen window last summer. It had landed in the spaghetti sauce she was stirring. "Not good surprises."

"You sure?"

Darren didn't know how he was so sure, some kind of instinct, but he was. He'd caught his mom looking at the picture of him and Jason she'd pulled off the digital camera, framed and hung on the living room wall. He was pretty sure her Christmas wish and his would be the very same. He thought she was in love with the driver. He knew this because the only other person, besides her parents, that his mom ever looked at that way, was him.

"Okay. I'm trusting you on this one."

"I got your back." Which was a line he'd heard on TV, but which sounded perfect.

"I'm flying in Christmas Eve. Do they still do the midnight service at church?"

"Uh-huh."

"Great. We've got a date. You got a pen? Write down my cell phone number. You can reach me anytime. If there's a problem or there's something you think I should know, give me a call or text me."

He scribbled the number down then folded the scrap of paper and stuffed it deep in the pocket of his jeans. For the first time he was glad they didn't have call display. His mom would never know who had called.

His gut was churning, but in a good way, as though he'd drunk too much soda in a hurry. This was going to be a great surprise.

CHRISTMAS WAS ALWAYS HARD, Emily thought as she tipped ginger into yet another batch of cookie batter. It was such a family occasion. From saccharine movies on TV to advertising in magazines, she was bombarded with images of rosy-cheeked, happy families. Mom, Dad, a few kids, the grandparents, the bungalow festooned with homemade cranberry wreaths, all reaching out to make her feel as though she'd failed. Even the grandparents had jumped ship, retiring to Palm Springs after her mother's arthritis got bad.

Emily was doing the best she could. The oven

timer dinged and she took a tray of gingersnaps out of the oven, filling the kitchen with their spicy scent. She was worried that Darren was feeling inadequate, too, because he'd been nagging her incessantly about decorating their house extra special this year, and whining for more kinds of home baking.

What worried her most was that he'd flatly refused to go to the Christmas Eve potluck hosted by his friend Ben's family. They were the calendar image of holiday perfection. If they weren't such nice people, she'd have to hate them on principle.

"But what will we do if we don't go to Ben's family?" she asked him. "It's a tradition. We go there for dinner and then we all go down to the midnight carol service."

Darren shrugged his bony shoulders. "I want to stay home this year."

She put down the spatula she was using to transfer the ginger cookies from the pan to a cooling rack and turned to look at her son already gobbling his first cookie, still floppy with heat, so he had to suck in cool air at the same time he was munching. Not a pretty sight. "Did you have a fight with Ben?"

He shook his head, swallowed, gulped milk and

said, "I want to do something different this year, that's all. Maybe we could rent a movie or something."

But he wouldn't meet her eyes, and she was always the one wanting to rent movies, not him. She nibbled at her lower lip trying to think what else would make her son so uncharacteristically antisocial. "Is this about your father?"

He did meet her eyes at those words. "No. He's in Texas, right? What's that got to do with anything?"

"I just wondered if maybe you were upset that he won't be here?"

"Mom, I haven't seen Dad at Christmas since I was four. He sent me a card and a check. I'll probably see him in the summer if he gets up here. It's fine."

And, she thought, if she knew her son at all, he was fine. She went back to her cookies and suddenly recalled what the counselor she'd seen after the divorce had told her. "Darren is his own person. Sometimes he'll go through things that have absolutely nothing to do with you, or your ex-husband or the divorce. Relax and enjoy him."

When Darren took his fourth cookie off the cooling rack she said, "Okay. This year we'll do it your way. What movie should we get?"

"I don't know. What do you want to see?"

"Well, I think we should get a movie for you and one for me." She paused to reflect. "I'm going to choose a Christmas movie. You know what I loved when I was a kid?"

He shook his head.

"*Miracle on 34th Street.* It's about a little girl who doesn't believe in Santa and who gets a Christmas miracle."

"Sounds like your kind of movie," he said without much enthusiasm. "I'll probably get *Space Heist 4.* We haven't seen it yet."

"That's a double bill you don't see very often," she said, feeling suddenly more cheerful. "I think it's a great idea. We'll have fun just the two of us. And you can pick anything you want for dinner."

"Pizza."

"Deal."

CHAPTER TWELVE

HE WAS GOING HOME, Jason thought. Odd how
Hammersfield was still the place he thought of as
home, even though he hadn't been back there in
more than a decade. And the thought of Christmas
in the snowbelt with Emily and Darren seemed
suddenly a lot more appealing than spending it in
his folks' town house in St. Pete, golfing with his
Dad on Christmas Day, dodging his parents' extremely unsubtle attempts to match him up with all
the daughters, nieces and sometimes marriage-aged
granddaughters of their friends and neighbors.

Of course, the only way he could stop his
mother from all but forcing him at gunpoint to
spend the holidays with her and his dad was to
admit the truth. He'd lost his heart to his high
school crush. His mom even remembered Emily as
"that nice Calder girl. Pretty as a picture, too."

"She still is. She's got a son. A nice kid. You'd like him."

"Are you going to marry her?" He couldn't decide if his mom was more excited about gaining a daughter-in-law or an instant grandson.

Damn. She wasn't his mother for nothing. "She doesn't know it yet, Mom, but if she'll have me, yes I am." He'd known that night on the beach that he couldn't let Emily go. But not until she and Darren had left, leaving a huge hole in his life, where he'd never noticed a hole before, had he realized how much he cared for them both. He thought maybe they needed him, too. Darren obviously lacked a man in his life, and recalling the way Emily kissed, she definitely shouldn't be letting all that sexy go to waste.

"Oh, darling. I'm so happy for you. Should we have the wedding here? Or at your house? Or—"

"Mom. She hasn't said yes yet."

"She will," said his mom in that tone that suggested only a born fool would turn down the chance to marry her boy. "Well, you bring her and her son to meet us as soon as things are settled."

"I will." Then he spoke to his dad for a few minutes, and after he hung up, immediately set about making his travel arrangements.

He bought a few gifts, checking his impulses to go all out since he didn't want to embarrass her. A racing simulator game for Darren, and the kind of geeky books he'd have liked himself at that age and truthfully still enjoyed. Emily was a lot harder to buy for. He wanted to give her everything, but he didn't want to freak her out. Or push her too fast. He hovered in front of jewelry store windows looking at diamond rings and then walked quickly on. Finally, on December 23, with time running out, he plunged inside a jewelry boutique and walked up to a glass display case of winking diamond rings.

"Can I help you?"

"Yes."

He stood there, feeling foolish. The clerk was about thirty, curvy with exotic good looks and a Cuban accent. He didn't think she'd recognized him, but he couldn't be sure. What if she blabbed to somebody in the media that he was buying an engagement ring? The news would be out on the racing blogs before he'd stepped on the plane.

"I'm looking for a pair of earrings."

She glanced down at the diamond rings he'd been studying. "Earrings?"

"Yes. For my cousin."

He ended up with a very nice pair of earrings

that he'd chosen for the stone. Some kind of rare sapphire, the jewel was the color of Emily's eyes. He had them gift wrapped.

Then he woke up on the twenty-fourth with a sense of anticipation that equaled the excitement he'd felt before his first NASCAR race. With some serious nerves thrown in.

As he packed his case, he knew suddenly that he couldn't wait. He wanted to ask Emily to marry him while he was in Hammersfield. He'd lost her once because he hadn't worked up the nerve to ask her an important question. He wasn't going to lose her again.

The same instinct that had impelled him to get Crystal to choose Darren's entry, the same instinct that had gotten him where he was professionally, told him to go for it. He would have said he didn't believe in love at first sight, except now he knew it had happened to him.

Twelve years ago.

He couldn't go back to the store where he'd bought the earrings. He couldn't chance going any-where he could be recognized, and because he lived in Florida he was pretty well-known in Miami.

Then it hit him. Bailey's. They had a jewelry de-partment and Crystal would make sure nobody blabbed. He threw his bag in the back of his car, figuring he'd head to the airport straight from Bailey's. Of course the traffic was murder. He'd rather drive a track at 180 miles per hour any day than navigate Miami.

On Christmas Eve.

At last Jason pulled into Bailey's parking lot, and by following a harassed-looking guy loaded down with shopping bags, nabbed his parking spot. Then he sprinted into the store.

The jewelry section was swarming with last-minute shoppers, mostly male. He wasn't the only one interested in diamond rings, either. He'd always thought it was sort of lame to get engaged on Christmas. As if the guy got out of buying a present by giving his girl the ring. But he already had the earrings, and doing it this way felt right.

"Ah, Jason, I'm glad to see you," said a booming male voice behind him.

Jason felt like cursing. He'd hoped the ball cap he was wearing would disguise him from his fans. He forced a smile, turned, ready to do the publicity thing and realized it wasn't a fan accosting him. It was the department-store Santa.

"Chris. Hi, how are you?"

"Oh, well, can't complain. Getting ready for my

annual holiday, though. I usually take one in January." He twinkled. "Christmas is my busy time."

"Right." Maybe Chris was a method actor or something. He was truly getting into the Santa thing.

"I wonder if you could do me a favor?"

"Sure. What?"

Santa handed him a flat rectangular box. "Would you give this to Darren when you see him?"

"How do you know I'll be seeing Darren?"

The broad shoulders, muscular as though they'd been carrying heavy sacks, rose and fell. "One hears things."

Paige must have mentioned it to Crystal for some reason, he decided. Though it wasn't like Crystal to gossip. "Sure." He stuck the package in his pocket.

"Can I help you with some last-minute shopping?"

"I, uh…" Oh, what the heck. He wouldn't mind some advice and Chris was a good guy. "I want to get Emily a ring. A diamond."

Santa didn't look remotely surprised. "That is very good news. I know you'll all be very happy." And he didn't say it in a way that suggested he hoped, it was as though he could see the future and really knew they'd be happy together. A sudden memory of that strange vision Jason had had of them as a family, with a baby girl in Emily's arms came back to him in a rush. There was something truly spooky about this guy. But in a good way.

Oddly, it took Jason less than five minutes to choose the ring. He knew the minute he saw it that it was the one. Not overly flashy, which he knew she'd hate, the ring was a solid platinum band with a diamond set flat into it. He imagined it would be more practical for a teacher who did a lot of crafts, and a mom with a baby. *Oh, boy.*

He didn't have this one wrapped. He simply slipped the jewelry box into his pocket.

He turned to Chris and said, "Thanks. I better get going or I'll miss my plane."

Santa was shaking his hand heartily and wishing him luck when his cell phone buzzed. It was Paige. "Hey, why aren't you home with your family? You're supposed to be on vacation."

"Jason, I've got bad news. Your flight is canceled."

"What? When's the next one?"

"I guess you haven't been following the weather. There's a huge snowstorm hitting the Midwest. Hammersfield airport is closed. I'm trying to get you on a commercial flight through Minneapolis, but most of those flights are being canceled, too."

Sudden and unfamiliar panic gripped him. "But I have to get to Hammersfield tonight."

"I might be able to get you on a train, but there are delays on the track. You could get there tomorrow, maybe the twenty-sixth. No guarantees."

"No. No. That's not good enough. Damn it, there must be something we can do."

"I'm doing everything I can, Jason, but it's crazy out there. It would take a miracle to get you to Hammersfield tonight."

How had he never even thought about weather? Because it was seventy-five degrees today in Miami, he'd forgotten all about the winter storms that were so frequent back home. He should have given himself extra time to get there. He should have—he should have realized that he didn't want to be apart from Emily and Darren on any of the special holidays from now on. Not Christmas or Halloween or the Fourth of July.

Chris watched him with a wrinkled forehead as he snapped his cell phone shut and briefly recounted what Paige had told him. "She said it would take a miracle to get me there tonight."

Chris nodded. "Yes. It will. Hand me your phone."

CHAPTER THIRTEEN

IT WAS NICE, EMILY THOUGHT, sitting cozily in front of a fire with snow swirling outside the windows and no need to hustle up boots and mitts and a casserole or dig her car out of one of the worst snowstorms of the season. Tonight was about her and Darren enjoying a special night together.

She lit candles, looked around at the decorations she and her son had hung everywhere. The tree was a monument to his increasing skills as an artist. From lumpy silver bells made out of foil and egg cartons done when he was three, to the latest ornament he'd brought home from school. It incorporated his school photo with a poem. Maybe he was no laureate, but his poem had made her cry.

Maybe her life hadn't turned out as the fairy tale she'd once imagined, but it was a good life.

Sure it would be nice to share all of it—the joys,

the responsibilities, the worries—with a man, but maybe that wasn't in her cards. Her thoughts immediately flicked to Jason Bane, as they did far too often lately.

To her surprise and delight, he hadn't given up on her. He called regularly and e-mailed her a lot. She wondered what people did before technology made it all so easy.

He was a pretty good writer, too. He told her funny stories from the road, sent her photos and sometimes they reminisced about their almost-but-not-quite shared past.

"How come you've never come home?" she asked him one night when she was sitting in front of her computer, thinking that a metal and plastic box with a screen was no substitute for face-to-face communication.

"I don't know," he replied. "I guess after my folks moved to Florida I didn't really have a good reason to come home. I miss some of my buddies and the places I used to hang out, but I don't want to be some jock who made good who shows up and expects a town parade, you know? But, maybe now, I've got a reason. I miss you."

Okay, so her skin shivered at those words. She was only human.

"I should warn you that Olaf's Diner features photos of you on all the walls, as well as your high school yearbook photo."

"What? You're kidding me. That is worse than I imagined. Anything else you need to warn me about?"

"The people who bought your parents' old house applied to the town council to get a plaque to put out front." She giggled as she typed, imagining his face. He replied immediately.

"Did they get permission?"

She laughed aloud in the quiet house. "Yep. It's one of those ornate plaques that announces your birthplace. Very elegant. Historic, even."

"I have to come up there to make sure you aren't making all this stuff up."

"Well, the golf tournament is in June. If you're serious. I sent Paige all the information." June seemed a thousand years away.

"Duly noted."

They chatted for a little longer and then he said he had to go. He hadn't wished her a Merry Christmas so she'd assumed she'd hear from him today. Maybe he was planning to call on the day itself, she thought. He hadn't asked her what she was doing, and she hadn't asked him. Maybe they both realized that their relationship existed outside their real worlds. It had to, that was the only possible way to make this work.

Jason had made her feel, for the first time since her husband had left, that she was a vital, attractive woman. If nothing else, meeting him again had reminded her that she had needs. Perhaps, one day soon, she'd be ready for a real relationship again.

"Let's watch your movie first, Mom."

"Okay. I'll go phone for the pizza."

If she hadn't been looking right at him, she wouldn't have noticed that Darren turned his head to check the clock on the table before shaking his head. "I'm not too hungry yet. Let's watch some of the movie first."

She'd known this kid for ten years—which made it easy to figure by now that something was up. He was still enough of a child that suppressed excitement made him a dizzy companion to live with. He bounced and ran all over the place, and he was definitely keeping a secret from her. Maybe someone had collaborated with him on a gift. Whatever it was, she'd go along with any kind of surprise he had planned. He was so sweet, her little boy. She wished he didn't have to grow up quite so quickly.

"We should call soon, though. The roads are getting bad with all the snow." She sent a quick glance outside. Her van was already a shapeless white mass. "I hope everybody's relatives got in okay."

"What do you mean?"

"Last I heard on the news, the main highway into town was closed and the airport's been closed for hours. With this storm I think a lot of travelers are going to be spending their Christmas in airports."

"Why didn't you tell me?" He practically shouted the words. Before she could think of an appropriate answer as to why she wasn't suddenly giving hourly meteorological reports, he'd jumped off the couch and sped to the window.

"I hate this!" he yelled at the swirling white stuff. "Snow sucks!"

Not knowing what else to do, she went to the phone and ordered the pizza. Maybe he had low blood sugar, she thought. She didn't think he'd eaten much today, with all the excitement over the holiday. Please let him not be getting sick.

She poured him some orange juice and made him drink it, which he did in sullen gulps.

"Shall we watch the movie?"

He shrugged, looking as tragic as he had when his hamster died. "Might as well."

"SANTA, IF I GET THERE tonight, I will never doubt you again. Give me the directions and I'll—"

"You'll never find it. I'm taking you. Come on."

So Jason found himself jogging out to the parking lot with a very conspicuous companion. When they got to the car they collided, heading for the driver's side.

"I'm driving," said Santa.

"I'm a professional," Jason argued.

"Trust me, boy."

And since Chris seemed to have found transport home against impossible odds, Jason figured he might as well. So he got into the passenger side and Santa got into the driver's side of Jason's black convertible.

"Put the top down," Chris ordered.

"This isn't a joy ride."

"Trust me," he snapped once more.

Jason put down the top.

As they roared out of the parking lot, the traffic was, if anything, worse than earlier. "We've got to get moving if you're to make it in time."

"Explain this to me again?"

"My old friend Rudy has a son, Nigel, who is a bush pilot for a forestry firm. Rudy was going to fly his floatplane to visit his son for the holiday anyway. He's waiting for you at the marina. He'll fly you into West Virginia, and Nigel will take you the rest of the way."

"But Hammersfield airport is closed."

"Yes, of course it is. Inconvenient. So Nigel will fly you out to the forestry company's private airstrip. It's just outside Hammersfield. He's an excellent pilot. You'll be in good hands. From there, he's arranged a four-wheel drive to meet you and take you where you're going." Chris made a growling sound. "But first we've got to get through this wretched traffic." Then he laid on the horn.

Jason slunk lower in his seat and pulled down his ball cap as low as he could. If only Chris would take off the damn Santa hat it wouldn't be quite so bad. But Chris had other ideas.

"Merry Christmas!" he bellowed, waving grandly, as he yanked the wheel and pulled the car out in front of shocked motorists.

"Find a radio station that's playing holiday tunes," he ordered, "and crank it up, boy."

"I don't know which one of us is crazier," Jason muttered, but he did as he was told. Sure enough, a Santa Claus tune was soon blasting the air. *Perfect.*

But it was working! Santa Ho, Ho, Ho'd while driving as if he was racing an obstacle course. He wove in and out of traffic like a maniacal stunt driver. Punk-haired and tattooed, blue-haired and poodled, the other drivers laughed and waved. He cut people off, didn't seem to care which side of the damn road he drove on, and drivers honked, not out of frustration, but in a cheerful way. As if being cut off by a red elf in a convertible was a good thing.

Soon they were barreling along the highway, palm trees whizzing past, beaches and high-rises a blur.

"Where did you learn to drive?" Jason had to ask.

Chris's eyes crinkled as he smiled. "I've had years of practice."

They screeched to a stop near a dock. The float-plane was ready, a man standing beside it consulting his watch.

"There you are. Now go."

"I can't thank you enough, Chris."

"No time for thanks. I've got to run. I've got a busy night ahead myself."

Jason grinned at him. "Of course you do. If there's ever anything I can do—"

"Give Darren his present. It'll save me a stop."

CHAPTER FOURTEEN

"WASN'T THAT WONDERFUL?" Emily sighed as the credits rolled. "That was always my favorite Christmas movie. The little girl was so cute when she pulled Santa's beard and discovered it was real. And then, in the end, when she sees the house she's been dreaming about, and you know she got her Christmas miracle…"

"It was lame. As if some department store Santa could ever be for real. What a crock."

"The pizza's late. Maybe they got held up on the roads. I can see what we've got in the freezer."

"Whatever."

She was heading for the kitchen when the doorbell rang.

"I guess the pizza made it after all." She picked up her wallet and headed for the door. A man's head showed, wavy through the frosted glass.

She opened the door and promptly dropped her wallet.

Jason stood there. Jason in a winter coat, his nose red from the cold, carrying a big bag of presents.

She couldn't even speak. She simply gaped at him, saw the happiness and maybe even a shade of doubt in the eyes looking back at her.

She had no idea whether she moved, or he did, but suddenly she was in his arms wrapped tight. His lips were cold; snowflakes melted against her hands as she hugged him to her.

Then somehow they were inside, and he'd kicked the door shut behind him, never letting her go. The bag of presents hit the floor with a thud and finally she pulled away, laughing.

"You got here," her son said from behind her, sounding as stunned as she felt. "I can't believe you made it."

"Merry Christmas, Darren."

She had no idea how it happened, but it seemed the most natural thing in the world for Darren to throw out his arms and get a Jason-size hug, too. The driver threw her son in the air as though he weighed no more than a pillow.

Her son's happy, laughing face turned to her

when he was once again back on the ground. His grumpy mood obliterated by the joy shining from him. "I totally fooled you, didn't I? Me and Jason planned the surprise totally behind your back."

He turned to Jason. "I almost blew it a bunch of times. I'd start to say, 'When Jason gets here' and then have to shut myself up."

She laughed, feeling light and happy and hopeful. Which should have been scary but wasn't. "Well, you two both fooled me." She couldn't help herself, she reached out and touched Jason's arm, almost to convince herself he was real—and really here.

"Let me take your coat," she said, suddenly leaping into hostess mode to cover her shyness. "All we have for dinner is pizza, if I'd known you were coming I'd—" She gasped. Turned to Darren. "That's why you didn't want to go to the potluck."

He grinned so widely she could have counted all his molars.

There was much laughter, and the two guys swapped stories of how they'd both almost blown the surprise. As she stood there watching them, it was hard to decide which of them looked the most boyish.

"Can I put these under the tree?" Jason asked, indicating the bag of goodies.

"Yes. Of course." She threaded her fingers together, almost wishing one of them had blown her surprise. "I'm so sorry. I don't have anything for you."

"Well, you didn't know I was coming, so why would you?" He grinned up at her from where he was kneeling beneath the tree. "I'm just happy to be here."

In that moment she knew. As hard as she'd tried not to, she'd gone and fallen smack in love with Jason Bane.

But, she realized, it wasn't the fancy driver with the fan club and huge sponsorship deals who'd stolen her heart, it was the boy she still remembered, who could look serious and humorous at the same time and who seemed to sense the connection between them as strongly as she did.

He drew a square, wrapped package out of the bag. "This one's for Darren from the Bailey's Santa, you know the one we posed with for that photo shoot?" He settled it under the tree. "Darren made quite an impression on him, I guess. In fact, that Santa is the one who got me here."

He'd turned back to settle the parcels to his liking. She couldn't help but laugh. Was he pulling their legs? "What? You hitched a ride on his sleigh?"

"No, but in case you haven't been watching, there's a huge snowstorm out there. The Hammersfield airport's closed. All the flights were canceled. When Chris tracked me down today, to give me that gift for Darren, he was there when I got the news. I could not find a way to get here in time for Christmas." He stopped, rose and said, "I told him it was really important I be here for the big day, and you know what he said?"

"What?" It was Darren who asked, his voice sharp with eagerness.

"He said, 'Oh, I know,' in that way he has, as though he'd read my mind." He shook his head. "There's something a little spooky about that guy. I think maybe he's got delusions that he really is Santa."

"Oh, yeah. I know," agreed Darren.

"So he stood there, looking down at his black plastic boots for a minute and I told him Paige had said it would take a miracle to get me here tonight. Then Chris said, 'Yes, that's what I was thinking.' As though a miracle was a possible solution.

"It was the weirdest thing but I'd almost given up hope, and a retiree in a red suit was getting me all fired up again."

The doorbell rang at that moment. "Now what?"

If it had been Santa himself in a sleigh pulled by reindeer dropping by to finish the story, she wouldn't have been a bit surprised.

It was the pizza.

"I would have cooked something special if I'd known you were coming."

"I love pizza."

"See, Mom? I told you. Pizza's perfect for us guys."

"Then I guess it's good enough for me."

As they chowed down, they all ended up talking and laughing over Jason's harrowing trip. "We landed in a lake in West Virginia. That was cool. Then they put me in a plane with skis on the bottom of it to get us here. The pilot radioed ahead to give the forestry guys our ETA and then told me not to worry because they were sending out snowmobiles to flatten the snow on the landing strip so we could land."

"I wish I'd been there," Darren said, his face alight.

"I wish you had been, too. And I could have been somewhere else. I'm telling you, when the bush pilot came down over those trees, snow swirling everywhere, the little plane bouncing against gusts of wind, I shut my eyes and prayed. I did. I've never been so scared."

"You should have waited and come later," she protested, half laughing because, despite his pretended fear, she could tell he'd enjoyed his unorthodox trip enormously.

He wiped his hands on a napkin. "Couldn't. I promised Darren I was coming." He grinned at Darren. "Besides, when we got off the plane, they let me drive one of the snowmobiles that was to get us to the main office where they had a four-wheel drive waiting. Those guys were great."

If she hadn't already realized she was in love with Jason Bane, she'd have fallen all over again right that minute. A man who would keep his promise to a boy, even if it meant traveling in floatplanes, bush planes and snowmobiles was a man to keep.

"Thank you," she said softly.

"Can I open one present tonight, Mom? Just one? Please?"

Certain he was going to choose whatever Jason had brought for him, she agreed. "Only one."

To her surprise, her son grabbed the one from Chris, Bailey's Santa.

He ripped open the wrapping to reveal a framed photograph. She recognized it immediately as one of the poses from the store's shoot. It wasn't the one that had appeared in the Miami papers, however. Santa didn't even appear in this pose. It was a grouping of the three of them. Jason with one arm around her and the other resting on Darren's shoulder. The three of them looked so right together, she thought, seeing their happy grins in triplicate. If she hadn't known those people, she'd have sworn they were one of thousands of happy families having their annual Christmas photo taken, the one that would go on their holiday cards along with the Christmas letter to friends and family.

The card with it read, "To Darren, Merry Christmas to you and your family. Chris."

She thought Darren might have been disappointed, but he read the message twice, yelled, "Sweet!" and put the photo carefully on the mantel.

"Is there some special significance to that picture that I'm missing?" she finally asked.

He gave her a look that seemed much older than his years. "It's kind of between me and Chris."

AFTER DARREN FELL ASLEEP on the couch, Jason picked him up and carried him into his bedroom, tactfully not mentioning the fan wall devoted to his racing career.

Back downstairs she and Jason sat side by side

on the couch in front of the fire. "I guess we won't be making it to the midnight carol service," he said.

"Do you mind?"

"Nope. We can always do it next year."

He leaned closer and put an arm around her, hugging her tight. "This is how Christmas should be. A roaring fire, your woman by your side, kids tucked up in bed, the dog at your feet." He looked around. "Wait a minute, where's the dog?"

"We don't have a dog."

"You don't have a dog? Why not?"

"Because Darren and I are both at school all day, and I have enough to do. Darren would love a pet, but the way things are now, it wouldn't be fair to the dog."

"What you need is a man around the house to do things like shovel the drive and walk the dog."

"And the garbage. Don't forget taking out the garbage."

"Why is that always the first thing a woman thinks of in terms of a man's job jar?"

"Because it's such a sucky job?"

"Okay, assuming I was willing to haul trash and other manly but possibly disgusting jobs, would you be willing to put up with me for a while?"

She looked into his eyes and saw everything she

needed to know. "I think I could manage to put up with you for a while."

He kissed her, long and slow, as if they had all the time in the world. "How long do you think you could handle me?"

"Indefinitely?"

He nodded. "The word I had in mind was *forever.*"

"Yes," she said, leaning in for another kiss. "Forever sounds perfect."

* * * * *

CHRISTMAS PAST

Debra Webb

To the loyal fans of the Colby Agency: Enjoy!

CHAPTER ONE

Colby Agency, Chicago
Four Days before Christmas

VICTORIA COLBY-CAMP STOOD at her window and admired the snow drifting to the city streets below. She hoped it would stay for Christmas. Her granddaughter was so excited about the coming holiday. A lovely blanket of white for Christmas morning would be perfect.

"Victoria."

Turning at the sound of her personal assistant's voice, Victoria shifted her thoughts from her granddaughter to the business of running her agency. "Yes, Mildred?"

"Mr. Harris is here."

"Thank you. Send him in." Victoria moved to her desk and waited for the famed NASCAR team owner to make his entrance. She had met Alonzo Harris for the first time two weeks ago when he came to Chicago looking for her agency's help with a somewhat personal matter for which he needed the utmost discretion. With a strategy in place, the news that he would visit again this morning had come as somewhat of a surprise.

Texas born and raised, Alonzo Harris swaggered into Victoria's office. The corners of his eyes creased as a broad smile stretched across his face. "I don't know how you folks survive in this cold." He'd already removed his coat and hat and left both with Mildred.

"The cold winters forge character, Mr. Harris, much like those scorching West Texas summers give a gentleman grit." He was every bit the charismatic man he was purported to be by the media. His love of racing ran deep in his bones.

Harris chuckled. "Touché, ma'am." He thrust his broad hand across her desk. "I sincerely appreciate you taking the time to see me this morning. I realize my visit was a bit impromptu."

Victoria gave his hand a firm shake. "When a man flies all the way from Texas on a snowy winter day, I can always make time. Please, have a seat, Mr. Harris."

Being the Southern gentleman he was, he waited until Victoria had settled into her chair before lowering his tall frame into one of the wingback chairs flanking her wide, mahogany desk.

"As you're aware—" Victoria cut right to the chase "—I have assigned Molly Clark to your case. She's an experienced climber and grew up in Colorado. She'll be right at home in Aspen."

Harris nodded. "I'm pleased for the most part with your choice. I read her dossier and she seems quite capable."

Something else Victoria liked about the man, he also preferred to get straight to the point. "She is very capable."

"My concern," he said, relaxing into his chair, "I suppose, is more her lack of experience with your agency. She's new, isn't she?"

Victoria smiled. "Brand-new. However, rest assured, no one is brought on board at the Colby Agency without undergoing rigorous reviews. Our hiring guidelines are unmatched in the business of private investigations. Molly Clark met every stringent requirement. And though she has no field experience per se, she has years of experience in mountain rescue and recovery. That makes her an invaluable asset under the circumstances."

Harris gave due consideration to her reasoning, then went on with his. "You understand that Jason isn't your typical celebrity. He closes himself off, particularly since the accident. I fear that Ms. Clark will have a difficult time getting close to him. He won't make it easy. She'll need a surprise attack, so to speak, or he'll cut her off at the pass."

Jason Fewell was the team's celebrated driver. His winning record had put him at the very top of the NASCAR prestigious list of drivers. But a mountain-climbing tragedy three years ago had sent his personal life into a tailspin. Though he managed to perform to his usual standards on the track, according to Mr. Harris, behind closed doors the driver grew more and more withdrawn. Two weeks ago Fewell had announced that he was going back to the scene of the tragedy to face his fears once and for all. Harris, as well as the entire Texas Thunder team, was concerned for his safety, since Fewell refused to allow anyone to accompany him.

The past was haunting Fewell. No one knew better how painful that could be than Victoria.

Harris's fears were legitimate, of course, two weeks ago and now. But he did not know Molly Clark. Once her sights were set on a target, she would not stop until the job was done. She would find the crack in Fewell's armor of self-exile and find a way in. Ensuring his safety would be her top priority.

"Trust me, Mr. Harris," Victoria assured him, "if anyone can get close to Jason Fewell, it's Molly. She's the younger sister of four brothers, all extremely competitive young men. Molly learned at a tender age how to hold her own with both difficult and determined men. You needn't worry about her ability to handle the situation."

Harris braced his elbows on the chair arms, laced his fingers and leaned forward. "I didn't come here to question your judgment, Victoria. Truly I didn't. But Jason is like a son to me. If anything happened to that boy, I don't think I could bear it. He's suffered so." Harris shook his head. "The counseling didn't do the trick. I'll be the first to admit that, just as I can understand he feels he has to do this. He needs to find peace. Soon. But I'm worried sick he'll get himself hurt…or worse."

Victoria knew firsthand that the need to find peace could drive a person to a point well beyond reason. Jason felt responsible for his girlfriend's death, though the investigation into the tragic accident had clearly shown equipment failure as the cause. His guilt and fear of again failing someone he cared about were eating him alive.

"I can't guarantee Mr. Fewell will find the peace he's so desperately seeking," Victoria allowed. "That part is up to him. But I can guarantee without reservation that Molly Clark will ensure his safety. And, if she can reach past those barriers of fear and guilt, she'll do all within her power to help him see the truth of what really happened three years ago. Perhaps recognizing the truth will be enough to set him on the right course."

Harris gave a thoughtful nod. "I suppose that's all I can hope for. That or a miracle."

Victoria smiled, hoping to reassure him. "It's almost Christmas, Mr. Harris. Miracles have been known to happen."

CHAPTER TWO

Aspen, Colorado

THE SNOW VALLEY LODGE was packed with ski enthusiasts, but Molly had already spotted her target among the mostly young and remarkably stylish crowd.

Five o'clock on the dot. Jason Fewell had arrived, surprisingly, without the fanfare she'd fully expected. No starstruck chicks right on his heels. No bodyguards. And only two bags.

Wow. He traveled pretty light for a celebrity.

She kept an eye out for a bellhop to show up pushing a cart with the rest of his luggage. But her primary attention remained on the man.

Even from across the room, he appeared taller than she'd gauged by his photographs and video shots. She'd watched several press coverage videos of his racing triumphs. He charmed the crowd, as well as the cameras. The man was a natural. Blond hair, blue eyes—though the latter couldn't be seen just now behind those designer sunglasses he wore. The all-American heartthrob. Born in West Texas, Jason Fewell had grown up dirt-poor. The proverbial rags-to-riches story that people from all walks of life loved to embrace.

But Molly wasn't fooled. She knew the type. All sweet talk and smiles for the public and the paparazzi. Turn off the cameras and close the doors, and he would no doubt turn demanding and unreasonable.

Spoiled by his stardom.

And that was the thing that annoyed her about her first field assignment with the Colby Agency. She had waited five months for it to come and then the assignment was *this*.

A babysitting job.

No mystery. No nasty villains to track down.

Just a rich guy who couldn't cope with loss.

Not fair, Mol. She sighed. Gave herself a mental kick for her lack of sympathy for Fewell's tragic loss. His girlfriend had been killed in that accident. It was a crying shame, no doubt about that. But a man with the physical and mental capacity to endure the rigors of his sport, should have the wherewithal to pull himself back together. That was the part she couldn't comprehend. Molly Clark was a survivor, as were the other members of her family.

When you got knocked down, you pulled yourself up by the bootstraps and went at it again.

Maybe dealing with the loss of her father at such a young age, and then her mother only a couple of years ago, had made her a bit less than sympathetic on the subject. But she wasn't one to wallow and had no patience for those who did.

Life was unfair sometimes. But you couldn't stop living just because it hurt. You sucked it up, and got on with it.

Fewell didn't seem to be able to do that. He continued to be a winner and to give his fans what they wanted, but according to the owner of his team, he'd grown more and more withdrawn on a personal level. He kept the world at a distance.

For Molly that meant one thing—drastic measures would be required if she was going to accomplish her goal. She'd also been forewarned about how difficult it would be to get anywhere near the guy.

She had a foolproof plan for that, too.

Fewell accepted his room key from the clerk.

Time for her to set phase one of her strategy in motion.

She couldn't use the usual tactics; those took time. Time was a luxury she didn't have. Molly had decided to limit Fewell's options to only one.

She smiled as she double-timed it up the stairs.

No way was this hotshot going to outmaneuver Molly Clark. Four older brothers had tried repeatedly and failed.

Babysitting job or not, she intended to not only get the job done, but to impress her employer.

That way maybe the next case she was assigned would be one she could sink her teeth into.

JASON CONSIDERED the stairs, but opted for the elevator. He'd stuffed his clothes and his gear into only two bags, making for a heavy load. The line at the elevator made him wish he'd gone for the stairs, but the lack of sleep the past few days had exhausted his usual endurance level.

He was dead on his feet.

The lobby was jam-packed. He was damned lucky he'd gotten a reservation at all when he'd called just over two weeks ago. A single cancelation, the only one the entire season, the reservation clerk had boasted, came only moments before Jason called. The Snow Valley Lodge was one of the smaller ones in the Aspen area. It pretty much stayed booked from November until July every year. That was the reason he and Cynthia hadn't stayed here three years ago. She'd seen this lodge on one of their previous visits and insisted they had to stay here one day.

Only one day had never come…for her.

He'd stopped experiencing the ache that had once accompanied the mere thought of her name. The shrink had told him that time healed all wounds. But the shrink wasn't entirely accurate. Part of him wouldn't be healed. At least not by the traditional methods, and drugs were out of the question. He'd gone through months of therapy sessions, had increased his physical workout to fight off the disabling panic attacks. He'd even attempted to focus on other personal activities, like volunteering in the off-season. But even if he worked himself into the ground each day, the nights were always the same.

He'd wake up in a cold sweat, his heart pounding, his muscles rigid with tension. Hours of walking the floors was the only way to calm himself enough to sleep.

His doctor and the therapist had insisted the panic attacks would go away in time. As suddenly as they came, the therapist had suggested.

But they hadn't.

They'd only gotten worse.

Jason had to do something radical.

For several weeks he'd been mulling over the idea of taking action. Finally, he'd realized what he had to do.

He had to come back here and face the fears eating away at his insides like a cancer.

A couple waiting on the fringes of the elevator crowd whispered to each other and glanced at Jason.

Not good.

The last thing he wanted was to be recognized.

He considered doing an about-face and heading for the stairs when the elevator doors slid open to admit the next group. His group, thankfully.

He selected floor four on the control panel and moved to the back of the car. Closing his eyes, he attempted to block the chatter of the other passengers.

Didn't work.

One couple was taking their first ski vacation. Another was in Aspen on a long-awaited honeymoon. The other man who had appeared to be alone announced that he and three of his friends were here on a professional challenge. As executives on an advertising team, they wanted to strengthen their cohesiveness with a physical challenge—mountain climbing.

Jason would bet his all-time best test-drive time that he was the only tourist in this town who'd come alone. No significant other…no friends.

Not exactly the best way to spend Christmas, but that was the way he had to do this. Alone. He'd figured out that no one could help him with this thing. No therapy, no encouraging friends. He had to overcome this himself.

There was only one way to accomplish his goal.

Climb back up on that damned mountain. Sit up high where the air was thin and the cold was a lethal enemy. And come to terms with why she had died and he hadn't.

Easy enough.

Yeah, right. He'd had to fight off a panic attack just boarding the plane to come here.

The elevator glided to a stop on four, the top floor of the lodge, and he was the only one left to exit. Funny, he hadn't even noticed the others getting off on the previous floors.

Room 403 was one of four luxury suites on the top floor. Fortunately the suite was located on the west side, which would allow for plenty of good light in the room. The dark was another thing he was having trouble with lately. He hadn't been afraid of the dark since he was a kid.

He shook his head as he slid the key into the lock. If he didn't get a handle on this out-of-control anxiety, he was going to lose the ability to walk out the door at all. He couldn't let that happen.

The green light blinked and he opened the door and stepped into the suite.

Two things struck him as odd the moment the door closed behind him.

The fruity scent of shampoo was in the air, and the television was set to some reality show he wouldn't watch in a million years.

Moving cautiously, he crossed the sitting room and entered the generous bedroom.

An open suitcase sat in the chair by the window, its contents hanging out as if there had been an explosion of silk and cashmere.

He dropped his bags on the floor and walked over to the chair. A pair of silky panties lay on top of the bag. He picked up the scrap of silk and lace and turned it around and around. Not much to it other than a little frilly lace with a tiny pink bow. The matching bra hung from the chair arm.

What the…?

He dropped the panties, turned around to survey the rest of the room more closely and noted other signs of occupancy. A shoulder bag sitting on the floor by the bed. Discarded jeans and sweater. Unlaced boots.

Another bag, this one stationed in the corner near the armoire, held climbing gear.

Had the check-in clerk made a mistake? Given him the wrong room.

He should just leave.

Go back down to the front desk and let them know that there was a mistake.

A lull in the sound on the television channel allowed him to hear the water running in the shower.

Definitely, he had to get out of here. The lady was in the shower. Having her come out naked and find him loitering about was as appealing as a blowout on the final lap.

He was halfway across the room when the bathroom door opened. Amid a billow of sweet-scented steam, a woman emerged wrapped in a towel. Outside of breaking into a full-throttle run, he wasn't getting away before she laid eyes on him.

She screamed.

Jason held up both hands, stop-sign fashion. "It's not what you think. There's been a mistake."

For a single second she stood there staring at him, big brown eyes wide with surprise or maybe fear, dark hair dripping, sending rivulets of water down her bare shoulders. Then she launched into action.

"Damn straight there's been a mistake." She grabbed a bottle of wine from the table next to the bed and held it up like a weapon. "And it was yours. Now get out of here before I call security!"

Jason backed up a step. "Look, I just came to the room the clerk gave me." He waved the key in his hand. "This *is* 403."

"That's right." She glared at him, lifted her chin defiantly. "And it's my room."

"I'm sure a quick call to the desk will straighten this out." Great. This was all he needed. If the woman recognized who he was, she could blow the whole thing out of proportion just to get some hush money. The team's attorneys warned him all the time about situations exactly like this.

"There's nothing to straighten out," she argued, tugging at her slipping towel with her free hand. "This is my room." She sent a narrowed glance at her purse on the floor. "Did you touch any of my stuff?"

There it came. "I did not touch any of your stuff." Except the panties. He swallowed hard. But she didn't have to know that.

She reached behind her for the phone. The towel slipped another inch. She quickly jerked the towel back up the inch or so it had slipped and glared at him for daring to look.

Still clutching the bottle of wine by the neck, she swiped a damp tendril of dark hair from her forehead. "I need a member of management in 403, please." She sent a suspicious glare back at him. "There's an intruder in my room."

Hell. "I'm not an intruder," he growled. "I have a key. One the clerk gave to me."

She ignored him, listened to whatever the front desk had to say. "Thank you." She sent him a triumphant look as she dropped the receiver back into its cradle. "The manager will be right up. He'll straighten this out, and then you'll see that you're in the wrong room."

Jason shook his head. "I'm in the room they assigned me. If—" he let his expression show the doubt he felt that this would be the case "—I'm in the wrong room, the clerk made a mistake. They'll give one of us another room and everything will be fine."

"It won't be me," she shot back. "I was here first. First come, first served, sir."

Jason removed his sunglasses so he could look her directly in the eyes. "That's fine. You stay. I'll take another room." Not a problem! He wasn't that hard to please.

"Wait." Those big brown eyes narrowed again. "I know you."

Defeat dragged his resolve all the way to the floor. Perfect. Now she would want to press whatever charges she could trump up. Or would insist that his Peeping Tom activities had permanently scarred her and generous compensation was essential.

"You're that kooky news anchor guy from CNN who jets around the country. I thought I recognized you even with the sunglasses. Maybe you need a teleprompter to understand this…"

He didn't argue, just let her think what she would.

"…they can't give you another room." She shifted the wine bottle to her other hand. "The place is filled to capacity. There aren't any other rooms. I guess you're out of luck."

Dread sat like a big, cold stone in his gut. She was right. He'd gotten the last room two weeks ago. And this one had only been available because of a last-minute cancelation.

Just great. This whole expedition was off to a spectacular start.

CHAPTER THREE

THE LODGE MANAGER, the concierge and the head reservation clerk were dumbfounded. The three gentlemen and Fewell stared at Molly as if she should admit defeat and forfeit possession of the room.

Not going to happen.

"Sorry." She folded her arms over her chest. To Fewell's obvious relief, she'd gotten dressed while they waited for the lodge powers-that-be to arrive. "No can do. I was here first."

Fewell shook his head. "Fine. I'll move to another lodge." He turned to the concierge. "Can you find me another room someplace else?"

The three staff members looked at each other.

"What?" Fewell demanded, clearly beyond frustrated.

"Sir," the manager confessed, "there are no other rooms. Anywhere."

Fewell looked from one to the other. "You've got to be kidding? In the whole city? That doesn't seem possible."

Victory sent a rush of adrenaline through Molly's veins. "Told you."

He glared at her. "You said there were no other rooms *here.*"

"I said," she countered, "there aren't any available. Period. Believe me, I was happy to get this room, even though I didn't really want to fork over the cost of a suite."

Fewell turned back to the lodge staff. "There's an easy solution to this." Fury simmered in his tone. "Just check your system and see who was first—"

"Are you out of your mind?" Molly demanded. He was determined, she would give him that. "I was already in the suite when you arrived."

The staff's collective gazes swung from Molly to Fewell in anticipation of what he would say next. It was their job to ensure all guests were satisfied with the accommodations and the service. This predicament was unacceptable…and completely beyond their control.

"I mean," Fewell rasped, "who made the reservation first. Surely that's annotated somewhere in the reservation system."

"Actually," the reservation clerk ventured, his hands wringing, "I already checked that. And it seems the reservations were made—" he moistened his lips "—simultaneously."

Disbelief claimed Fewell's face. "Is that even possible?"

"I've never seen it happen before," the manager hastened to assure, "but it does appear to have occurred in this instance." He shook his head grimly. "Madam, sir, I do apologize. I can offer you both a complimentary stay at some other time. But there's simply nothing more I can offer at the moment. One of you will have to accede to the other. We will gladly attempt to find other lodging in a nearby village."

"I'm not leaving," Molly announced, her words in perfect time with the exact ones Fewell uttered.

They stared at each other.

"We'll leave this to the two of you to resolve," the manager offered. "Again, you have our sincerest apologies."

The three men were out the door before the announcement stopped echoing in the room.

Molly would have to call her friend and thank him. His little visit into the lodge's reservation system had not only worked like a charm but had been completely undetectable. As pleased as she was that her old high school buddy's hacking skills were so primo, it was a rather scary thought. Good thing he was one of the good guys.

"All right." Fewell set his hands on his hips in finality. "What's it going to cost me to get this room, Ms. Clark?"

Molly adopted a properly outraged expression. "Who do you think you are? This is my room, fair and square. You cannot buy me off, Mr. Fewell."

"Ten thousand dollars," he announced. "That's as high as I'll go."

Her eyes widened. Was he for real? "You're out of your mind. Just because you're evidently rich doesn't mean you can push the little people around. It took me all year to save up for this vacation. I've always wanted to do Christmas in Aspen. I'm not about to ditch it all for a guy who can take a fancy vacation anytime he chooses. No way. The room is mine."

That hit the spot she'd hoped for. His fury seemed to rush out of him as quickly as it had come.

"I'm sorry. I didn't mean that the way it sounded." He plowed his fingers through his hair. "You're right. That wouldn't be fair to you."

She was almost there. "Look." She took a big breath. "We should be rational about this. We're both adults. It's a huge suite." She spread her arms wide apart in emphasis. "There's no reason we can't share. I'll bet the lodge will even let us have the place for free, considering the obvious error."

He was shaking his head before she finished speaking. "I can't do that."

She looked him up and down as if he'd just insulted her. "Why? If I'm willing to share the space, what makes you above my company?"

He closed his eyes, heaved a disgusted breath. When he met her gaze once more, he said, "My presence here may become an issue... If the press hears about it, there could be a less-than-comfortable situation."

Her mouth dropped open in an oh-my-god reaction. She looked him up and down once more. "You *are* some TV personality."

He held up both hands. "Not a TV personality."

"You don't look like any politician I've ever seen." Her gaze tapered as if assessing her memory banks. "Are you that big Wall Street guy suspected of embezzling all that money?"

Now he was the one wearing the oh-my-god face.

"Right. Right." She shook her head. "He's way older than you. But with all the *Botox* you celebs use, who can tell?"

"My name's Jason Fewell," he explained since the lodge staff had addressed him as Mr. Fewell. "You really don't know who I am?"

She shrugged. "Sorry. Never heard of any Jason Fewell." Her brow furrowed as she feigned further consideration. "How do you spell that?"

He waved her off. "Never mind. I'm a NASCAR driver."

"NASCAR. Oh." She nodded knowingly.

"Oh? You're not a fan?"

"Well." She laughed, going for the appearance of embarrassment. "I mean, if you're asking if I watch the races, I'd have to say no. I mean, I'm not really into all that *for show* competition stuff."

He let the roundabout insult pass. "Got it."

"So…reporters follow you around?"

A skeptical look shot her way. "Not all the time." He shrugged those broad shoulders.

She frowned.

"Never mind." He threw up his hands again. "Let's just get past that, okay?"

"Why did you pick Aspen?" Molly dropped on the sofa. She was starved. She hadn't eaten since well before lunch and it was nearing six now. "A guy like you could go anywhere. I guess you like to ski."

The pain that blanketed his face made her gut tighten. Oh, yeah. This guy was still deeply disturbed by the three-year-old tragedy. One would expect the memory to still be a tender one, but if in fact it had slowly but surely started to paralyze him on a personal level, that was a whole different issue. And not the normal course of the grief process.

"I used to. My first love is climbing."

A smile tilted her lips. "Me, too. I'm here to climb. Forget the skiing, that's for all those people who don't have the courage to go after the real adrenaline rush."

He stared at her for a long moment, his expression completely unreadable. "I don't know if this arrangement you're proposing will work, Ms. Clark."

She had to tread carefully here. She didn't want to scare him off. "To be honest, I won't be here much. I have a full itinerary planned. By the time I come to the room at night I'll probably just collapse in bed. You'll hardly know I'm here."

"But there's only one bed." He jerked his head toward the bedroom.

"But there's the couch. It makes a bed. Looks expensive so it'll probably be comfortable. And there are two bathrooms. One in here with a shower and then the larger one in there with the soaking tub."

He walked over to the wall of windows and stared out.

At least he hadn't said no…yet.

Molly joined him at the window, not getting too close. The view over the gorgeous village was awesome. "Look, Mr. Fewell. I waited a long time for this vacation. And you seem to have your own reasons for needing to be here. Let's just make the best of it. We'll hardly see each other. If you get friendly with a lady, you'll just have to go back to her room. I'll do the same."

He smiled as he turned to her. "You get friendly with the ladies?"

That was the first real smile she'd seen, and man-oh-man was it something. The cameras did not do that smile justice. "You know what I mean."

"Where are you from, Molly Clark?"

"Chicago." That was where she lived right now. She didn't dare tell him she had three brothers living just down the road. The oldest was in Denver now.

"What do you do in Chicago?"

Now he wanted to check her out, did he? "Research."

"What kind of research?" A flicker of suspicion darkened those blue eyes.

"For companies who need background checks on people." She bit her bottom lip. That was part of her job, so she wasn't telling a total lie. "I'm not really supposed to talk about it, though."

He nodded. "Okay." His gaze collided with hers once more. "You don't have a boyfriend or husband who's going to make something out of this?"

"Nope. Never been married and probably never will. I don't really trust men."

A frown etched its way across his brow. "You don't trust men, and yet you're willing to share this suite with me?"

"I don't trust men as boyfriends and husbands. Considering you're a big celebrity and all, I figure you'll behave yourself. Otherwise I might cause you a lot of bad publicity. That would not be in your favor."

"Definitely not."

"So you respect my space, and I'll respect yours, and we'll get through this just fine."

"I have to consider what the media would make of this arrangement," he countered.

"Discretion is my middle name," she assured him. "Deal?" She thrust out her hand.

He hesitated only a moment before closing his hand around hers. "Deal."

That was the moment she realized that she'd made a serious tactical error.

The tingle that accompanied those long fingers wrapping around hers buzzed right up her arm and seemed to ignite along every nerve ending.

She, Molly Clark, who had kicked the butt of any boy who'd ever tried to get fresh with her, was attracted to this guy.

Impossible.

It never mattered how cute a guy was or how charming. She was, of course, a woman and on some level acknowledged those assets. But not once had she ever experienced a truly visceral reaction to any man.

Until now.

CHAPTER FOUR

Three Days Until Christmas

INCREDIBLY, THE NIGHT had passed without any trouble to speak of. Molly had gone out to dinner and hadn't returned until Jason was already in bed. He'd watched her slip through the dark sitting room on her way to the bedroom. She'd closed the door and run a bath.

He'd tried to go back to sleep, but sleep had proven impossible. He'd kept imagining her naked. Hadn't been that difficult since she'd been wearing nothing but a towel when they met. Flashes of those long, toned legs and all that curly dark hair cascading over her shoulders had kept him tossing and turning for hours. He had imagined her stepping from that tub with the water slipping down her skin. Her soft fingers smoothing the towel along that same path.

The only good thing about it was the fact that he hadn't been slammed in the gut with a panic attack. Not to mention he hadn't felt that kind of attraction in three years. Maybe it was a sign that coming here had been the right step toward recovery.

That was what his shrink called it. Recovery. Recovering himself and his ability to face each day with whatever trials it brought.

"Yeah right." Just because some parts still worked didn't mean he was anywhere near *recovered*.

There was something else he wasn't supposed to do—expect failure.

Where the hell had his confidence gone? The only place he felt like himself was on the track. Would the time come when he lost that, too?

Opening the door as soundlessly as possible, he stepped out of the bathroom. He was dressed and ready to go. All he needed was his gear—

"Good morning." Molly had one hand on the door, obviously on her way out. "You were so quiet I thought you were gone already."

He couldn't speak for a moment. He could only stare at her. Dressed all in black—sweater, cold-weather slacks that fit her toned legs like a second skin, mountain boots and heavy-duty parka. The necessary gloves stuck out of her pockets. That mass of wild curls was tucked into a ski hat. A bag of gear hung from her left hand.

She was ready for an expedition, as well.

Just like Cynthia had been that final morning... the day before Christmas.

"You had breakfast?"

He mentally scrambled to regain his bearings in the present. "No. I..." He what? Planned to go out without fueling up? Not a smart move. Saying it out loud would be even dumber.

"Great. We can have breakfast together." She smiled. "Management feels so bad about what happened, they'll probably spring for our meals, too."

He walked across the room and pulled on his parka, then stuffed the gloves into the pockets. "I'll get something later." He grabbed his gear.

"Okay." She smiled. "Have fun."

She had a nice smile. And the cutest little freckles sprinkled across her nose.

What the hell was he doing? Last night he'd been frustrated and travel weary. He hadn't been thinking straight. He should never have agreed to this arrangement. The action was wholly out of character for him...even since he'd started losing his mind.

This was about the most ridiculous situation he'd ever gotten himself into.

He didn't try to catch up with her as they moved down the corridor outside the room. She stopped at the elevators and pushed the call button. He kept going, heading for the stairwell. The longer he was with her the more questions she would ask. They'd already shared enough personal information.

More than he'd shared with a stranger in… three years.

Funny—he reached for the stairwell door—it seemed that most everything about his life had either ended or ground to a near stop three years ago.

Right here in Aspen.

Maybe that was the problem. He was disoriented to some degree…making decisions he wouldn't usually even entertain.

He slung the backpack over his shoulder and took his time descending the stairs. Maybe by the time he'd reached the lobby, she would already be out the main entrance or in the restaurant.

There were far too many mountain trails around here for them to end up attempting the same one. But he didn't want to risk running into her again in the lobby. He'd been wrong when he arrived yesterday. He wasn't the only person here alone. Molly was alone, as well. Unlike him, she didn't appear to want to stay that way. If he encountered her in the lobby, she would no doubt suggest they go climbing together.

That was something he had to do alone.

Assuming he could do it.

That was the crazy thing. He could push his car around the track one hundred and eighty miles per hour, but he couldn't put one foot in front of the other to do one damned thing else considered even remotely dangerous without breaking out in a cold sweat.

He paused as he reached the lobby. Strange. He hadn't had the usual nightmares last night. Hadn't awakened in a cold sweat with his heart beating out of his chest. Once he'd gone to sleep, he'd slept straight through until the alarm went off on his cell phone at five this morning.

Must've been crazy tired.

Being tired certainly hadn't helped before, but maybe he was finally turning that corner toward acceptance and recovery.

However minimal, it was progress.

The lobby was crowded with skiers prepared for adventure. All ages and all sizes. Some clearly total amateurs, others obviously seasoned pros.

He pulled his sunglasses from his pack and pushed them into place. If he was really lucky, no one would notice him. But Aspen was one of those places that drew celebrities. The Hollywood types loved coming here, especially during the holidays, and wherever celebrities gathered, so did the paparazzi.

All he had to do was get across the lobby without running into one of their spotters.

MOLLY LINGERED NEAR the massive fireplace and scanned the crowd milling about in the lobby. Still no sign of Fewell.

Wait.

There he was.

He'd ventured across the lobby but hadn't made it out the main entrance. Instead, he had stopped at an ATM machine.

Had he noticed the two spotters chatting in the center of the room? A large gathering place with comfy sofas and chairs all grouped into conversation areas was designed to give guests a place to meet and make plans. But the two men filtering back and forth through the crowd were not guests. She didn't know either of them, but she recognized the tactics. One would chat while the other, seemingly involved in the conversation, scouted for prey. Their body language, more than anything else, gave them away. The false smiles and disingenuous laughter. They were pros, too. The little game they played didn't miss a beat.

The hands-free cell phone accessories each wore didn't set them apart from any of a number of other guests sporting the same technology. But Molly watched the two. Even as they seemingly spoke to each other, their body language warned that another conversation was going on with a third party. They were keeping someone informed of the goings-on in the lobby while they received the latest information on airport arrivals.

One of the guys had noticed Fewell, was watching his movements at the ATM. If Fewell didn't get moving soon, he was going to give himself away. How long did it take to make a transaction?

Fewell had been a public figure plenty long enough to be better at this.

One of the spotters moved through the crowd, weaving his way in the direction of the ATM station.

Molly bolted into action. She skirted around the throng of guests, making it to Fewell's position with scarcely a second to spare.

"Baby!" She threw her arms around him when he turned to her in surprise. "I thought you were never coming down. You ready to go?" She guided him away from the ATM, keeping an arm curled around his shoulders.

He didn't resist as she ushered him out the main entrance into the bitter cold.

"What the blazes was that all about?" he asked as they cleared those gathered at the valet parking stand.

"A spotter almost made you."

He stared at her. Molly wished she could see his eyes behind those dark glasses, determine if he was annoyed, relieved or suspicious.

His jaw tightened. "How would you know about spotters?"

Well, that answered her question. "I run checks on people," she reminded him as she glanced beyond his broad shoulders. "We should get out of here if you don't want to draw attention."

"My SUV's in valet parking."

"You hang around here and you'll be made for sure." She tugged him away from the line gathered at the valet desk. Before he could decide whether he was going to believe her or not, she leaned in close and said, "Come on. I'm parked in the garage. I can get us out of here."

He hesitated.

She didn't give up, tugging a little more firmly.

"Besides, I know a great place off the beaten path that serves a terrific breakfast."

He relented.

Molly hadn't used the valet parking for precisely this reason. She had to be prepared to go on a moment's notice and waiting in a line for her car to be delivered to her was not conducive to that kind of exodus. Using the valet parking would be routine for guys like Fewell. He could learn a few things from her.

When they'd settled into the SUV and she'd started the engine, he broke his silence. "What does running security checks on people have to do with picking a spotter out of a crowd?"

He was still suspicious. "Okay, the truth is—" she backed out of the parking slot and headed for the exit "—I don't just work from an office. I interview neighbors. Lots of legwork, following up on the answers people provide on their résumés and applications. Body language is a key element in determining what's fact and what's fiction. You know what I mean?"

"Maybe." He didn't completely buy her story.

She braked for the garage exit. "Duck down until we're out of here."

He didn't argue, since another clutch of skiers

poured out of the lodge's main front entrance. He wasn't about to risk being spotted by the celeb stalkers.

She let off the brake and eased down on the accelerator. "You won't be sorry," she said, hoping to make him feel better about having followed her instructions. "Mama Jo's has the best coffee for a hundred miles."

When they were far enough away from the lodge entrance, she gave him the all clear. "It's safe for you to get up now." It was still dark, but the village lights made the ice and snow sparkle. A winter wonderland. That was Aspen. God, she'd missed this part of the country. It snowed in Chicago, but the landscape was nothing like this. The only mountains seen from her apartment view were skyscrapers.

He sat up, twisted around to glance out the rear window. "You do this often?"

She navigated the increasing village traffic. Tourists were already out in force. "I have to admit, I've never facilitated an escape."

"Could've fooled me."

She was going to have to watch her step or he'd figure out she was a little too helpful. A little too *around*.

The roads were in good condition despite the recent snowfall. A definite plus when maneuvering the busy streets of the picturesque village. The early hour didn't deter anyone. They'd come here for the slopes and they weren't wasting a single moment. The village folks went all-out for Christmas. Lights and greenery in every window. New York's holiday window displays had nothing on Aspen's.

Add the ambience to the great skiing, and tourists flocked to the area. During the winter season the population of Aspen skyrocketed, making for close quarters on the streets and sidewalks and in every other space thereabouts.

As she left the city streets behind, her passenger spoke up. "Where exactly is this Mama Jo's?"

"A few miles outside town." She'd eaten there a million times. As a kid, her family had often gone for Sunday brunch.

Then she realized just how deeply she had thrust her booted foot into her mouth.

"How do you know the place has the best coffee for a hundred miles? You've been here before? I thought you said this was your first visit to Aspen."

She didn't have to look at him to know he'd just

put two and two together and come up with five. It was inordinately clear in his voice. Not to mention he was staring a hole through her.

"Don't you do your research before you take a vacation?" She did look at him then, as if she couldn't believe he would be so careless. She was skating on thin ice here. She'd taken her cover over the top, given him way too many avenues to question. And just as many for her to stumble over.

"What do you mean?"

"Honey—" she turned her attention back to the road "—I check out every restaurant, shop and accommodation I think I might be even remotely interested in. I work too hard for my money to waste it. When the better part of a hundred reviews say Mama Jo's is the best breakfast stop for a few hundred miles, I believe it's in all likelihood so."

Molly's fingers tightened on the steering wheel. She'd seriously screwed up there. If he didn't buy her excuse…this whole setup could crumble and her first field assignment would be blown. Not a good way to cement her fledgling career as an investigator at one of the top agencies in the nation.

If they could just get past these sorts of questions, she would be good to go. He'd accepted the whole "we have to share a room" setup. And, until now, he'd seemed to be satisfied that she was who she said she was.

The more experienced investigators at the Colby Agency had warned her about giving too much information when developing a cover. *Keep it simple. Give only the absolutely necessary.*

First time out, she'd failed.

Idiot!

"I guess," he finally said, "I prefer taking the risk."

Relief made her shoulders sag. Thank God. She'd dodged the bullet on that one. She glanced at him. "That could be because you can afford to. Those of us who can't, don't like risks that involve our bank accounts."

Stop there, Molly. Answer his questions, don't dole out any additional information.

"Well, I hope your sources are right," he commented. "I could use some serious coffee."

"Me, too." She flashed him a smile. "Can't hit the trail without serious coffee."

CHAPTER FIVE

"YOU'RE SURE THIS IS the trail you want to take?"

Jason had already answered that question. Twice, in fact. "You said you'd considered it yourself." He remembered distinctly her saying so at the coffee shop. And she'd been right about the coffee. It was the best he'd ever had.

"I'm okay with it." Molly opened the SUV's rear hatch. "Any one of the fourteens is fine by me."

Hadn't she mentioned this one? Maybe he was confusing what she'd said with…three years ago.

Flashes of Cynthia laughing as they geared up that day three years ago kept twisting his gut. She would point at the mountains in the distance and sigh. *Beautiful. Hurry, Jason! We're wasting the day!*

She'd wanted to take this route, even though it wasn't recommended in the winter season. With the heavy snowfall only days before their arrival, he'd urged her to reconsider. She'd teased him, reminding him that the route was only a class three. Was he afraid?

But it had proven a strenuous eleven-hour trek to the summit.

Would he have noticed something wasn't right if he hadn't been so physically exhausted? Could he have done more to talk her out of going over that last cliff face for a photo opportunity?

The answers were no. He understood that. And yet the fear continued to haunt him. To paralyze him at the most inopportune times.

"…helmet?"

He blinked. "What?" He'd missed whatever Molly was rambling on about.

"Do you have a helmet?"

"Yes." Safety First was his motto. He had worn one, as recommended, the last time. So had Cynthia. It hadn't made a difference. The mountain had still claimed her life as it had so many others.

Stop.

He had to focus on now. His palms were sweating. His heart rate had sped up to a ridiculous level. Panic was already clawing at his insides.

Ten minutes later, they were fully geared up,

crampons included, and tramping across the landscape. It was damned cold. Maybe colder than last time. The wind was brisk and the sky was clear, keeping the temperature hovering about the same as it had been at dawn. The snow was packed fairly hard, making for an easier go than he'd expected considering the fairly recent precipitation.

Molly pointed out the various peaks and the breathtaking scenery as they followed the trail toward Crater Lake. Jason nodded whenever she glanced his way and attempted to come up with something intelligent to say in response. Mainly he focused on trying to slow his heart rate. The increasing speed of the traitorous organ had little to do with the cold and the physical exertion... This was the beginning.

Slow, deep breaths. Hold it. Release.

He would not let this happen.

"Almost there." She pointed out their goal, the couloir soaring toward the ridges above.

Because of the extreme mental focus required for forward movement and to keep his heart from bursting from his chest, Molly ended up in the lead. She chattered on about how she'd been planning this kind of adventure for months. That she'd climbed in other places many times. At this point he couldn't summon a response at all, but she didn't seem to notice.

They moved to the right of their destination along climbers at the base of the headwall, then left to avoid some of the more treacherous cliffs. The climbing had begun in earnest.

His legs felt like leaden clubs. He stumbled once. Couldn't shake the overwhelming sensation of impending doom.

Molly did a quick turnaround and ended up on her butt for her trouble. She slid a few feet, picked herself up and laughed it off. He choked out a laugh at her good-natured reaction. Didn't help the tension pounding in his veins, swelling in his throat.

Molly stopped, dropped her pack on the ground. "I don't know about you, but I need a breather."

He couldn't see her eyes or her face around the sunglasses and ski mask she wore. No reason to believe she'd taken this stop for his benefit.

"A break would be good." His words sounded tight and breathless. He worked at swallowing back the lump of pulsing panic lodged in his throat. Couldn't.

She sat down on the rocky and snow-packed ground, dug through her pack and pulled out her ice axe. "I understand it gets a little tougher from here."

He stared at the ice axe; those moments before the latch on Cynthia's harness had given way completely rushed past his retinas. She had tried desperately to hang on to the axe she'd buried to the hilt as her body hung precariously in the air.

The band around his chest tightened to the point that any sort of breath was impossible.

He'd reached for her. Urged her to grab hold of his hand.

But fear had paralyzed her.

When he dangled half over the ledge and grabbed for her…it was too late.

He'd clung to that ledge…in shock…devastated. He didn't even remember pulling himself back up. It was a flat-out miracle he hadn't fallen. Apparently instinct had taken over and he'd dragged himself up.

Pay attention. Molly was talking again. He could see her lips moving, but the words didn't make it past the haze of extreme anxiety swaddled around his brain. *Reach into the pack and get the necessary equipment.* The order echoed in his mind but he couldn't move. He could only watch Molly prepare. Her lips continued to move with her excited chatter.

Blood roared in his ears.

Don't do this.

"You okay?"

The question exploded in his ears.

He blinked. Gave a jerky nod.

Coming here with her had been a mistake. He shouldn't have let this morning get out of his control. What the heck was wrong with him? He'd let the woman stay in his room. He'd gone to breakfast with her, and now they were here…starting out just as he and Cynthia had three years ago.

How had this happened?

MOLLY DIDN'T NEED TELEPATHIC abilities to know this guy was terrified. His breathing was far too rapid. His responses too slow and vague—if he responded at all.

According to the information the agency had been given, he had no physical condition that would create these symptoms. He appeared to be suffering from the panic attacks Mr. Harris had warned Victoria about.

Molly had never experienced a panic attack, but she'd done her research before coming on this assignment. His blood pressure and heart rate would be out of bounds. Cold sweat would break out on his skin. Shaking hands. The inability to interact appropriately. And the worst…a feeling of imminent doom beyond his control.

She looked around at the sky. "You know we got a pretty late start today. Maybe we should check out the area a little more, plan our ascent a little better and come back tomorrow. I'm starting to get uneasy." She shifted her attention back to him. "Will you be mad if we go back now?"

He stared at her for a full ten seconds. She wished she could see his eyes. Like her, he wore those dark glasses and the ski mask.

"If that's what you want," he finally offered.

The words were strained, loaded with tension. How was it that a guy as young and healthy as this could be totally paralyzed by a fear that wasn't tangible? At least not yet. They hadn't gotten to the really dangerous climbing. She wanted to understand, but she just couldn't grasp the concept. Coming here, climbing to the summit of this mountain again was a good decision, in her opinion. But how could he possibly hope to accomplish his goal if he couldn't make it past this point without freaking?

She should cut him some slack. Obviously, to him, the fear was real. "You're sure you don't mind?"

He pushed to his feet, reached an unsteady hand

for his pack. "If you're unsure, to carry on would be a mistake."

She surveyed the sky again. "Looks like snow clouds moving in, too. Maybe it'll be better tomorrow." They had avalanche beacons and every other essential safety device recommended. And the weather forecast hadn't mentioned snow. But he didn't know that she understood they were fully prepared, certainly had time, and that the conditions were safe enough for this time of year.

Mountain climbing came with some amount of danger. Winter expeditions upped the danger factor. Adrenaline junkies liked it that way.

But this adrenaline junkie had crashed and burned.

Jason Fewell was afraid. It was difficult to watch. She had four older brothers, two close to his age. She couldn't imagine any one of them suffering this kind of setback. But it could happen to anyone if the conditions were right. The situation had to be devastating.

The descent was easier going. Fewell made no attempt to lead the way. Just like on the trek in, he said practically nothing. She kept the one-sided conversation going in hopes of giving him something besides his inner thoughts to dwell on.

She had to find a way to turn this around. Molly

was no psychologist, but she had a fair under-standing of the male psyche.

Men like Fewell considered themselves above fear. This uncontrollable reaction would call into question all that he believed to be true and right about himself. Particularly the ability to protect others.

She needed a diversion.

Something that would allow him to feel heroic. Like the protector he instinctively needed to be. Even if for only an instant.

She'd already busted her backside once. What was one more tumble?

With a glance back at him, she said, "When we get back to town, let's have an early dinner. I could—"

She toppled to her right, hoping like everything there were no sharp rocks hidden in the snow. She hit the snow with a soft grunt, then slid a few feet. By the time she stopped, he was crouched next to her.

He snatched off those dark glasses and looked her over. "You okay?"

For a moment she got lost in those blue eyes. The sincere concern for her well-being quickened her pulse. "I'll live."

He helped her to her feet, not an easy task with

the pack hanging to one side and throwing off her balance.

"That was stupid," she muttered, testing her weight on her right foot. She groaned.

"You twist your ankle?"

"Think so." Truth was, she had, but it wasn't enough of an injury to mention.

He took her pack and moved around to her right side. "Hold on to my arm. Lean on me as much as you need to. We'll take it slow."

"Thanks." She really could've walked without any assistance, but the maneuver worked like a charm. Fewell was so focused on helping her that he forgot all about the panic that had obviously been clawing at him.

The trek back to the trail on the valley floor was slow going. The cold was invading her bones despite the layers of insulating clothing. The physical exertion of carrying her pack and moving at a faster pace would have prevented the cold from sneaking up on her like this. But the sacrifice was necessary. She needed him to see that he could defeat this enemy.

"You're sure you're up to the challenge of a fourteen?" he asked out of the blue.

He hadn't spoken in so many minutes, the sound

of his voice startled her. "Yeah, sure." She wanted to tell him she'd climbed to her first summit of 14,000 feet when she was a teenager, but that wasn't part of her cover. So she didn't. "I haven't done any climbing in a while, but I've been preparing for months. Increased my usual workout considerably. After all that, I go and do something this dumb. I promise I'm not usually this clumsy."

"Maybe you're just having an off day."

Yeah. "Good thing you were here."

He didn't respond to her comment.

The rest of the trek back to where they'd left her rental was made in silence. The route was a few miles longer since the parking area beyond Maroon Creek Road was closed in winter. But the magnificent view made every step worth the effort.

At the SUV, she fished for her keys and handed them to Fewell. "Maybe you'd better drive."

He dropped their packs to the ground, then helped her into the passenger seat—which was completely unnecessary, but she allowed him to continue playing the hero.

When he'd loaded their packs into the cargo area, he slid behind the wheel. "A hot soak is what you need for that ankle."

She could definitely use a hot soak, twisted ankle

or no. "We can order room service." She was starved.

"That'll work."

A smile tugged at the corners of her mouth. So far, she had him eating out of her hands. The question was, could she get him to trust her enough to talk about the accident?

Just maybe.

As he drove, she studied his profile. The turn-around was amazing. He'd clearly been on the verge of a full-blown panic attack back there, and now he was as cool as a cucumber.

How could he climb into the hot seat of a race car and fly around that track for a few hundred miles and not be able to climb that first vertical ridge that required only a little technical expertise?

A mental block, she decided. He had to find a way through it or around it.

At the lodge, the crowd outside had thinned. Most of the guests were either on the slopes or shopping, Molly would lay odds on it. Any lurking paparazzi would be doing the same in hopes of spotting a story.

Fewell parked the SUV in the garage and got out. By the time she'd unfastened her seat belt and opened her door, he was there waiting to help her.

She let him. It was dumb. She was fine. But if it made him feel better, she could deal with it.

Or did she deal with it because it made *her* feel better?

He'd taken off his gloves, as had she, and the feel of those strong fingers curled around her hands made her a little giddy.

Unfortunately, that was not part of the plan.

CHAPTER SIX

JASON BRACED HIS HANDS on either side of the window and peered out at the mountains all around the eclectic village setting.

He'd failed.

One look at that ice axe and he'd lost it. Felt paralyzed. The panic had consumed him completely. He wasn't sure he could have made the trek back if Molly hadn't fallen. Somehow he'd been able to push the fear aside and help her back to civilization.

By the time they'd tramped halfway back to the SUV, his heart rate had returned to normal, as normal as one would expect with the physical exertion required to make the journey. The cold, bitter sweat of panic had given way to the clean, healthy sweat of physical exertion.

But the fear of making the technical leg of that climb, the more dangerous part, had shut him down.

Three years. *Three long years.* The situation had worsened in recent months and it was escalating.

Therapy was a joke. His friends and teammates didn't understand. They tried. But they couldn't possibly. When a man reached out to the woman he loved and couldn't save her from falling to her death, it changed something inside him. That change had somehow set off a domino effect. Each time he found himself in a precarious situation, the panic started its slow creep up his spine. Sometimes it came out of nowhere.

He closed his eyes and forced away the memories.

How had he thought coming here would change anything?

The day would come when settling behind the wheel of his car to win the race would prove an insurmountable obstacle.

What would he do then?

"A long, hot soak was exactly what I needed."

He turned at the sound of Molly's voice. She crossed to the sofa and curled up at one end. "I feel like a new woman. You should try it."

"A shower was sufficient." He gestured to the cart waiting in the center of the room. "I ordered room service. I wasn't sure what you would want and I didn't want to disturb you, so I ordered a variety."

She pushed up, a flash of thigh showing where her robe wrapped. "Great. I'm starved."

He watched as she lifted the elegant silver lids and checked the entrées beneath. She inhaled deeply and moaned her pleasure when she reached the spaghetti. He'd never met a woman who admitted she loved to eat. Or who dug in with the vigor of Molly Clark. He liked that about her. Her honesty was refreshing.

"This is the one." She set the lid aside and claimed the plate. "You're not eating?"

"I was waiting for you."

After leaving her plate on the table next to the sofa, she went back to the cart in search of silverware and a bottle of water. "You're such a gentleman."

He wandered to the cart and surveyed the offerings. He wasn't really hungry, but he understood he needed to eat. "Except when it comes to giving up the last room at the lodge."

Her laughter tinkled in the air. He liked her smile. Liked her laughter, too.

"You compromised," she said in his defense. "That's something."

While she twirled her fork in the pasta, she

watched him pick at the bowl of stir-fried veg-
etables with rice. "Sorry about ruining your plans
for the day. I guess I wasn't as ready as I thought."

He was the one who needed to apologize.

"No problem. I…" What did he say? He was
damaged goods? He couldn't have continued anyway, because he had been too terrified?

She held his gaze, hers expectant.

"You can try again," he suggested. The advice
was more for him than for her.

Molly shrugged. "Probably won't be as much
fun alone."

The rice tasted like cardboard in his mouth. He
swallowed. "There are guided events."

"Yeah, right." She stuffed a forkful of spaghetti
into her mouth and chewed, then said around it, "If
you want to do the wimpy stuff."

A smile tugged at his lips. "Wimpy?"

She nodded. "You know how it is. This time of
year all the good routes are closed unless you're
willing to attempt the trek on your own. The Forest
Service recommends staying away from the tough
climbs. I didn't come here to tromp around in the
snow with a bunch of designer-clad tourists."

He had to laugh. "It won't be the end of the
world if you don't do a fourteen this time."

She swallowed. "Are you kidding? That's why I'm here."

The woman had her heart set on claiming a fourteen-thousand-foot summit. "Your vacation's not over yet. It could happen."

"What about you?" She captured another forkful of pasta. "You going out again?"

His fingers tightened on the fork in his hand. The mere thought had his heart rate climbing. "Maybe."

"You should." She downed a gulp of water. "You're here. Might as well, right?"

"Yeah." If it were only that easy. He couldn't eat. He set the bowl aside.

"You look tense." She licked her fork. His gaze followed the movement as if he'd never seen a woman do that before. "You really should take a soak. The tub jets are fabulous."

Images of her in that big tub reeled through his mind. "No, thanks. I'm good."

"Too girlie for you?" She set her plate aside and studied him.

"Something like that."

"What made you decide you wanted to be a driver?" Molly asked, not because she needed to but mainly because she wanted to know the answer.

One corner of his mouth lifted in a smile—it was

the sexiest thing Molly had ever seen. *Slow down, girl, you're going about this all wrong.*

"I didn't exactly make the decision. It just sort of happened." He sipped his water. "I started out as a flunky for the team. Doing pretty much whatever needed to be done. Worked my way up. Al, my team owner," he explained, "noticed my instinct when driving was particularly good. He pushed me to challenge myself and I did."

"Sounds like you and your team owner are close." She fluffed her drying hair, combing her fingers through the damp curls.

"The whole team's like family," he confirmed.

"So you've been here before?" Molly shifted the conversation back to the here and now. "Done that same climb we started today?"

"Yes. I've been here before." The tension he felt at the question showed in his posture.

The room phone rang.

Jason was thankful for the interruption.

Molly picked up the receiver. "Hello." She listened a moment. "Sure. Okay." She got up, held the receiver out to him. "It's for you."

Jason pushed up and walked over to the sofa and took the phone. "Thanks."

She got up, grabbed her plate and wandered

back to the cart. To give him some privacy, he supposed.

"This is Jason Fewell." Jason listened as the desk clerk explained there was a problem with his rental car. The agency had left a document at the desk for him to review and sign. "Sure, I'll be right down." He placed the receiver back in its cradle. "There's an issue at the front desk with the rental car. Some kind of form. I'll be right back."

"God, the fruit is marvelous." She moaned as she sank her teeth into a strawberry.

A new kind of tension tightened in Jason's belly. A few minutes out of the room would be a good thing. This lady was getting under his skin way too fast.

"I'll save some for you," she called after him as he headed for the door.

"I can always order more," he reminded her before slipping out.

The corridor was empty. Who would hang around their room when on vacation in a snow-covered paradise like this?

Other than him?

And his roommate?

Jason shook his head. He wasn't sure if she was

staying close because she felt sorry for him or because she was lonely, too.

Too… That truth rattled him.

He was lonely.

That admission had been a long time in coming.

He hustled down the stairwell. Tomorrow morning he should run. The thinner air would be somewhat limiting, but staying in shape was essential. Too hard to come back from a few days of laziness.

After pushing through the door to the first floor, he strode across the grand lobby and bellied up to the front desk.

"I'm Jason Fewell. You have something here for me to sign."

Two female clerks stood behind the counter. They exchanged a look that said they had no idea what he was talking about.

"I'm sorry, sir. Did someone call you?" the one named Carrie asked.

Jason nodded. "He said his name was Austin."

Another of those looks passed between the two.

"Sir, we don't have an Austin at the front desk."

Confusion tugged at his brow. "Maybe he works in the manager's office or in reservations?"

Both heads shook. The one whose name tag read

Ellen confirmed, "No, sir. We don't have an Austin on staff at all."

"But the call," Jason countered, "was from inside the lodge."

"If the caller knew your room number," Carrie explained, "he could use any of the house phones." She gestured to a table in the lobby. "Maybe a friend is playing a prank on you."

Realization tingled at the base of his skull. He didn't bother explaining that he didn't have any friends here. He knew exactly what was going on.

MOLLY PULLED A SWEATER over her head. She had a bad feeling about this call to the front desk. Why would a rental agency drop off a form at the lodge without calling Fewell first?

They wouldn't.

She shoved her feet into her boots and headed for the door.

This was a setup.

Walking wasn't an option. She ran for the stairwell. Plunged down the four flights of stairs. Her ankle stung but not enough to slow her down.

When she burst into the lobby, the front desk had already called security.

A male cameraman and a female reporter were

still shouting questions at Fewell even as security hauled them toward the door.

"Come on, Jason," the woman urged, not ready to give up her quest, "tell me why you came back here after what happened three years ago."

The security guards were making quiet promises to have her hauled into the police station if she didn't cooperate and leave the premises.

Fewell stood there, unmoving, unblinking.

"Do you still feel responsible for Cynthia's death?" the reporter shouted, getting in one more jab before the guards got her out the door.

The few guests that had wandered in during the commotion stared at Fewell, whispering among themselves. One even going so far as to point.

"Come on." Molly took Jason by the arm. "Don't give them anything else to talk about."

He glared at her, his face pinched in pain.

"Come on." She tugged at him. "Jason," she urged. "Just…come on."

Molly hauled him to the elevator since it was closer than the stairs and the doors on one had just slid open. When the doors had closed, she asked, "What happened?"

"It doesn't matter."

The hell it didn't. "It does matter."

He sent a deadly look down his shoulder at her. "I do not want to talk about this."

"Okay."

The silence thickened, making the elevator feel as if the walls were closing in.

When the doors opened, he waited for her to exit. A gentleman to the end.

She shoved the key card into the lock and opened the door to their suite. "I'm filing a complaint with the manager." She kicked off her boots.

"It wasn't the staff's fault." He wandered to the window and stared out at the darkness.

The view in Aspen was beautiful, that was true. But he spent way too much time at that window. Like a prisoner who longed for freedom.

"I know you said you don't want to talk about the things that reporter said, but sometimes it helps to talk."

"Not for me."

"Well—" she moved in next to him at the window "—if you're referring to therapy, that doesn't count. Not in my book."

He glanced at her, his face grim. "It's supposed to help."

"Sometimes it does, sometimes it doesn't." She leaned against the window frame and studied him.

"But it always helps to get it off your chest with someone who'll really listen."

"Lady—" he shook his head "—my team, my family, they've all been there for me, but no amount of talk has changed anything."

Molly took the plunge. "Who's Cynthia?" She held her breath.

"I guess you're one of the few who didn't read about it. Or watch it on the entertainment news shows."

She shook her head. "No. Sorry."

He braced a hand on the window frame. "Cynthia O'Neal was my girlfriend. We came here three years ago for the Christmas holidays."

"Oh my gosh." Molly shook her head. "I feel terrible for giving you so much trouble about the room. I had no idea."

"The room…" He shrugged. "It doesn't matter."

"What happened?"

"We had climbed all over the country. Here, too. She loved the mountains here better than any place else."

Molly waited patiently for him to continue. She knew this was difficult for him.

"The trail you and I started today was one of her favorites."

"I can understand that. It's a beautiful place."

"The weather had been particularly bad that winter. We shouldn't have gone."

He fell silent again.

She didn't push him. She already knew the story. But that he would tell her about it indicated some amount of trust.

"We went anyway. We reached the summit. She…her harness gave out. Faulty equipment they said."

"You tried to save her?" That would be an easy guess for anyone.

He nodded. "But I failed."

"Do you feel responsible for what happened?"

He closed his eyes, took a breath. "Logically—" he opened his eyes once more "—I understand that it wasn't my fault, but I can't say that I don't feel responsible."

"That's normal, I think."

He searched her eyes as if trying to understand the reasoning behind her pursuit of the subject.

"My mom had a heart attack," she went on. "I feel guilty to this day that I stopped at a convenience store on the way home and didn't get there in time to help her before it was too late."

"Sorry about your mom." He turned his attention back to the view out the window.

"The point is," she added, "I don't let that guilt stop me from going on with my life. My mom wouldn't want that."

"You should know," he said quietly, "I have these…panic attacks. Whenever I'm in a stressful situation, they hit. I keep checking off activities from the list of things I can do. Pretty soon there's going to be nothing left."

"Did that happen today?"

His gaze collided with hers. "Yeah. I froze. Couldn't do what I knew exactly how to do. What I'm fully capable of doing. I just couldn't do it."

"But you haven't had to check off racing? You can still do that."

He laughed; the sound was strained. "That's the strangest part. That's the only place I really feel normal. When I'm behind that wheel flying around the track, I feel like me. The old me."

"I can't say that I've ever had a panic attack, but it seems to me that it's a mind-over-matter thing. Kind of like getting back on the horse that threw you."

"Sounds easy, doesn't it?"

He was right. "I'm certain it's not easy. I didn't mean to insinuate that it was. But you have to keep trying. If you stop—" her gaze collided with his "—then you'll never get started again."

"You really think it's that simple?"

"No." She shook her head. "But it's like that whole trust thing they do, when you fall back and let someone else catch you. It's really hard at first, but once you've done it a couple of times, it's easy. Maybe if you climb that mountain, the way you started to today, maybe you'll break through some kind of barrier and the panic won't have control anymore."

"I tried to do that today, in case you've forgotten, and I failed."

"But you didn't have a coach today." She smiled broadly when his gaze met hers once more.

"I'm not sure I want to know what that means."

"I tell you what, Fewell," she challenged. "You go back out with me tomorrow and I guarantee you'll climb that mountain. We won't come back until it's done."

He searched her eyes for a long moment, a glimmer of hope in his. "We'll have to start early. Be prepared for every possible scenario."

"All good climbers are prepared," she countered.
He offered his hand. "Deal?"
She smiled and placed her hand in his. "Deal."

CHAPTER SEVEN

Two Days before Christmas, 9:00 a.m.

JASON STOOD STONE STILL.

The traverse from the trail proper had been pure hell. Molly had kept a gung-ho attitude despite his foul mood. The local papers had slashed his name across the headlines with questions about the accident three years ago.

He shouldn't have come back here.

"Let's get moving, Fewell," Molly said, coming up beside him. "We've got a long ways to go and daylight is running out." She pulled her ice axe from her bag. "Don't back out on me now."

His movements stilted, he reached into his pack and retrieved his own ice axe. The climb would move from the sloped basin to the east face couloirs upward to the ridges above. Achieving the Bell Chord proper was the next goal.

She moved forward.

He forced his feet to follow her movements.

"Stay focused on what's right in front of you," Molly called back to him. "Don't look beyond your next few moves."

Jason rolled the details over in his mind. They had all the equipment they needed. Rope, pickets and gear for bunking down for the night if necessary. He knew the drill. Understood exactly what each move should be.

His heart rate escalated with each step. Sweat leached on to his skin beneath the layers of protective wear.

Comfortable angle, he told himself. About forty-five degrees. Keep moving. *You can do it.*

They hit a narrow, treacherous section of the couloir, moved cautiously beyond it.

And they climbed.

The alternating sounds of ice axes digging in, gloves ferreting out handholds, boots finding traction and footing reverberated around him.

"Hear that," she said. "It's a rhythm."

Crack, rub, grind.

"Focus on the rhythm," she prompted. "Focus on the next step."

They climbed and climbed, stopping for occasional breaks to rest their muscles and catch their breaths.

Jason's heart rate slowed to a more expected level for the physical exertion. His ability to concentrate cleared, allowed for better focus.

He saw the head of the couloir and the sky beyond. Relief trickled inside him. They'd made the first major hurdle.

"Sit," Molly instructed. "Let's enjoy the view."

Jason settled next to her. He allowed his respiration to slow naturally. No extra effort required. *Just breathe.* Felt…good.

"Here." She passed him a granola bar and bottle of water. "Brunch."

He smiled at the small granola bar. "I hope there's more." He tore open the wrapper and took a bite. The taste of oats and cherries filled his mouth. Tasted better than anything he'd forced himself to chew in a really long time.

She passed him another bar. "How you holding up?"

"Good." He settled his attention on her. All geared up with her face protected by dark glasses and a ski mask. But he knew the line of her jaw by heart…the shape of her soft lips. Looking at her was far more appealing than the magnificent mountain views all around them. He hadn't enjoyed looking at anything other than the finish line for a long time.

"Let's leave some of the stuff we won't need here," she suggested. "We can do a pickup on the way back. The next stretch is tough. Light is better."

He suffered a twinge of panic but refused to let it take root. "You're the boss."

She laughed as she shoved aside their crampons and other nonessentials for the next leg of the trip. The sound of her laughter prompted his determination. *He could do it.* He tucked his water bottle back into his pack and stood.

"Let's do this thing." The words were strong. It felt good to say them.

A few feet of ice was the first challenge. The going was, as she said, tough. The ground beneath the snow was ledgy with lots of loose rock and snow, a ready mix for slides. Handholds were few and far between and less than optimal. The wind had picked up, whipping with enough force to steal the best balance. Slow but steady progress finally gained them the summit.

The eyewear came off and for long moments they stood there, high atop the valley below and with some of the most breathtaking mountains on the planet sprawling before them. Snow-covered and grand.

Truly magnificent.

Molly smiled at him. "You made it. You conquered the beast."

He pulled off his helmet and ski mask. She did the same. The wind sent wisps of hair across her cheeks; he removed his glove and brushed them away.

"Thank you, Molly Clark."

She stared into his eyes, her own filled with satisfaction. "Don't thank me, Fewell. You had it in you all along."

He kissed her. There was simply no other way to properly show his gratitude.

Thanks to her undying spirit and ambitious belief in him, he had conquered the beast.

MOLLY DIDN'T WANT the kiss to end. But the wind was freezing their faces.

When they drew apart, they quickly donned their ski masks once more.

Gloves and eyewear in place, he took the lead. "When we get back to town," he called back to her, "we're celebrating. Dinner, champagne, the works."

"Sounds good to me. I'm always hungry."

They made a slow and careful descent, burying their ice axes as necessary. Fewell stayed in the lead. Molly was proud of him. Truth was, she'd gotten way too close to this guy in the past forty-eight hours.

And that kiss…well, she was reasonably sure she had never been kissed quite like that. Definitely not fourteen thousand feet above sea level.

They picked up their gear on the way down. Once they reached the gentler slopes, they moved a little faster. Molly was pumped. The day had gone off without a hitch. Surely this accomplishment would allow Fewell to get a hold on the panic attacks.

The beginning, she decided. The beginning of finding his footing in life again.

BACK AT THE SUV, they stripped off their parkas and the other outer gear no longer needed. He stole another kiss and Molly let him. She liked the way he kissed. Liked the feel of his lips moving over hers. She could get used to this…all too easily.

It was dark as they reached town. He gave her the directions to a restaurant that didn't require reservations.

Molly parked the SUV and climbed out. Her

legs were a little stiff. She would be sore tomorrow, but the outcome had been worth every step of the climb—and the couple of slides she'd taken.

"You're sure this place is good?" she queried. This was one place she'd never been. Carlo's was a little off the beaten path and without the panache of Aspen's high-class offerings.

"If you like Mexican food, you'll love it."

She definitely liked Mexican food. Could eat her weight in it. Especially tonight.

Tonight felt special.

It was crazy. They barely knew each other. In fact, he didn't know her at all. Would never know her. As much as she was enjoying spending time with him, anything beyond this time together was, in the cold harsh light of reality, out of the question.

She had lied to him.

Repeatedly.

She would just have to enjoy tonight and maybe tomorrow, then it would be over.

Inside the cozy little restaurant it felt warm and smelled heavenly. She inhaled deeply. Her stomach rumbled.

"Told you it was good," he said, noticing her dreamy expression.

As the hostess led the way to a table, he held

Molly's hand. She felt as if she was back in high school and out with the captain of the football team after a game. His training to stay in shape for racing kept his body lean and muscled. He had a great body.

Fewell ordered a feast of several items on the menu. Soft drinks and water completed the list.

"We'll have the champagne when we get back to the lodge," he explained. "I made a call. It'll be waiting in the room."

"Very good, Fewell. I can see why you're a winner. You stay ahead of the game."

He was also smart. Drinking, even a glass of wine, and driving was risky business. She liked that he took that into consideration.

Jason Fewell was a really nice guy. Nothing like the celebrity, self-absorbed personality she had expected.

"When do you have to go back to Chicago?"

She dragged herself back to reality. There was a question she would just as soon not answer. "A couple of days, the day after Christmas I guess. I have the rest of the week off. How about you?"

"I thought I'd stay through New Year's. Maybe even do some skiing."

The waitress delivered their drinks.

Molly took a sip of water, then laughed. "You'd

better not do any more climbing without me. That wouldn't be fair at all." Not to mention, she would worry about him going alone. That was never a good idea, no matter how experienced the climber. Mountaineering was not meant to be a solitary sport. Particularly this time of year.

"You could stay." There was that hope glimmering in his eyes again. "The room is ours. For free." He grinned. "Might as well milk it for all it's worth."

"Is that an invitation, Mr. Fewell?" That same hope she saw in his eyes had her pulse fluttering.

"It is exactly that."

The waitress showed up again, bearing platters of steaming entrées. God, it smelled good.

"Well." Molly dished samples of everything onto her plate. "I might just take you up on that, hotshot." She searched his eyes. "You'd better make sure you know what you're asking."

His gaze was steady on hers, real and open. "I know exactly what I'm asking."

"Then the answer is yes." She shoved a chunk of enchilada into her mouth. Her eyes closed and she moaned with delight.

They ate. They laughed. She wasn't ready to go but the restaurant was closing.

Even the cold air felt somehow warm when they

walked to the car. She hadn't felt like this, ever. Not over a guy. Maybe over a career accomplishment, but never over a guy.

This one was nice. Truly nice. Smart. And he loved all the outdoor activities she loved.

Was there nothing they didn't have in common?

The answer was yes. They didn't have the whole truth in common.

He'd been totally honest with her the last twenty-four hours.

And she was still lying about why she was here and where she worked.

When he'd parked in the garage at the lodge, she sat still for a few moments, her eyes closed. She wanted to hold on to this feeling a little longer. It wouldn't be long until it would be over... He would have to know the truth.

And those warm, fuzzy feelings he had for her would be gone for good.

He opened her door and she turned to look at him. "I could sleep right here, I think. I'm beat."

"Come on." He offered his hand to help her out. "We'll unpack all this gear tomorrow. We have champagne waiting."

That was something else she loved. She wasn't much of a beer drinker. Or cocktails, either, for that matter. A nice wine, bubbly and sweet, that was her weakness. He had, without knowing it, touched on another of her favorites.

As usual the lobby and bar area were brimming with activity. Skiers and hikers sharing their adventures of the day. The occasional leg or arm cast could be spotted where someone had taken a nasty spill.

"Jason Fewell!"

A chill rushed up Molly's spine.

"Keep walking," Jason whispered.

They'd almost made it to the elevators when three camera-wagging dirtbags and a reporter caught up with them. Molly recognized the one as a reporter since he was the one shouting questions.

"Any comment on today's headlines?"

Jason stabbed the call button, and didn't respond.

"I see you're getting along with your babysitter."

Dread detonated inside Molly.

The elevator doors slid open and Molly tugged at his arm. "Let's go."

But he didn't budge. He turned back to the reporter. "What the hell are you talking about?"

And that was the beginning of the end.

CHAPTER EIGHT

Christmas Eve, 9:00 a.m.

YOU LIED TO ME.

The words kept echoing in Molly's head.

She stared at the champagne now floating in a pool of water in the ice bucket.

Jason had left the lodge last night and he hadn't come back. The concierge's staff had packed his belongings and taken them away.

Molly had tried to explain that, yes, she had misled him. That his team owner had hired her to come here and see that he didn't get hurt.

But that was before.

Before she'd known the man behind the name.

Before she'd let her heart get involved.

He hadn't listened.

She didn't blame him.

If she'd told him the truth, would he have climbed that mountain with her?

That part didn't matter. He could only see the lies.

The telephone rang. Molly shuffled across the room and picked up the receiver, part of her hoping it would be him.

"Molly?"

Not him. Her employer, Victoria Colby-Camp.

"Good morning, Victoria."

"Are you all right? I heard about what happened. Mr. Harris called."

Molly explained the details of how they'd been ambushed in the lobby by the paparazzi and a rogue reporter. She should have considered that once the press had seen her with Jason they would dig until they found out who she was.

But she hadn't been thinking.

Not the way she should have anyway.

She'd gotten too close to the man she was supposed to be keeping safe.

"When are you coming back?"

She didn't know how to answer that question. She'd tried getting an earlier flight, but with the holidays everything was booked.

"Maybe in a couple of days. Flights are all booked."

"Take your time, Molly. Tomorrow's Christmas. Enjoy Aspen. Visit your family."

She could do that.

Since their mother had died, they didn't get together nearly often enough.

"Mr. Fewell told Harris how you helped him achieve the goal he'd set out to accomplish. Well done, Molly."

Great. At least he'd recognized that some part of their time together was worthwhile. "He conquered his fear that once," Molly agreed. She was happy for him, but she couldn't work up any real enthusiasm just now. "If he can do it once, he can do it every time."

"This isn't your fault, Molly. You did your job. And you did it well."

Molly thanked Victoria and placed the receiver back in its cradle. She plopped down on the sofa and sat, her head in her hands.

She had been so excited about this assignment. Her first chance to prove herself.

Was Victoria right? Had she done well?

The mission was accomplished. Molly supposed that she had done her job to the best of her ability.

She should be ecstatic.

Somehow she wasn't.

She felt empty. Lost.

Like a traitor.

No point sitting here feeling sorry for herself.

She got to her feet, dragged to the table where her cell phone lay and put through a call to her youngest brother. He was happy to hear from her. Of course, she should come home for Christmas, he insisted.

With that out of the way, she packed.

It didn't take long. She had traveled light. Like always.

She looked at the wasted bottle of champagne one last time and left the room.

The door closed behind her, the thud echoing in the empty corridor.

Alone again.

Funny, being alone hadn't bothered her at all until she'd met Jason Fewell.

Now she was pretty much obsessed with the idea.

She wouldn't be alone for long. Her brothers would all congregate at the family home. The next to the oldest lived in the house they'd grown up in. There would be a massive Christmas tree. Lots of amazing food, since his wife was an awesome cook.

They would reminisce about their childhoods. Have a few glasses of wine in front of the roaring fire.

Christmas would come and go and she would be off to Chicago.

To her little apartment.

The place where she'd thought she was happy.

11:50 a.m.

JASON OPENED THE DOOR and stared into the eyes of the man he considered a father.

Alonzo Harris swaggered into the room without a word.

Jason closed the door behind him. He didn't know why the man insisted on flying up here the day before Christmas.

It wasn't as though anything he was going to say would make a difference.

Jason would still be furious with him.

The concierge at the Snow Valley Lodge had found him a cabin last night in another village, after calling in a number of markers. Then he'd had Jason's bags sent over.

"You have some kind of nerve, young man," Harris announced, launching his counterattack before Jason so much as said a word.

Jason turned to him. "Look who's talking. You set me up. Hired a *babysitter.* What were you thinking?" That's what that damned reporter had called Molly, and he'd been right.

"I was thinking about keeping you safe," Harris growled. "Or don't you care about that anymore?"

Jason didn't want to hear this. He held up his hands. "I've said all I have to say. I understand your motive and as much as I appreciate your concern, this better not happen again."

Harris looked properly chastised. The big bear of a man loved the members of his team as if they were his own kids. "It worked, didn't it? You said as much yourself."

Jason turned away. Stared at the fire. "Yeah. It worked."

Molly had lied to him at every turn. She had grown up just a few miles from here. She'd been climbing these mountains since she was a kid.

She had coaxed him up that mountain. Made him forget all about the fear.

But he couldn't get past the lies. Even after they'd kissed, she still hadn't told him the truth.

"That doesn't make it right," he argued, not about to let Harris have the final say on the matter. "This was wrong on so many levels, I don't know where to begin."

Harris lowered into a chair. "I'm going to tell you the truth, Jason."

Jason didn't look at him. He was still too ticked off.

"You sit down here and listen to me," Harris ordered. "I know you're madder than blazes. But you're going to hear me out."

Jason turned to face him, but he wasn't sitting down.

"We've all been worried about you for the past three years. We watched you go through the pain of losing Cynthia and the agony of coming to terms with your responsibility. It's been hard as hell on every member of this team. You know that."

Jason couldn't deny his words. His team was his family. They cared about him. As much as any family. The NASCAR ties might not be blood, but they were every bit as strong.

"When you announced you were coming here to climb that mountain, we were all scared to death." Harris shook his head. "We couldn't let you take that kind of risk alone. But you refused our help. I had to find a way around that hard head of yours. And by Job I found it."

Jason shook his head. "You didn't have to do it this way."

"Son, it's like when you take that final lap around the track. You sort of feel bad at the idea that you're out in front because your closest competition hit the wall, but when you win, it's a win all the same. However you got past that checkered flag. It's a win."

"But..." Jason braced his hands on the mantel. Stared into those dancing flames. "I thought I had met someone who understood me for me."

"I see."

Did he? "This was about more than climbing that mountain, Harris. It was about bonding. Something I haven't been able to do in three years."

"You liked that feisty gal, did you?"

A smile haunted Jason's lips. "I did...I do."

"She's a pretty thing, rightly enough," Harris noted. "A real go-getter, I hear."

She definitely got Jason.

"Until I found out how easily she could lie." The anger lit inside him. He'd been struggling with it since that damned reporter outted Molly.

"She wasn't meaning to lie to you, Jason. She was just doing her job. The job I hired her to do."

"That makes it so much better." He turned to his team manager and friend. "She was paid to keep me company."

Harris folded his arms over his chest and eyed Jason a moment. "Did she lie to you about anything other than why she was here and where she worked?"

Jason shook his head. "According to what you told me, the rest of her story was fact. Who knows?"

"Then she only stretched the truth where she had to, not where it counted. Not where it was real."

What kind of answer was that? "And just how am I supposed to know what parts are real?"

Harris smiled. "Oh, I think you know exactly what part's real." He pushed to his feet. "You study on it awhile. Take your time. It'll come to you. I'm heading back to Texas. Too damned cold here."

The big guy gave Jason a hug before leaving. He never failed to squeeze the air out of Jason's lungs.

Jason sat down before the fire and did as his mentor had instructed. He studied his memories of the time he and Molly had shared. The way she smiled. The sound of her laughter. Sweet, genuine.

The way her nose turned up just slightly. The sprinkling of freckles that cascaded over the bridge of her nose. The taste of her lips.

His chest tightened, but not with the tension of a coming panic attack. With the desire to taste her lips. To hold her hand.

To know all of her.

Maybe Harris was right. Maybe Molly had been completely truthful with him on all the things that mattered. Like trusting his instincts on the mountain when he'd long ago thought his instincts were unreliable.

Right now his instincts were urging him to find her.

To tell her the truth.

CHAPTER NINE

7:00 p.m.

MOLLY COULDN'T EAT another bite. She sat on the sofa with her niece and groaned. "Your mama is too good in the kitchen."

"That's what Daddy says."

Molly hugged her niece. She didn't know why she'd hesitated about coming here. With family was the place to be at Christmas.

The snow, the fire, the food…and family. Family was what really mattered in life.

Jason Fewell had a life. A busy one with a demanding career. He likely didn't have time for anything else.

He was probably on his way back to Texas. The idea made her breath catch.

Unless she got a glimpse of him on the news, she doubted she would be seeing him again.

She wished she could feel that he would at least have pleasant thoughts about her as he looked back on their time together.

The idea that he might have bitter feelings toward her was nearly more than she could bear.

But there was nothing she could do.

He'd made up his mind and walked out.

In a couple of days she would go back to Chicago, and this whole trip would be filed away along with her expense report.

Robert, the next to the oldest, stuck his head in the door. "Mol, you have company."

"What?" She couldn't have company. No one knew she was here.

"Get the door, Mol," someone else shouted.

"Fine." She scooted up from the couch, much as she abhorred the idea of doing so, and slogged to the front of the house.

She frowned when she realized the visitor had been left on the stoop. "Great manners," she called back to her brother.

Molly opened the door and Jason was standing there, like a mirage in the falling snow. But he was real. She reached out and touched him. Couldn't help herself.

"What're you doing here?"

"I came to apologize."

It was freezing outside. Where was her brain? "Come in."

He stepped across the threshold, and she closed the door.

Her heart had already taken off. He looked good. She was so glad to see him.

But she couldn't get her hopes up.

He was here because he had something to say. An apology. He was too much of a gentleman to leave the hard feelings to fester.

He shouldered out of his parka and gloves. She took the parka, shoved the gloves into the pockets. When she'd hung his coat in the closet, she faced him.

"Why did you really come here?" He could have apologized on the phone.

"Because I didn't want to make another mistake."

Now she was even more confused. "What mistake?"

"Three years ago, I let Cynthia talk me into going along with things I shouldn't have agreed to. She's dead, and maybe I'm to blame to some degree. I should have said no. But I didn't."

Wow. He had come a long way. "I'm glad to hear you're focusing on the *you* in this equation."

"Actually—" he stepped closer "—I'm completely focused on you."

Joy kicked her heart into overdrive. "Why would you be focused on me?" She had to hear him say the words.

"Because you gave me back my courage."

Her hopes fell. Not the words she'd wanted to hear.

"But more than anything, you gave me a little glimpse of you. It wasn't enough. I want to know everything about you. I want to know you, inside and out."

Now he was talking. She tiptoed, put her arms around his neck. "Does this mean we're going to take the time—*time* being the key word—to get to know each other better? See where this goes?"

He nodded. "Absolutely."

Then he let his lips explain the rest. They captured hers. He kissed her long and deep.

Jason Fewell really was a winner.

He'd definitely won her heart.

* * * * *

SECRET SANTA

Gina Wilkins

To my daughters, now pursuing careers
on opposite coasts, and my son,
whom I'm going to keep at home for as long as possible!

Merry Christmas, kids.

CHAPTER ONE

ROBERT JOHN SANGER—Rob to a few close friends and R. J. to the rest of the world—adjusted the faux-fur-trimmed, red velvet hat on top of his white-bewigged head and admired himself in the full-length mirror. His brown eyes peered through round wire glasses perched on the end of his nose. A thick, curly white beard and mustache hid most of his face. His red suit was made of a luxurious velvet edged with the same white faux fur as his hat and belted around the padded middle with a wide black leather belt that matched his just-below-the-knee boots.

He thought he looked great.

The custom Santa suit had cost a small fortune, but it was worth it. He planned to wear it many times. He still remembered how threadbare his dad's Santa suit had become after too many charitable appearances to count. Yet his dad had never looked happier than at Christmas, when he had volunteered his services to any organization that needed an appearance from Santa Claus.

Rob had idolized his dad. All his life, he'd tried his best to emulate him. Even as he'd focused intently on his career as a NASCAR Sprint Cup Series champion race car driver, he had always intended to follow in his father's footsteps at Christmas. Of course, his dad, a tax accountant, hadn't had to contend with fame. With the media. Or with speculation that his good deeds had been designed for maximum publicity.

The racing season had ended only a couple of weeks earlier, and as usual, Rob was exhausted after the grueling schedule. Though he had hoped to capture his second NASCAR Sprint Cup Series championship in as many years, he'd finished second this season. Not bad, of course, but for a fierce competitor like him, second place would never be good enough. He needed to focus on something else for a while. To concentrate on people less fortunate than himself. To do something totally different from his usual routine.

When he'd thought of his dad's annual Santa appearances, he'd realized that this was the year he wanted to take up that tradition. And he'd wanted to do so without calling media attention to himself. So, he was making his first appearances as Santa Claus completely anonymously. Thanks to his cousin, Eileen Marcus, who was active in just about every charity in North Carolina, he had several appearances lined up during the first couple of weeks of December. If all went well, no one would know who he was beneath the beard.

Not even Mrs. Claus.

He had arrived in full costume, but had taken a moment to double-check his appearance in the men's restroom of the community center where this event was being held. Hosted by a local charity organization on this first Saturday in December, it was one of the earliest parties of the season, the date chosen to avoid scheduling conflicts as the month progressed. As Rob entered the foyer, he could sense the excitement inside as the volunteers geared up for the arrival of the underprivileged children for whom the party was being held, a group of first through third graders all enrolled in an after-school tutoring program. The whole place seemed to glitter with tinsel and garland, the smells of peppermint and fresh-baked cookies filled the air, and holiday music rang heartily from speakers arranged throughout the main room.

The door into the foyer opened, letting in a gust of cold air along with a gaily dressed duo. He grinned behind his fake beard when he recognized his "wife." Though he couldn't immediately see her face, Mrs. Claus had one fine figure, displayed modestly, but quite nicely, in a long, red velvet dress trimmed with white faux fur.

She was accompanied by a pint-sized elf—a little girl with red hair pulled into a curly ponytail, pointed plastic ears fitted over her own, a sweetly freckled face, and a green elf dress worn with green-and-white stockings and curly-toed, bell-tipped shoes. The child held a big, beribboned basket filled with small peppermint canes.

Spotting him, the little girl widened her eyes and pointed. "There's Santa!"

Mrs. Claus turned with a smile to greet him.

He felt the breath leave his padded body with a stunned whoosh.

Maybe it was her eyes. So green he wondered if the color could possibly be natural, they gleamed with intelligence and humor behind a little pair of wire-framed glasses similar to his own. Her face was a perfect oval, creamy and unlined, belying the color of her upswept white hair covered with a white lace cap. Little ringlets from the wig just brushed her rosy cheeks. He wondered what color her hair really was. Her nose was perfect, her mouth soft and delectable, tinted with a glossy, candy red. She couldn't possibly be older than thirty.

Realizing that he was simply standing there, staring at her, he cleared his throat and tried to speak lightly. "Mrs. Claus, I presume."

She nodded. "I hope we're not late. We got into a bit of traffic."

"No, you're right on time. The kids haven't even arrived yet."

"Oh, good." Placing a hand on the little girl's shoulder, she said, "This is my daughter, Kylie, who'll be assisting us today."

Her daughter. Which probably meant she was unavailable. Telling himself it was foolish to be disappointed, he held out a white-gloved hand to little Kylie, whom he guessed was six or seven. "Nice to meet you, Kylie. I'm—"

"I know who you are," she assured him, giving him a smile that revealed a charming gap where a baby tooth had once been. "You're Santa."

"Now, Kylie, remember what I said," her mother admonished. "This isn't the real Santa. He's one of Santa's helpers—just as we are today."

Rob knelt to bring himself to the girl's level. "Your mom's right. You can call me Rob. But not in front of any of the other children, okay? For them, I'm Santa today."

She gave him a big wink. "Okay, Santa."

Smitten, he grinned at her. "That's the spirit."

"I'm giving out candy canes," she told him, hefting the basket. "I have to make sure everyone gets one. It's a very important job."

"Yes, it is. Santa would be proud to have such a responsible helper." Rising, Rob turned to her mother and offered his hand to her. "Great kid you've got here."

"Thank you," she said, clasping his hand for a moment. He regretted they both wore gloves. "My name is Leanne, by the way."

"Nice to meet you, Leanne. I'm Rob." The fact that she hadn't offered a last name made it easier for him to do the same. He was pretty sure she hadn't recognized him, and he would just as soon keep it that way for now.

"Oh, good, you're all here." A middle-aged woman bustled through the door that led into the main room, nodding in satisfaction when she saw the three of them. "The children should be arriving any minute, so maybe you should set up inside. I'm Jane, by the way, if you need anything at all. And thank you so much for donating your time today. You all look wonderful. I know the children will love you."

Still chattering, she led them into the lavishly decorated party room. Two huge trees, sparkling with lights, tinsel and ornaments, dominated the decorations. Wrapped gifts were piled beneath them. A red-velvet-covered armchair sat on a dais cornered by large plastic candy canes. A camera sat on a tripod nearby for photos of the children with Santa. On one side of the room, long tables were filled with food and smaller tables were decorated with red tablecloths and green-and-red center-pieces. Green-and-red balloons floated above each table. Judging by Kylie's entranced expression, Rob figured the decorations would be a hit with the soon-to-arrive guests.

"This is where you'll sit, Santa," Jane said, ges-turing unnecessarily at the big chair. "The children will line up to speak to you, and we have a person-alized gift for each one, which Mrs. Claus will hand to you to give them. Remember, chat with each child, but we don't encourage you to ask what they want for Christmas, since we don't want any child to be disappointed on Christmas morning. We certainly don't want you to make any promises."

"Of course." He had already been given basic instructions, but there were some things he would have known on his own, he thought wryly.

He took a seat in the chair, settling into a comfortable position.

The first ripple of nerves went through him at the thought of the horde of children who would soon descend upon his knee. He was good with kids, he reminded himself in a mental pep talk. He could do this.

Kylie leaned against the arm of his chair. "You look just like the real Santa Claus," she assured him.

He grinned behind his beard. "Thanks."

"Do I look like a real elf?"

"Absolutely. You're brimming with elf-confidence."

After only a momentary hesitation, Kylie dissolved in giggles. "I got that. You're funny."

It was easy to amuse one well-behaved seven-year-old with a stale pun. He just hoped the rest of his audience would be so cooperative.

"She likes you," Leanne commented when Kylie ran off to examine an intricate Victorian gingerbread house set up on a table across the room.

"Of course she does. What kid doesn't like Santa Claus?"

Smiling a little, Leanne shook her head. "What I meant was, maybe you can get her to tell you what she wants for Christmas. I asked her last week, so I could get a little head start on shopping, you know? I could sense there's something special she wants, but she wouldn't tell me. It's odd, usually she tells me everything—it's always been just the two of us, you see, so we're in the habit of confiding in each other. But she's being very secretive about this. I wouldn't want her to be disappointed if she has her heart set on something."

Unreasonably cheered, Rob smiled at her. "I'll see what I can do—but I'm not supposed to ask what the kids want for Christmas."

"That's for the kids who might not get what they ask for. If Kylie has her heart set on something, I'll make sure she gets it—well, if I can, of course. She asks for so little. So, if she happens to tell you what she wants, let me know, okay?"

"I'll do that."

Kylie ran back to join them, her basket of candies bobbing at her side. "Mommy, you should go look at the gingerbread house. It's even got gingerbread furniture inside, like a real dollhouse."

"That sounds interesting. I'll go look. Stay here by Santa, Kylie. The guests will be arriving any minute."

Knowing what he was supposed to do, Rob smiled at the little girl when her mother crossed the room to examine the gingerbread house. "So, Kylie, is there anything special you want for Christmas? Maybe I could put in a word for you with the real Santa."

He knew immediately why Leanne had gotten the impression that Kylie had something specific in mind. It was written all over the child's instantly wistful expression. He held his breath, hoping she would confide her desire to him, but instead she shook her head, making the little bells at the tip of her elf's cap jingle. "That's okay. I'll tell him, myself."

"Um—when are you going to do that?"

She shrugged. "As soon as I see the real Santa."

"Yeah, but, Kylie—"

A burst of noise drowned out his words—not that he knew what he would have said to somehow convince her to confide in him. Leanne hurried to take her place at his side as a group of children scampered noisily through the doors, herded by the charity volunteers. Several kids squealed and dashed in his direction, only to be firmly stopped and arranged into four groups of ten by Jane, the organizer.

"Group one, get in line to visit Santa," she instructed them in a friendly, but no-nonsense tone. "Each of you will have a picture taken with Santa and receive a gift, which you may then take to the table marked with the number one. Groups two, three and four, line up now at the refreshment tables and you'll be served whatever you like by the ladies there. Everyone will get a chance to talk to Santa, and everyone will receive a gift, so just be patient and enjoy the party until it's your turn, okay?"

"What do you want to bet she used to be a schoolteacher?" Rob asked Leanne in a low, amused voice.

"No bet," she replied with a smile. "I happen to know that she was. She told me earlier, when Kylie and I arrived."

The first child—a boy with a bright smile and eager, dark chocolate eyes—headed straight for Rob's knee when he was given permission to approach. "Hey, Santa."

"Well, hello, there." Rob tried to speak in a cheerfully booming voice suitable to his character. "What's your name?"

"I'm DeMarcus. That's my sister, Nevaeh," he added, motioning toward the little girl shifting her feet impatiently at the head of the line. "I'm six. She's seven."

"And have you been getting along with Nevaeh this year?"

After only a momentary hesitation, DeMarcus nodded. "Pretty good. Most of the time," he added.

"What grade are you in, DeMarcus?"

"First grade. Ms. Rogers is my teacher. She's nice, but she gets loud sometimes."

"Are you being a good student?"

The boy nodded again. "I'm real good at math, and Ms. Rogers says I'm getting better at reading."

"Good for you." They chatted a couple minutes more and then Leanne handed Rob a wrapped package with DeMarcus's name written on the tag.

Rob had been told that each child had been given the opportunity to request one special gift, and the volunteers had purchased and wrapped those items. Rob had given a generous donation to that cause, though he had done so anonymously through Eileen, who was working the refreshment table today. As they'd agreed, she hadn't acknowledged him, in the hope that no one would connect him with her race car driver cousin.

He gave the gift to DeMarcus, who beamed as he clutched it to his chest.

"Say thank you, DeMarcus," Jane reminded him.

"Thank you, Santa," the boy parroted obediently.

Rob lifted a white-gloved hand. "High five."

Laughing, the boy slapped his palm while still clutching his gift. He climbed down from Rob's knee, accepted a candy cane from Kylie, then hurried off to the refreshment table.

"Good job," Leanne murmured as Nevaeh moved forward to take her brother's place on Rob's knee.

Rob looked up at her hopefully. "I was okay?"

"You were great," she assured him.

Much too pleased by her praise, Rob turned with an extra-bright smile for young Nevaeh.

SANTA HAD ONE SEXY SMILE. Despite the lush beard that covered most of his face, Leanne suspected that a very nice-looking man lurked behind those synthetic whiskers. It was something about his eyes, a warm, rich brown that gleamed when he smiled. Something about the way his lips quirked when he was amused, causing those warm eyes to crinkle a little at the corners.

She guessed his age to be early thirties. She

couldn't tell anything about his build beneath the velvet suit, but she had a feeling the suit was well padded. The way he stood, the way he moved, indicated to her that he was in pretty good shape under there.

He seemed like a nice guy, too. She enjoyed watching him interact with the children. He acted so genuinely interested in each one of them. He didn't talk down to them, and he paid close attention to the things they said to him in return. He was even able to coax a few words out of the shyest children in attendance, the ones whose natural inclination was to duck behind someone they knew when it was their turn to visit with Santa. But of course he liked kids, or he wouldn't be volunteering to portray Santa Claus for this and several other upcoming charity events.

She wondered if he had any of his own.

"I'm too old to believe in Santa Claus," a boy of about eight in group four informed Rob somewhat defiantly. Standing in front of Rob's knee, he scowled at "Santa" with his best tough-guy expression. Some of the other kids had been a bit naughty that afternoon, trying to tug at Santa's beard or shock him with a curse word—these were, after all, at-risk kids—but Santa had handled them all in stride.

"What's your name?" he asked, just as comfortable with this boy.

"Everyone calls me Streak. 'Cause I'm the fastest runner they know."

"A runner, huh? I used to be on the track team in high school. I was a sprinter."

Streak eyed him skeptically, taking in the snowy beard and soft middle. "You were a runner?"

Chuckling, Rob lifted a shoulder. "Don't judge by appearances, Streak. I was pretty fast. I even thought about going to the Olympics, but I, uh, chose to concentrate on another sport, instead."

"Reindeer races?" Streak asked with a sneer.

Rob laughed, and Leanne tried to hide a smile. She thought it was a pretty clever dig, actually.

"Yeah, something like that," Rob agreed. "Anyway, you keep training, Streak. Your talent could get you a college scholarship, and maybe you'll be an Olympian, yourself."

Looking a bit thoughtful, Streak shrugged. "I could do it. I'm really fast."

"I'm sure you are. Mrs. Claus, we have a gift for Streak, don't we?"

Leanne stepped forward with the shoe-box-size package Jane had handed her for this boy. "We certainly do, Santa. Here you go."

Winking at her, Rob took the gift, then turned to present it to Streak. "Merry Christmas, Streak. I'll be watching for you in the 2020 Summer Olympics."

A reluctant smile tugged at the boy's lips. "Yeah. Maybe."

Taking the gift, he stepped away, already ripping into the paper. "Oh, man!" he hooted a minute later, pulling a pair of sleek-looking running shoes from the box. "Sweet."

"Tell Santa thank you, Streak," Jane called to him, the schoolteacher in her determined to teach lessons even during this holiday event.

Leanne watched as the boy met Rob's eyes. After a moment, he moved closer to say, "I still don't think you're really Santa. But, anyway, thanks for the shoes, man."

"You're welcome," Rob assured him. "And you should thank every volunteer here today before you leave. They all had a part in providing you with this event and your gift."

But the boy was already gone, dashing across the room to show off his new running shoes to his friends.

"Wait!" Kylie called out, running after him while waving a candy cane in her hand. "You forgot this!"

"She takes her responsibilities very seriously," Rob murmured to Leanne as he motioned for the next child—one of only three left in line—to come forward. "She's being amazingly patient. I would think she'd be bored by now."

Still a little flustered from the wink he'd given her, Leanne replied, "Kylie's having a great time."

"Yeah. So am I. How about you?"

"Of course," she replied, before turning to collect the next child's gift.

By the time she turned back, Rob's attention was already fully focused on the little girl sitting on his knee, who was telling him how much she loved playing dress-up because she wanted to be an "actoress" when she grew up. Leanne suspected that there were dress-up costumes in the big, wrapped box she held for the girl.

When the final child had seen Santa and received a gift and a candy cane, Jane consulted in a low voice with Rob, and then made an announcement that Mr. and Mrs. Claus and their elf helper had to leave. "But first," she said over the chorus of disappointed groans, "Santa's going to lead us in a song. Everyone knows the one about Rudolph, right? That just happens to be Santa's favorite song, and he wants you all to sing it with him before he goes."

A bit surprised, Leanne turned to look at Rob as he stood on the dais prepared to lead the singing. She thought his face looked a little pink, as if he might be flustered at the idea of leading singing, but it was hard to tell beneath the beard.

He needn't have been concerned. He had a very nice voice. It carried as he led the children in a noisy, enthusiastic version of the old holiday standard. She and Kylie sang along, and then Jane escorted them through a back door and into a smaller meeting room where they could relax while the party concluded in the other room. One of the volunteers brought them all plates of goodies and glasses of punch.

Rob popped a bit of cookie into his mouth. "I'd better pass on that red punch," he said, patting his snowy white beard.

"You could always take off the beard," she suggested. She had to admit she was curious about what he looked like beneath the costume.

After a brief hesitation, he shook his head. "I wouldn't want one of the kids to accidentally see me without it. It would spoil the whole afternoon. I'll just wait until later to change. I'm not thirsty, anyway."

For a moment she wondered if he was reluctant

for her to see his face. But since that made no sense at all, she decided to take him at his word.

Kylie was making good headway on her own cookies and candy treats. She had no reservations about the red punch, which left faint red stains around her mouth. Handing her daughter a napkin, Leanne asked Rob, "So, how did you get roped into this gig?"

He chuckled. "I volunteered, actually. My dad always, um, helped Santa at this time of year," he explained with a glance at Kylie. "It's something I always wanted to do when I had the opportunity. What about you?"

"My next-door neighbor, Eileen Marcus, is very active in a lot of local charities," she replied. "I work full-time as an office manager for an insurance salesman, and I take care of Kylie when I'm not working, so I don't have a lot of extra time for charity work, but this was something Kylie and I could do together, so I accepted. I think it's important for Kylie to learn about volunteering and helping those who are less fortunate."

Something she'd said seemed to have startled him, but he merely nodded and commented, "It's always good to start instilling those values at an early age."

She was pleased that he agreed with her in that respect. "I think so, too."

He popped a piece of chocolate into his mouth, carefully avoiding his whiskers, and she had to laugh at how funny he looked with his beard bobbing up and down when he chewed. That made him grin, too.

Very nice guy, she thought again. Since she was scheduled for three more appearances with him, she was glad she found it so easy to be with him.

It had to be the Santa suit. As Rob, himself, had asked, who didn't like Santa?

TWENTY MINUTES LATER, the party was over, and the guests had been escorted away with their gifts and goody bags. Leanne, Kylie and Rob were thanked repeatedly by charity volunteers as they made their way to the exit. Rob escorted Leanne and Kylie to their car, a sensible, no-frills white sedan parked close to his own gleaming black sports car.

"I did good, didn't I, Santa? I mean, Rob?" Kylie asked, hopping up and down as her mom unlocked their car doors.

"You did great, Kylie," he assured her. "You should be very elf-satisfied with your performance."

Leanne groaned, but Kylie giggled. "I have high elf-esteem," she assured him, and he laughed, figuring she'd been waiting for a chance to say that.

Really cute kid.

"I'll see you both next Saturday, I guess," he said, glancing at Leanne as he spoke.

The smile she gave him made him swallow hard. He was charmed by little Kylie, but her mother made his pulse race.

He found himself looking forward to the next appearance with the intriguing "Mrs. Claus."

CHAPTER TWO

"SERIOUSLY? YOU'RE GOING out like this?"

Adjusting his beard, Rob laughed. "Yes, I'm going out like this."

His crew chief and best friend, Bill Ross, shook his head dubiously as he studied Rob in full Santa costume. "You look—"

Rob patted his middle. "Like Santa Claus?"

"Well, I was going to say like a goofball, but okay." Bill had stopped by the house for an off-season meeting that afternoon, bringing with him a three-inch stack of paperwork he and Rob had to go through and discuss. They'd spent two hours talking about work before Rob had announced that he had to get ready for his Santa appearance late that afternoon. Amused, Bill had insisted on staying to see his driver decked out in full Santa regalia.

Rob made a slow turn, holding out his arms to

give his friend the full effect. "How can you not like Santa Claus?"

"Yeah, ask me that again when you've got three kids, all with five-page lists of stuff they want for Christmas."

"Come on, Bill, your kids are the least spoiled I know. You and Paula have done a great job of raising them with money, but without turning them into greedy, entitled little monsters—like a few others I could name."

Bill nodded gratefully. "Gotta give Paula credit for a lot of that. She's the one who makes sure they know just how fortunate we are as a family. She's insisting that each one of them narrow their list down to just three special items. We'll fill in with some smaller things, but she's determined not to ruin them with material excess."

Settling his cap more snugly on his head, Rob spoke approvingly, "I've always thought Paula was one of the best mothers I know. She's much too good for you, of course."

"No argument here. Uh, your eyebrows are crooked."

"Thanks." Peering into the mirror, Rob made an adjustment to the bushy white eyebrows he'd attached with spirit gum. "There. Is that better?"

"Yeah. I guess. So, you're having a good time with this, huh?"

"A great time. The kids seemed to really enjoy the party last weekend."

"Tell me more about this woman who posed as Mrs. Claus. You said she seemed nice?"

"Very nice. Her name's Leanne, and she's a single mom to a cute little girl named Kylie."

"Good-looking?"

"I've only seen her in costume, but, yeah, she's pretty."

"Going to ask her out?"

"I've only spent a couple of hours with her. But, maybe."

Bill nodded in satisfaction. "That's good. It's been too long since you've been out with anyone interesting. Paula's been threatening to fix you up again, and you know she always puts me in the middle when she does that."

"Please. No more fix-ups," Rob responded with a groan. "I love Paula, I really do, but she and I don't necessarily agree on the perfect match for me."

"Yeah, I haven't forgotten the giggly blonde she brought to dinner with us last month."

Groaning again, Rob shook his bewigged head.

"Let's not talk about that evening right now, okay? I'm trying to stay in a jolly mood."

"Can I hear you say Ho, Ho, Ho?"

"Sorry." Rob reached for his keys. "I'm saving all my Ho, Ho, Hos for the kids."

Bill tagged behind Rob as he headed for the door of his palatial, yet spartanly furnished lakeside mansion. He'd bought the place on Lake Norman a year earlier, after he'd won his NASCAR Sprint Cup Series championship—the first of several, he hoped. At the time he'd purchased the house, he'd hoped to turn it into a real home, the kind he'd lived in as a kid. This place was a lot bigger than his family home, of course, but he'd wanted it to have that same warm, welcoming feeling his parents had instilled in their modest Mooresville bi-level.

He'd discovered that it was hard for a place to feel like a real home when he was the only one living there. And when he was on the road thirty-four weekends a year. He'd furnished the house with the essentials needed for his comfort on the rare times when he was there, and told himself that he would get around to the rest later. In the back of his mind had been the thought that he would like to find someone to share this place with him, to make a home with him here, but finding time for relationships wasn't easy for a busy driver. Regardless of Paula's efforts to introduce him to every single woman who came within her orbit.

He wondered how Leanne felt about race car drivers.

"Do me a favor, will you, Bill?" he asked as he locked his doors behind him.

The keys to his own car in his hand, his friend cocked his head curiously. "What do you need?"

"Don't mention Leanne to Paula. I mean, you know how Paula gets. She'll hear I've met someone nice and she'll be throwing dinner parties for us. Give me a chance to find out first if Leanne and I even get along during a second meeting, okay?"

Looking amused, Bill nodded. "You have my word. I won't mention her until you've had at least a second date."

"I'd appreciate that."

"No problem." Taking one last look at his disguised friend, Bill laughed softly and turned toward his car. "Don't drive stupid on the way to your gig, okay? That would be one embarrassing mug shot in tomorrow's paper."

Laughing, Rob opened the door of his sports car. "I'll keep that in mind."

THE PARTY ON THIS SATURDAY afternoon was being
given at a private kindergarten for children with
learning disabilities. The event was being held in
the school dining room, which had been suitably
decorated for the occasion. The schedule was a
little different this time. Santa and Mrs. Claus and
their helper elf would make a grand appearance
after games and refreshments. They'd been instructed to park in the teachers' lot at the back of
the school so the children wouldn't see them arrive.

Leanne saw Rob climbing out of his low black
car just as she turned her own economy sedan into
the sparsely occupied back lot. Kylie spotted him
at the same time from the backseat. "Mommy,
look. There's Rob. I mean, Santa."

Leanne smiled indulgently. Kylie had been quite
taken with Rob. She had been practicing elf puns
all week. "I see him. We're all right on time."

Having recognized their car, he waited until
Leanne parked, then came around to open her door
for her. He carried a bag filled with stuffed animals,
an arrangement he had made with the organizers
of today's party. "Nice to see you both again."

"Hi, Rob!" Extricating herself from the seat belt,
Kylie climbed out of the car, bells jingling from her

hat and shoes. "Look, I got a new necklace. It has a candy cane on it. Ms. Eileen gave it to me."

"Eileen's our next-door neighbor," Leanne reminded Rob as he bent dutifully to admire the little candy cane charm on a thin gold chain.

"It's very nice," Rob assured the child. "Looks good enough to eat."

She shook a little finger at him. "You can't eat it. You have to use elf-control."

He grinned. "You just couldn't wait to use that one, could you?"

She giggled. "I have some more. But I'm not going to tell you all at once."

"I'll brace myself for them." Straightening, he turned to Leanne. "Ready to face our fans?"

Nodding, she fell into step beside him, with Kylie jingling along on his other side. "It has occurred to me that Mrs. Claus gets overshadowed by her more famous husband," she remarked lightly, just to make conversation as they crossed the parking lot and circled the building to the front entrance.

He chuckled. "Sorry about that. I guess it's just the price of having a famous spouse. So, uh, how do you feel about that?"

She smiled. "Fortunately, I'm not the type to

crave the spotlight. I'm perfectly content to stand back and let you take the bows. Kylie, however…"

She let her voice drift off as Kylie climbed the stairs with enough force to cause every bell on her costume to ring out. Kylie was definitely not shy about seeking attention.

One of the teachers met them just inside the door. "Oh, you look wonderful," she said, addressing the compliment to all three of them. "The children are going to be so happy to see you."

"I have candy canes," Kylie announced, holding up her basket as evidence.

The teacher smiled down at her. "The children all love candy canes."

She glanced at Rob then. "The bag of toys is just right. Exactly as the children expect Santa's bag to look."

The big red toy bag was trimmed with white faux fur along the opening. Big stuffed animals of every species and in a rainbow of improbable colors filled the bag and peeked over the top. Grinning behind his beard, Rob slung the bag over his left shoulder. "How do I look?" he asked, meeting Leanne's eyes.

Returning his smile, she assured him, "You look perfect."

"Why, thank you, ma'am."

Laughing, she moved to his side and motioned Kylie to fall in behind them. After confirming that they were ready, the teacher who had greeted them threw open the doors into the party room. Holiday music and babbling voices spilled into the entryway, and the teacher had to raise her own voice to be heard over the merriment. "Children, there's someone here to see you," she said loudly.

Stepping out of the way, she revealed the guest of honor.

"Santa Claus!" a dozen little voices squealed at once.

Obviously reveling in his role, Rob moved forward, Ho-Ho-Hoing and beaming at the eager children who surged around him.

IF POSSIBLE, THIS PARTY was even more fun for Rob than the previous one. The children, most of whom had Down syndrome, were well-behaved, happy and affectionate. They seemed to be delighted with the stuffed animals Leanne distributed from Santa's big bag. Kylie was in her element again, skipping around the room in her jingly shoes to make sure everyone had a candy cane.

One little girl with strikingly blue eyes and dark

blond pigtails tugged shyly at the hem of his coat. Remembering her from earlier, he leaned over to smile at her. "Did you forget to tell me something, Violet?"

She nodded, her round face wreathed in a smile. "She's pretty," she whispered loudly, clutching her new pink teddy bear to her chest.

"Um—?"

"Your wife," she clarified, pointing a chubby finger at Leanne, who was chatting with a little boy in a wheelchair as she helped him select a stuffed dog for his gift. "She's pretty."

A funny feeling went through him at the reference to Leanne as his wife, even though he knew the child was only referring to the roles they were playing for the day. He was sure he would have felt the same way if anyone else had been posing as Mrs. Claus; he wasn't accustomed to thinking of anyone as his wife.

Still, marriage and kids had been on his mind for a while now as he'd watched his married teammates and competitors with their families at the tracks. It would be nice to have someone there when the races ended and the roar of the crowds died away, someone to share his luxury motor home on the road and his nice house on Lake

Norman. He didn't know that Leanne was the woman he'd been looking for—but he didn't know that she wasn't, either. She certainly made a great first impression.

"Yes," he agreed. "She is very pretty. And so are you," he added, tugging gently at a swaying pony-tail. "Has anyone ever told you that you have beautiful blue eyes?"

"Yes," Violet replied with a charming smile.

He laughed. "Well, they were right."

She impulsively hugged his knee. "Thank you for my teddy."

"You already thanked me," he reminded her. "And you're still welcome."

The party organizers began to signal that it was time for the guests to be on their way. "Say goodbye to Santa Claus, everyone," one of the teachers instructed.

"Goodbye, Santa Claus," they recited in unison.

"And Mrs. Claus, too," someone else said, prompting a chorus of "Goodbye, Mrs. Claus."

On an impulse, Rob took Leanne's hand and tucked it beneath his arm as they turned toward the door, waving to the children on their way out. Kylie followed with her nearly empty candy basket.

Out in the entryway, Kylie tugged at her mother's

dress, motioning her down so she could whisper in her ear. Leanne smiled and pointed to a door on the left. "I'll wait for you out here."

Kylie handed her basket to her mother, then slipped into the restroom and closed the door, leaving Rob alone with Leanne for a moment. Never one to miss taking advantage of an opportunity, he smiled at her. "Good party, wasn't it?"

"Yes, I had a lovely time. The kids were so cute."

"Did you get to talk to Violet much? She's a real sweetheart."

"Yes, I remember her."

"She told me I have a very pretty wife."

The color in Leanne's already rosy cheeks deepened a bit. "Did she? That was nice of her."

"I agreed with her, of course."

Glancing down at the candy-cane basket she held, Leanne murmured lightly, "Why, thank you, sir."

"So, maybe, after all this holiday craziness is over, you and I could have a drink sometime? As ourselves, I mean."

Her eyes widened so dramatically that he wondered if it had really been so long since anyone had asked her out. He found that hard to believe. Maybe she just hadn't expected to be asked out by Santa

Claus. He was trying to figure out a way to tell her who he really was when she stopped him by shaking her head.

"Thank you," she said, "but I don't really date right now. Between work and Kylie, I just don't have any spare time."

"You, uh, don't date. At all?"

"No." Lifting her chin, she met his eyes. "It's just not a good time for me. But I do thank you for asking, and I hope this doesn't make things awkward between us at the other holiday appearances we have lined up this month."

"No, of course not," he assured her hastily. "Nothing's changed. It was just a thought."

The restroom door opened and Kylie emerged. "Okay, I'm ready."

Doing his best to mask his stinging ego, Rob opened the door for them. "After you, ladies."

They were crossing the back parking lot with Kylie skipping and chattering between them when they heard another child squeal, "Santa Claus! Look, Cruz, it's Santa Claus!"

Rob glanced up to see a dark-haired, dark-eyed boy of about fourteen carrying a grocery bag in each arm. He was accompanied on the sidewalk that skirted the back of the school by a boy of perhaps nine and a girl around Kylie's age. Both the younger children had shaggy, dark hair and bore a marked resemblance to the teenager.

It was the little girl who jumped up and down and pointed at Rob. "It's Santa, it's Santa!"

Amused by her enthusiasm, Rob took a step toward the trio. "Hello, there," he said in his jolly voice. "Would you like to talk to Santa Claus?"

The child looked up beseechingly at her older brother. "Can I go talk to him, Cruz? Please?"

"I'll give you a candy cane," Kylie offered eagerly, waving her basket.

Cruz hesitated a moment, then motioned for his sister to stay put while he moved forward to speak with Rob. His body was still adolescent-lean in a somewhat shabby gray hoodie and faded jeans with holes in both knees. A silver cross hung from a leather strip tied around his neck. He was obviously prepared to defend his little sister from these colorfully dressed strangers. "What's going on here?"

Intrigued by the young man's protective attitude, Rob motioned toward the school where the party was still winding down. "We just made an appearance at a Christmas party for the children in this school. I'd be happy to visit with your little sister for a moment. And if it's okay with you, I have a couple of extra stuffed animals left over for your sister and your brother, too, if he'd like one."

"Yeah?" Cruz looked warily at the almost-empty toy bag. "How much?"

Rob shook his head. "Santa doesn't charge for toys. I do this for fun. I just like to make kids smile, you know?"

"Well…okay," Cruz conceded. "Ana will get a kick out of it. But don't make any promises to her for Christmas presents, okay?"

"I never make promises," Rob assured him.

Stepping back, Cruz nodded toward his little sister. "Okay, you can talk to Santa."

Thrilled, the little girl dashed forward. She was at that cute age between being too shy to talk to Santa Claus and too jaded to believe in him. "Hi, Santa," she said, catching his hand in hers. "I just wrote you a letter, but I haven't sent it yet."

"I'll look forward to getting it," he said, bending down to her level. "Your name is Ana, right?"

"Ana Osorio. And those are my brothers, Cruz and Victor."

"I don't have to ask if you've been a good girl. I can tell that you have."

Ana beamed. "I do everything Cruz tells me to, just like Mama says I should. And I don't fight with

Victor—well, not much. And I clean my room and I dry the dishes after dinner."

"That's very good. I'm sure you're a lot of help to your mother."

She beckoned him down closer so she could whisper in his ear. "There's something I want very much for Christmas."

Remembering Cruz's request, Rob cleared his throat. "Um, Ana—"

"I don't know if it's something Santa can do or not," she added quietly. "But I want my Mama to get a good job so she doesn't have to clean so many houses and offices and I can see her more. And then Cruz wouldn't have to take care of Victor and me all the time and he could play baseball."

"Oh. Well, I— Isn't there anything you want for yourself for Christmas, Ana?" he stammered, caught off guard by her request.

She shrugged. "Anything's okay with me."

Straightening, he reached for the bag he'd given to Leanne to hold for him. "I bet we have something in here for Ana, don't we, Mrs. Claus? Just to hold her over until Christmas?"

"I'm sure we do," Leanne replied with a bright smile for the little girl. "And our little elf has a candy cane for you before you go."

Rob pulled a yellow teddy bear, a realistic-looking stuffed tiger and a purple elephant from the bag. "Which would you like, Ana?"

Her eyes lit up. "I can have one? Really?"

She looked quickly at Cruz, who nodded somberly. After only a moment's thought, she chose the elephant, hugging it to her slender little chest. "Thank you, Santa Claus. I like him a lot."

"You're welcome. Step right over there and get a candy cane from my elf friend. I'll talk to Victor, if he likes."

"Okay." She skipped up to Leanne and Kylie, showing them her elephant before accepting a candy cane.

Victor was a bit shyer than his little sister, and obviously considered himself too old to talk to Santa. But he had his dark eyes fixed on the stuffed tiger as he stepped forward slowly.

"Hello, Victor. How are you?"

"I'm good," the boy replied in a quiet voice, peering at Rob through a curtain of shaggy bangs.

"How's school?"

"It's okay. I got a B on my math test Friday."

"Hey, that's great. I always liked math."

"Yeah, me, too. Uh—aren't you going to ask what I want for Christmas?"

"If you want to tell me," Rob replied.

Slanting a quick glance at his brother, Victor murmured, "I know you aren't really Santa, but I can tell Ana I told you stuff I wanted. She'll like that."

Amused by the reasoning, Rob nodded. "I'm sure she will."

"Anyway, if you really could bring us stuff, I wish you could get a ballerina dress for Ana. She wants one really bad, and Mama is trying to find one for her, but I don't think she has yet. And Cruz needs a new coat. He doesn't like to wear his because it's getting too little, but he won't let Mama buy him a new one because he says we can't afford it."

"And what about you, Victor?" Rob asked, touched by the picture of proud poverty the boy was unconsciously drawing for him. "Don't you want anything?"

Victor shrugged. "I'd take a new backpack if you find an extra one in your sleigh Christmas Eve," he quipped.

Smiling, Rob handed him the stuffed tiger. "Will this do for now?"

"That's pretty cool. I like tigers." Victor accepted the toy with a shy smile. "Thank you."

"You're very welcome. Go get a candy cane from Kylie. She loves giving out candy."

When Victor joined his sister, chatting with Leanne and Kylie, Rob moved closer to Cruz. The teenager looked at him with a wry smile. "I'm a little too old to sit on Santa's knee."

Rob chuckled. "I know. I just want to tell you what nice kids Victor and Ana are. They're very polite."

Cruz nodded, his dark eyes gleaming. "They are good kids. Thanks for talking to them and giving them the toys. You made Ana's day."

"Cruz." Rob hesitated a moment, searching for tactful words. "I got the impression your family is going through a difficult time."

The boy frowned, looking older than Rob suspected he really was. "We're doing okay. It's just— well, our dad died two years ago, and my mom got laid off from her job. She's got some part-time jobs now while she looks for another. I'd work, too, but I have to take care of the kids."

"You seem to be doing a very good job with that."

Cruz shrugged. "Like I said, they're good kids. Still, as soon as I'm old enough, I'm going to get a job so I can help Mama out more. I want to work for a pit crew someday, but maybe I can work in one of the shops first. I hear they hire people to sweep floors and stuff."

"Yes, they do. When you're a little older, I'm sure you can find something in one of the shops. In the meantime, would you mind if I help your family out a little this Christmas?"

Cruz straightened his thin shoulders. "We don't take charity."

"It isn't charity, exactly," Rob assured him quickly. "I'd get a kick out of doing something for Ana and Victor, and maybe I could help your mom find a job. I've got a few strings I can pull."

"Why would you do this?" Cruz asked, suspicion born of difficult times reflected in his dark eyes.

"Because I'm Santa Claus?"

His lips twitched with a slight smile, but Cruz didn't seem overly reassured.

Rob sighed. "Because people have done nice things for me when I've needed help in the past, and now it's my turn to help some other people. Besides, I don't have any kids of my own, and I really like Christmas. Obviously," he added, motioning toward his costume.

"That's not your little girl?" Cruz asked, nodding toward Kylie.

"No. She and her mom are making appearances

with me at some Christmas parties this month. So, what do you say, Cruz? Will you let me give you a hand? For the kids?"

That wasn't exactly a fair argument, since Rob suspected Cruz would do almost anything for his younger siblings. After only a moment, Cruz asked, "You really think you can find a good job for my mom?"

"I'm pretty sure I can."

"Okay. It'd be all right, I guess, if it's okay with my mom."

He recited his address and phone number, and Rob made a note of them in his personal-assistant phone, which he then slipped quickly back into his pants pocket. "I'll be seeing you around, Cruz."

"Okay, uh—what do I call you? Other than Santa, I mean."

Lowering his voice to a conspiratorial tone, he replied, "Just call me Rob."

Still looking a little concerned about what he'd agreed to, Cruz jerked his head to summon Victor and Ana. "We gotta go. I gotta put these groceries away before the frozen stuff melts."

Hugging her purple elephant, Ana skipped after him. "Bye, Santa, bye, Mrs. Santa, bye, elf," she called behind her, waving.

Rob turned to see Leanne studying him intently. She stood close enough that he wondered exactly how much of his conversation with Cruz she had overheard.

"You're taking this Santa role very seriously, aren't you?" she asked, letting him know that she'd heard at least a little.

He shrugged self-consciously. "They seem like a nice family in a tough situation. It's the least I can do to see if I can help them out a little."

"And you really think you can find a job for their mother?"

"Like I told Cruz, I have a few strings to pull. I'll find out what she's looking for, and then see if I know anyone with the right connections. It won't hurt to try, anyway. In the meantime, I can buy a few Christmas gifts for the kids. It's just something I want to do."

"Mama, can we go now?" Kylie asked. "My nose is getting cold."

It was pretty chilly, but the child hadn't wanted to button her coat and hide her elf costume. Warm enough in his own velvet coat and pants, Rob watched as Leanne helped Kylie get buckled into her seat.

"I'll see you tomorrow," he told her when she

closed the car door and moved around toward the driver's side. They had three more appearances scheduled, one at a children's hospital the next afternoon.

She nodded, her expression so studiedly serene that he couldn't get even a hint of her thoughts. "See you tomorrow, Rob."

She drove away without glancing back, leaving him alone with his bruised pride.

CHAPTER THREE

"SHE SHOT ME DOWN. In flames."

"Dude." Bill laughed heartlessly, despite his friend's gloomy tone. "When's the last time that happened?"

"I, uh, don't remember. Exactly."

Leaning back in the chair behind his desk at team headquarters Saturday evening, Bill crossed his hands behind his head. Rob had to resist the urge to tip the chair backward, so that his crew chief would fall flat on his back.

"Let me get this straight," Bill said. "You gave her one of your patented smiles. You asked her out. She said no."

Regretting now that he'd been so candid, Rob nodded. "Yeah. Something like that."

Bill laughed again, making Rob slump into his

chair with a scowl. He'd had to hurry to get home after the party, change into regular clothes and make it to the shop for a meeting with his owner, crew chief and PR rep. They'd discussed several publicity events scheduled for the weeks between Christmas and the first race of the new season, synchronizing their calendars to make sure everyone was available when needed. Rob hadn't mentioned his current charity activities. His owner wouldn't care, would probably strongly approve, but he'd have his hands full keeping Maddie, his PR rep, from jumping on the publicity angle.

Now it was late and Rob was tired and he should be headed home for some rest, but instead he'd chosen to confide in his friend. Great idea.

"So," Bill murmured, still grinning, "were you dressed like this when you asked her out or, uh—"

Rob winced. "I was dressed like Santa Claus."

"And did you tell her who you really are, or did you ask her out as St. Nick?"

"She knows me as Rob. I haven't mentioned what I do for a living."

"So, some guy in a Santa suit, who she knows only by one name and knows absolutely nothing about, asked her out and she turned him down. I've got to say I can sort of see where she's coming from. Especially since she's got a young daughter to worry about."

Rob supposed he hadn't looked at it quite that way. He'd enjoyed the time he'd spent with Leanne, and he'd believed they'd made a connection. But maybe to her, he really was still just a stranger behind a fake beard. Maybe he'd gotten a little spoiled by all the positive attention he received as R. J. Sanger, champion NASCAR driver. Maybe all his talk about wanting to be anonymous and ordinary was just that—talk. Maybe he liked the perks that came with fame. The way people seemed predisposed to like him because of who he was.

Pathetic.

"Maybe you'll ask again, once she gets to know you a little better?"

"She said she doesn't date. At all."

Bill nodded sagely. "That's because she hasn't been exposed to the full power of the lethal Sanger charm. Give her a couple more exposures, pal, and I bet her answer will be different."

Though Rob wasn't so sure, he decided he hadn't quite given up yet. Maybe he just needed to approach this a different way.

LEANNE AND ROB MET in the lobby of the children's hospital. He wasn't hard to spot in his Santa Claus costume, of course, but she thought she'd have been able to pick him out of a whole lineup of Kris Kringles. She'd have known those warm brown eyes with the charming little smile lines anywhere.

His bag of stuffed toys slung over his shoulder, he moved forward to greet her. "Hi. Where's Kylie?" he asked, looking behind her.

"I thought it best for Kylie not to come today. Young visitors are discouraged around the patients, just in case Kylie's carrying any bugs she picked up at school."

His whitened eyebrows rose. "How'd she take that?"

"She wasn't happy about it, of course, but I've told her all along she wouldn't be making this appearance. My neighbor, Eileen, offered to take her this afternoon. They're making Christmas cookies, and Eileen promised Kylie she could decorate as many as she wanted. Kylie loves to bake and decorate cookies, so that appeased her somewhat—even though she said this morning that she would miss seeing you."

"Tell her I missed her, too. But I'll see her next Saturday."

"I will."

"Did you ever get her to confide in you what special thing she wants for Christmas?"

"No," she answered with a slight sigh. "I still have a feeling there's something she isn't telling me, but she's not budging. Maybe she'll confide in Eileen today."

A middle-aged woman with shoulder-length salt-and-pepper hair and purple scrubs decorated with cartoon characters crossed the lobby to greet them. "I don't have to ask if you're the people I've been watching for," she said with a laugh. "You both look great."

"Thank you," Leanne and Rob said almost in unison.

"I'm Gayle. I'm to show you to the party room where the ambulatory patients are waiting for you. After you've visited with them for a while, I'll take you to some rooms of patients who aren't well enough to move around. You're going to put smiles on a lot of little faces today."

"That's what we're here for," Rob replied.

They were already getting attention from visitors moving in and out of the hospital lobby. Several children pointed and squealed, and Rob spent a moment chatting with them before following Gayle. He even stopped at the elevator to converse with an elderly woman in a wheelchair being pushed by a young orderly; the woman seemed delighted to talk to Santa, and even asked for a hug from him, which he happily supplied.

"You feel better soon, okay, Ms. Helen?" he said to her.

Giggling like a schoolgirl, the frail little woman nodded. "I suppose I have to now, don't I? I've been visited by Santy Claus."

He laughed. "There you go."

Leanne was beginning to think Santa Claus was the wrong character for Rob to be playing. He should, instead, be dressed as the pied piper. All he had to do was flash that bearded grin and twinkle those chocolate eyes and people just seemed to respond to him. Young or old, it didn't matter. They liked him. And she didn't think it was all about the suit. She'd seen other men in Santa Claus costumes who didn't elicit nearly as strong a response.

He was having entirely too strong an influence on her. He was the first man in a long time who tempted her to forget her no-dating rule and tell him she'd changed her mind about meeting him for drinks or dinner.

She was relieved that he didn't seem at all awkward with her today. Actually, he acted as if his invitation and her refusal had never even happened. He was warm, friendly, cheerful. Exactly as he'd been before. So maybe it hadn't bothered him at all that she'd turned him down. Maybe he'd asked as an impulse, and hadn't given it another thought. Maybe he figured it was just as well she'd said no.

She was no more immune to him than anyone else. She liked him. She really did. If things were different, maybe she would consider spending more time with him. But she had to put Kylie first, and she had decided it was best for Kylie if she didn't date for now. She certainly wasn't going to change that policy for a man whose last name she didn't even know, no matter how nice and genuine he seemed.

Gayle hesitated for a moment outside the big playroom where the children and their families were gathered. "Have both of you visited a children's ward before?"

"Many times," Rob surprised Leanne by responding.

"Only once or twice," she said, wondering why he had spent so much time in hospitals. She'd gotten the impression that he was fairly new at the Santa thing, so she didn't think it had been for that purpose.

Gayle nodded. "That's good. After you've been a few times, it's easier to control your emotions and treat them like any other kids. That's all they want."

Both Leanne and Rob nodded to indicate they'd gotten the message. Their eyes met for a moment, and Rob gave her an encouraging smile. Then he held out his right arm for her to take so she could enter at his side. He carried the toy bag slung over his left shoulder.

Sliding her white-gloved hand beneath his elbow, she noted again the muscles that lay beneath the soft suit. Despite the lecture she had just given herself about why she didn't want to get involved with him, she was woman enough to respond quite predictably to the feel of those firm biceps in combination with the warm look he gave her.

Telling herself she had more important concerns on which to focus at the moment, she pushed those inconvenient reactions to the back of her mind and walked with him into the room behind Gayle.

Being greeted with delighted smiles never got old, she decided, as a ripple of excitement went through the patients and their families that filled the room. Quite a few of the patients were in wheelchairs, while others sat in the red wagons in which they'd been brought to the room. Others were able to walk, but still looked frail. Some looked healthy, except for casts or bandages. Parents hovered around their children, smiles tinged with worry, faces lined with weariness.

It was all too easy to imagine how difficult this must be for them, to put herself in their place. But because that level of empathy made it harder for her to be relaxed and cheerful in her role for today, she refused to allow herself to dwell on thoughts of Kylie being in this situation.

As was his practice, Rob didn't ask what these children wanted for Christmas. He had no ability to provide what these families wanted most. Still, the children seemed happy to talk to him and looked pleased with the stuffed toys he distributed.

Following behind him, chatting with the parents and other children, Leanne noticed again how good Rob was at this. As if there were nowhere else in the world he would rather be, he took his time with each child. Once again, she noted that he truly listened to each one, without a trace of condescension or insincerity. He seemed to be a genuinely kind-hearted man who loved both kids and Christmas.

He was actually starting to seem a little too good to be true. There had to be some reason he was apparently single and unattached. She was sure that behind the suit was a regular guy with flaws and failings like anyone else. It was just that she was seeing him at his best, she assured herself.

When every last child in the party room had had a chance to talk to Santa, Gayle led them onto the ward and into the rooms of patients who were too ill to leave their beds, but still able to accept a special holiday visitor. The smiles that wreathed the pale little faces broke her heart, but Leanne was able to keep her own smile firmly in place. And Rob continued to be awesome with the kids.

If someone told her he was the real Santa Claus, just doing a little charity work in the Charlotte area for kicks, she would almost believe it, she thought whimsically.

When they had given out the last stuffed toy and accepted the last grateful hug, they made their way toward the hospital exit. Gayle walked them to the lobby, thanked them both with grateful hugs, then left them there to return to her work.

Rob let out a long breath. "That's not exactly easy, is it? I feel so darned sorry for the kids. It's hard sometimes not to let it show."

"You were amazing with them," she said candidly.

"Thanks. So were you. I was impressed that you

got that one little girl to open up to us. The really shy one who kept hiding under her sheets."

She smiled. "She was cute, wasn't she? Once she started talking, she didn't seem in any hurry to stop."

"I noticed."

He escorted her through the automated doors, nodding and waving to passersby who smiled and pointed at them. He seemed perfectly at ease being the center of attention in his costume, she noted. She wondered if he would be so comfortable if he weren't hiding behind the fake beard.

She glanced at her watch. She still had almost an hour before she needed to pick up Kylie, which would give her time to stop at home and change first. Her mind on her plans for the remainder of the day, she was a bit startled when Rob laid a hand on her arm as they walked toward their cars.

Having gotten her attention, he dropped his hand quickly. "I wanted to ask you something before you go."

Was he going to ask her out again? Even after she'd thought she'd made it quite clear that she didn't date? She really hoped not, because she hadn't changed her mind and she didn't want to spoil the rest of the appearances they had scheduled together. "Um—what is it?"

"Where do you suppose would be the best place for me to shop for the Osorio kids? You know, a place that would have the best clothes and toys and stuff for them?"

The unexpected question made her blink in surprise. She actually felt a little foolish that she had thought he intended to ask her out again. Obviously, he'd accepted her rebuff and moved on. That was just what she wanted, wasn't it?

After a moment, she asked, "You're planning to shop for them, yourself?"

"Yeah. I talked to their mother this morning."

"Really?" He'd surprised her yet again.

He nodded. "I called the number Cruz gave me and she answered. The kids had told her about running into Santa, and Cruz had warned her that I might call. She was a little suspicious at first. It wasn't easy to convince her that this wasn't a scam or that I had no ulterior motives. I told her I just really liked her kids when I met them the other day and I wanted to do something nice for them, and she finally agreed. She seems like a nice lady, down on her luck. Very proud, but she was pleased with the idea of doing something special for her kids."

Leanne could identify with that. After all, wasn't

she eager to find out what Kylie most wanted for Christmas? "What else did you say to her?"

"I asked for the kids' sizes and a list of things she thought they might like. She was a little shy about asking for too much, but she gave me a few ideas. So, where do you suggest? The mall?"

"Yes, probably." She pictured him buying clothes and "girl toys" for Ana and she couldn't help smiling. "Do you have someone to help you shop?"

He shrugged. "No, but how hard could it be? She said all the kids need clothes and shoes and warm coats. And of course, I'd like to throw in a few toys and games. Christmas gifts shouldn't all be practical."

She bit her lip, trying to talk herself out of the offer she was tempted to make. She certainly didn't want to complicate things between them, but ultimately she couldn't resist asking, "Would you like me to help you choose some things for them?"

She wasn't suggesting a date, she assured herself. This had nothing to do with him asking her out, and she hoped he understood that. It was just that she thought he could use some help with this project from a woman who had experience shopping for a child, especially when it came to buying clothes for Ana.

His brown eyes lit up behind his little wire glasses. "You'd be willing to help? That would be great. I mean, I think I could manage, but I'm sure you'd be better at putting outfits together and that sort of thing."

She was rather amused by his assurance that he could do this on his own, if necessary. A touch of pride, perhaps? But still, he seemed genuinely grateful for her offer.

"I was as taken by those kids as you were. They seemed so polite and well mannered. Cruz was so protective and responsible with the younger ones. I would enjoy helping you give them an extra-nice Christmas. I can't contribute a lot financially, but I can buy a few of the gifts, and I can certainly donate a few hours to help you make selections."

Something she'd said made him frown a little. He started to speak, hesitated, then nodded. "So, when can you do this? I'm free pretty much all week."

Which made her wonder what he did for a living that left his schedule so flexible. Money didn't seem to be too much of an issue for him, either, though that was just a feeling on her part. This didn't seem like the right time to ask about his job, but she supposed the subject could come up during their shopping trip.

"I can meet you at the mall Wednesday after work. That's the last day of school before the holidays, and Kylie's going home with a friend for a birthday sleepover, so I'll have the evening to myself. If that's convenient for you."

"Wednesday?" He took a moment to review his mental calendar, then nodded. "Yeah, I can shop Wednesday."

It wasn't a date, she reminded herself yet again. She only hoped it wasn't a mistake. "Okay. Wednesday. So, we can meet at the front entrance at—say, five-thirty?"

"Yeah, okay. That sounds good."

She had just opened her car door when another thought occurred to her. "Wait. How will I know you? I mean, unless you show up in your Santa suit."

"Nah. I wouldn't want to invade the mall Santa's turf. But don't worry," he said, opening his own door. "I'll know you."

He climbed into his car and gave her a little salute before starting the engine.

Sliding behind her own wheel, she fastened her seat belt. She entertained herself on the drive home imagining what Rob might look like behind the beard.

ROB ASSURED HIMSELF that he was not using the Osorio kids to spend more time with Leanne. After all, she had offered to accompany him on this shopping outing, he reminded himself as he waited at the main mall entrance, having arrived fifteen minutes early. So maybe he'd thrown out a few hints to encourage her to do so, but she'd been the one to set the time and place.

He'd been unaccountably nervous all week thinking about this appointment. He was careful not to think of it as a date, since Leanne had made it clear how she felt about that, but still, they'd be spending time together. Alone. As themselves.

Would she recognize him? Not only as the man she knew as Santa Claus, but as R. J. Sanger, NASCAR driver? He had already been recognized by a few shoppers entering and exiting the mall. No one had actually approached him yet, but he knew the signs. He recognized the double takes or vaguely confused looks of recognition that turned into aha! expressions.

He had dressed as generically as possible for the evening in jeans and a plain white oxford-cloth shirt and a brown leather jacket. No team logos or colors to call attention to himself. He'd even worn his silver-framed glasses instead of his contacts this evening, as much because he'd overworn the lenses that week as for an attempt at a disguise. But still, people noticed.

Would she? And if so, would she be annoyed with him for not telling her before?

He'd been confident that he would know her, but he scanned the milling crowds carefully, looking for a familiar face. He'd feel pretty foolish if she walked right past him and he didn't know her after his boast. He could kick himself now for not giving her his cell phone number; he hadn't thought of it at the time. It wasn't like him to be so scatterbrained.

There was just something about Leanne that rattled him. Had from the start.

But she didn't date. And he'd do well to remember that tonight or risk losing the tentative friendship they had established.

He shouldn't have worried about recognizing her when he saw her. He spotted her immediately. Maybe it was the way she carried herself, even though she looked very different than she had the previous times he'd seen her.

Without the white wig, her hair was as red and as curly as Kylie's, though Leanne's looser curls were cut in a more sophisticated, just-above-the-collar style. Like Rob, she wore jeans, hers with a soft green sweater that flattered her slender curves. She wasn't wearing a coat, probably because she didn't want to be burdened with one inside the mall, and her face was pink from the cold. She walked quickly toward the light and warmth of the mall entrance.

Rob stepped in front of her. "Hi, Leanne."

She paused in midstep, staring at him in what looked like surprise. Suddenly self-conscious, he wondered if he looked at all as she had imagined. "Rob?"

He nodded. "I told you I would know you."

She smiled a little, though a faint frown creased her eyebrows. "I'd have known you, too, if I'd only seen your eyes. You had an advantage, since I haven't been covering my face while we've been together."

Cocking her head, she studied him more closely. "Um, you look a little familiar, actually. We haven't met, other than as Mr. and Mrs. Santa, have we?"

"No." He escorted her inside the bustling mall, moving with her out of the path of the doors. Scents of baking cookies from a nearby vendor swirled around them. Decorations gleamed from every corner, and Christmas carols wafted from hidden speakers. With only eight days remaining until

Christmas, the shops were crowded. People talked and milled around them, some laughing, some focused almost fiercely on their shopping. Rob was only peripherally aware of all of that as he studied the woman in front of him.

He'd thought she was attractive in costume. He was even more drawn to her now that he saw her as herself. He'd have been intrigued by her no matter how they'd met, he thought. Even if he'd seen her across this crowded mall. There was just something about her....

"You're staring at me," she murmured, tucking a curl behind her left ear. "Do I look so different?"

"No. You look...great." He cleared his throat. "I guess I should tell you—"

"Excuse me." Two women had approached them, one short, plump and bleached blonde, the other taller, thinner and brunette. Both appeared to be in their mid-thirties, and both were staring at Rob with disbelieving eyes. "Are you R. J. Sanger?" the one who'd spoken earlier—the blonde— asked.

CHAPTER FOUR

GIVING LEANNE A QUICK LOOK of apology, Rob forced a smile as he turned toward the women who had approached them. "Yes, I am."

Falling back in surprise, Leanne watched the blonde poke her companion. "See, Nita? Didn't I tell you?" she said with a smug look.

Nita nodded slowly. "I didn't believe her," she confided to Rob, totally ignoring Leanne. "But Jan said she'd seen you in your glasses before, at the track, so she recognized you right off. You should wear glasses more often," she added with more than a hint of flirtation. "They look great on you."

He took a step closer to Leanne. "Thanks. It was nice to meet you both—"

"Wait." Jan was digging frantically in one of the many shopping bags dangling from her arms. "I just bought my son an R. J. Sanger cap at the sporting goods store. Would you sign it for me? Man, that would just make his Christmas!"

She pulled out a baseball-style cap in a bold red-and-black color scheme, with a lightning bolt slashed in shiny gold fabric across the bill. "Please? He's your biggest fan."

"I'd be happy to sign it, but I don't have a— Oh. Thanks." Rob accepted the permanent marker Nita practically shoved into his face and scrawled his name on the lightning bolt. Then he signed a scrap of paper for Nita, who had no licensed merchandise on hand for him to autograph.

"Thank you so much." Jan clutched the cap as if the lightning bolt really were made of gold. "Oh, man, my Jason is going to go nuts when he sees this. He's got a couple of autographed pictures of you and a T-shirt you signed at the car dealership last summer, but he doesn't have a signed cap. He'll love it."

"I hope so." Taking Leanne's arm, he almost pulled her into step beside him. "Merry Christmas, ladies," he said over his shoulder.

"Keep walking," he muttered to Leanne, ducking his head a little so he didn't make eye contact with any of the onlookers who'd noticed the encounter. "If we stop and I look too approachable, we're liable to be stuck here for a while."

"You're R. J. Sanger." She heard the accusation in the foolish statement even as the words left her mouth.

He nodded. "Yeah. Rob to my closest friends."

Since she hardly knew him, she couldn't imagine why she was in that group. "Why didn't you tell me?"

"Because I didn't think it was important."

She frowned at him, and he sighed. "Okay. Because I was trying to stay under the radar with the Santa thing. I don't want any media attention or recognition from the kids or their families. I just wanted to have a good time, make the kids smile a little and keep it all low-key, you know?"

"So no one involved with the charities knows who you are?"

"Well—"

She looked at him in question.

"My cousin," he admitted. "Eileen Marcus. She set up everything for me."

He had managed to surprise her yet again. "Eileen. My neighbor. The one who got me into this," she murmured.

"I guess she thought you'd enjoy it, too."

Leanne had a few theories of her own about why Eileen had arranged for her to play Mrs. Claus to

Rob's Santa. Eileen had been blatantly hinting for some time that Leanne needed to get out more, put her disappointing romantic past behind her and meet some nice men. Leanne had made it clear that she wasn't interested in fix-ups, but apparently Eileen had found a sneaky way around that policy.

"Eileen mentioned a couple of times that she was related to R. J. Sanger—to you—but I didn't make the connection when you introduced yourself as Rob."

"Like I said, I use Rob only with family and close friends. R. J.'s my racing nickname. It sort of helps me keep the two sides of my life, private and public, separate."

Considering how many people were eyeing them and whispering, she didn't imagine that would be such an easy thing to accomplish. And this was Charlotte, where driver spottings were commonplace. That only showed what a big star in the sport Rob was, and how zealously he guarded his privacy. She didn't know how he could stand the constant attention. It was certainly making her self-conscious. This was different than appearing in public as Mrs. Claus. This felt like opening her private life for scrutiny and comment.

"Just ignore it," Rob advised. "Most of them will

leave us alone. They've got their own shopping to do. It's not like I'm not seen around town often enough, even though it's been a long time since I've visited a mall when I wasn't making a PR appearance."

She imagined he had people to do his shopping for him. Wasn't that what rich people did? She gulped as she realized that he was, indeed, a very wealthy man. And she had offered to help him purchase gifts for the Osorio kids. That must have amused him.

He pulled a sheet of paper from an inside pocket of his leather jacket. "This is the list Esther Osorio dictated to me when I spoke with her last Sunday. I have everyone's sizes and a couple of things each of the kids would like other than clothes."

Trying very hard to act as she always did with him, though it required an effort, she took the list and studied it. "I hope we'll be able to choose clothes Cruz likes. Teenagers can be picky sometimes."

"Somehow I didn't get the idea Cruz has had the luxury of being picky. But anything he doesn't like, he can always return and swap for something else. I'll work that out with his mom."

She nodded. "That should do it. We saw what he was wearing before, a hoodie and jeans. That's probably his usual style."

"Esther said Victor likes those long-sleeve polo shirts over tees. And she said Ana doesn't care what she wears as long as there's pink or purple on it somewhere. Her favorite colors, apparently. She's also crazy for princesses."

"Most little girls her age are. Kylie likes to play princess, herself, sometimes."

Rob chuckled. "Kylie was born to play a princess."

She couldn't help smiling in return. "That's true, of course."

"Any luck on finding out her secret Christmas wish?"

"Not so far. Eileen had no more luck than we've had."

"She said she would only tell the 'real' Santa Claus. Have you taken her to see the mall Santa? Maybe she'd tell him."

"She's seen two different mall Santas," Leanne replied drily. "She was delighted to see them both, chattered like a little magpie to both of them, told me afterward that they were both very nice—but neither was the 'real' Santa, so she didn't tell them her wish."

"Man. The kid's giving you a challenge this year, isn't she?"

She nodded. "I've already bought everything I know she wants. There's just that one last thing. I wish I knew whether it's even something suitable. Or realistic."

Dodging out of the way of a woman with infant twins in a side-by-side stroller, Rob suggested, "Maybe you could get her to write a letter to Santa. On the computer. Save it and read it when she isn't looking."

Leanne frowned. "You mean, deliberately invade her privacy?"

Looking flustered, he stammered, "Uh, well, it was—"

"I've already tried that," she confessed, taking pity on him. "She said she'd already written a letter and put it in the mailbox, herself. I never saw it. It's sitting someplace where Santa letters are taken at the post office."

"Maybe you should just level with her. Tell her that unless she clues you in, she won't be getting whatever it is she wants. That Santa needs you to act as his liaison."

"Tried it. She just shrugged and said it didn't really matter. If she was meant to get it, she would."

He laughed wryly. "She's something else. Have I mentioned how much I like your kid, Leanne?"

Her heart warmed, even though she told herself to behave. It was just that she was such a sucker for compliments about her daughter. And Rob sounded as though he really meant it. A particular talent of his, she reminded herself.

She waved toward the doorway of a large department store. "We should look there for some clothes. They carry some nice, affordable brands that are popular with kids."

"Okay, sure. We can look there."

Clearing her throat, she looked up at him. "I think it would be best to get them some good, quality clothes that look good and are easy to care for, rather than expensive, designer label things that would call too much attention to them. I don't believe in spending ridiculous amounts of money on name-brand items."

"Neither do I," he assured her. "Trust me, I'm not in the habit of trying to impress anyone with the latest trends or the fanciest toys. I've got better things to do with my money."

Budget shopping was a necessity for her, of course, but Leanne had always wanted to believe that, even if she came into a fortune, she wouldn't fall into the trap of keeping up with the flashy crowd. She had seen too many wealthy children spoiled by senseless consumerism and excessive greed. She wanted Kylie to grow up grounded in her faith, her compassion for others and a sense of self-worth that was measured by her accomplishments and not her possessions.

Rob was surprisingly interested in helping Leanne select individual items for the Osorio children. He was particularly interested in choosing things for Cruz. He chose several nice hoodies, eschewing any that bore pictures or words neither he nor Leanne found suitable for a young teen, and several pairs of stylish, but practical jeans.

Saying every boy needed at least one nice outfit, he also selected a versatile sport coat, a button-down dress shirt and a coordinating tie. Though the sport coat would look just fine with jeans, he threw in a pair of nice khakis, just in case the occasion arose when Cruz would need them. He selected similar items for Victor, in addition to the polo shirts and jeans the boy favored.

"I have a feeling the boys will be wearing these outfits to church soon," Leanne commented, remembering the silver cross necklace Cruz had worn tucked inside his hoodie. Maybe it was just a fashion statement, but she suspected that the proud and hardworking Esther Osorio made sure her children attended church at least occasionally.

"Probably. That's the way my mother liked me to dress for church."

"Is your mother still living?"

"Yeah. She and Eileen's mother are first cousins."

"I wondered how you were related. Does your mother live in this area?"

"She sold her house in Mooresville and moved into a condo here in Charlotte after Dad died. She's made a lot of friends, and stays busy all the time with activities and volunteer work. My sister's an optometrist here, so the whole family's pretty close."

"That's nice for you." She tried not to let him hear her slight wistfulness. It sounded as though he was close to his family.

Rob let Leanne make most of the choices for Ana, who was about the same size as Kylie. Making sure she chose several shades of pink and purple, mixed with several coordinating colors, Leanne put together a cute, mix-and-match wardrobe of easy-care cottons and knits. Like Rob, she selected a couple of outfits for dressier occasions—two pretty little dresses with matching tights and hair bows. A very nice Christmas wardrobe, Leanne thought, hoping the children would be pleased with their choices.

Leaving that store, they made a trip out to Rob's car to lock the packages in the trunk before heading back into the mall empty-handed. They still had coats and shoes to buy, and hadn't even started on toys.

After another hour of shopping, they'd found everything on their list, including a pink ballerina dress for Ana, to Rob's relief. That had been the one gift he'd seemed most determined to locate, and they'd snatched the last one when they'd spotted it in the toy store. Rounding out Ana's gifts with the toys her mother thought she'd like, along with a few other things they found on their own, they made another trip to the car, then returned yet again to the mall to finish shopping for the boys.

"How about a break before we do any more shopping?" Rob suggested, making a show of wiping his brow.

Though she had known to wear sensible shoes, Leanne's feet were begging for a rest. "Sounds good," she said. "We've got a little over two hours before the mall closes."

"Two hours." He nodded doggedly and said,

"Okay, I can handle that as long as I get something to eat first. How about that pizza place over there? Do you like pizza?"

"Sure. Pizza sounds good. But sitting down for a few minutes sounds even better," she admitted with a smile.

He grinned. "I'm glad you said that. I thought I was the only one getting tired. It was making me feel pretty wimpy."

Eyeing the muscular body outlined by his leather jacket and close-fitting jeans, she bit back a laugh at the very suggestion that there was anything at all "wimpy" about this lean, fit athlete.

While they shopped, it had been easy enough to concentrate on the merchandise and the task they'd assigned themselves. Now that they faced each other across a small, somewhat secluded booth in the back of a mall pizza shop, Leanne was all too aware of just who he was. She wondered if anyone around them had recognized him. If anyone was watching them, wondering who she was and what she was doing with R. J. Sanger.

"Don't do that."

She blinked a couple of times and looked up from her plate, catching Rob's eyes across the small table. "Don't do what?"

"You're thinking about it again. About who I am, I mean."

Sighing, she reached for her paper cup of diet soda. "How did you know?"

"It's something in your body language, I guess. You seemed pretty comfortable with me when you knew me only as Rob. Is it really any different now?"

Swallowing a sip of her drink, she set the cup back down. "If you thought it wouldn't change anything, you'd have told me your full name when we met."

He conceded her point with a slight nod. "Come to think of it, you've never told me your last name."

"Baker. Leanne Baker. And, no, that shouldn't ring any bells for you. I'm not famous for anything."

He frowned. "It's only my job, Leanne. Just like yours is managing an insurance office."

A little surprised that he'd remembered that offhand remark she'd made the first time they'd met, she shook her head. "It's hardly the same thing. I don't have television and print cameras focused on me while I work. No one ever sticks a microphone in my face and asks my strategy for getting my filing done. I don't have a whole team of people to keep me on schedule and make sure I

have everything I need, nor am I flooded with of-
fers to endorse products. And I have never once
been asked for an autograph."

"All of that stuff is just part of what I deal with
in order to do what I really love to do. Drive fast
cars," he said with a little laugh. "It's all I've
wanted to do since I was a kid racing midgets. My
dad was an accountant for a race team—not the one
I drive for now, but he had enough connections to
get me a start. He was my biggest supporter, and
my biggest role model."

"You really loved your dad," she murmured,
studying his face. Even his voice changed when he
referred to his late father, growing deeper and
warmer.

Rob shrugged. "I pretty much idolized him. I
just hope my own kids will feel that way about me
someday."

"You don't have any children, right?"

"No, not yet. I've been too focused on my career
to this point to settle down. But who knows. Maybe
that'll change soon."

She took a big bite of pizza to avoid having to
respond to that. She doubted that he meant the
comment as anything more than making conversation, but she was still aware that he had asked her

out only a week earlier. If he was looking for someone with whom to settle down soon, she was sure he'd realized by now that she wasn't a suitable candidate, even if he'd impulsively offered an invitation that one time.

"What about your family, Leanne?" he asked after they'd eaten in silence for a few minutes. "Are your parents still living?"

"Yes. I don't see them often."

"Oh? They live far away?"

"They're divorced. My dad lives here in Charlotte, but he travels quite a bit. My mother remarried and moved to West Virginia with her husband, who's a contractor there. I talk to her a couple of times a month and see her around the holidays."

Searching her face, he set down the crust of his pizza slice and asked gently, "You don't get along?"

She shrugged. "She never quite forgave me for getting pregnant in college and ending up an unmarried mother. Not only did it make her a grandmother much sooner than she would have liked, it was embarrassing for her that her daughter had been so stupid. It might have been somewhat easier for her if I'd married Kylie's father, but he panicked and took off as soon as I told him about her."

"He doesn't know Kylie?"

"He's never been interested in knowing her."

"Very much his loss."

"I think so, too, but I'd never want to push her on someone who doesn't want her. I'd never want her hurt like that."

"Neither would I. Is that why you don't date? Because you aren't sure another man would want Kylie in his life?"

Deciding abruptly that she'd said too much, she frowned and shook her head. "You really are very good at this Santa thing, aren't you? You've even got me telling you my life's story."

His mouth quirked just a little at the left corner. "Maybe you'd like to tell me what you want for Christmas?"

She laughed shortly and reached again for her soda. "Like my daughter, I think I'll keep some things to myself."

"Fair enough. Do you want any dessert?"

He had insisted on paying for the inexpensive meal, and she'd allowed it because she didn't want to argue with him in public, but she shook her head in response to this offer. "I'm full, thank you."

"I think I'll have one of those macadamia nut cookies. I need the sugar rush to finish our shopping," he quipped. "I'll be right back."

She wasn't the only woman who watched him saunter across the dining room to the order counter. And she wasn't sure the others were all watching him because they'd recognized him. He was simply the type of man who drew attention when he walked into a room. Something about the way he held himself. The way his slender hips rolled when he moved. The way his glossy, dark hair fell across his forehead. His smile lit up his face when he spoke to the teenager girl behind the counter, leaving her smiling and blushing a little when she handed him the cookie in exchange for his money.

Would Leanne have known him if he hadn't stepped in front of her earlier? He certainly looked different without the costume. She hadn't known the color of his hair, or his true size beneath the padding. She certainly hadn't realized the man behind the beard was the face she'd seen often on TV selling a popular soft drink and representing his sponsor, a national home improvement store. But she thought she might have recognized him, anyway, just from the effect he had on other people.

He returned with his cookie and slid back into the booth. "So, we still need to find a cool backpack and a handheld video game for Victor and I want to get an MP3 player for Cruz, and maybe a gift card for some music downloads. What do you think?"

"Shouldn't be too hard to find any of those. And they're great ideas." Like Rob, she figured every teenage boy would enjoy an MP3 player and she doubted that Cruz had one. "I'd like to stop in the bookstore before we're done. I want to buy all three kids a couple of books. I'd like that to be my contribution to their Christmas."

"Books, huh?"

"Yes. I love to give books for gifts. I'm sure we can find something suitable for each of their ages."

"Cruz said he wants to work for a pit crew someday. There are a couple of pretty good books about that."

"Good suggestion. Um, did he know who you were when he mentioned that?"

"No, I just told him Rob. But it's certainly not uncommon in this area for a kid to want to work for a race team."

"Most of them seem to dream of being drivers."

He shrugged. "A lot of them dream of being crew chiefs. I have a feeling that's what Cruz has in mind."

"He's much too young to start working for NASCAR."

"Well, yeah. But when he turns sixteen, he'll be able to get some part-time work in one of the shops, maybe. And once I tell him who I am, I'll give him some pointers—like how making good grades in school and getting a college degree are always advantages to someone with ambitions in racing."

She smiled. "I'm sure his mother will appreciate that."

"It's what we tell all the kids who ask us for advice. It also happens to be true."

Hearing a nearby clicking sound, Leanne turned her head to investigate. A giggling teenage girl had taken Rob's picture with her cell phone. He nodded pleasantly enough at her, but immediately began to gather his trash and make signs of being ready to leave. "Are you rested enough to get back to our shopping?"

"Yes." It seemed his strategy for avoiding too much attention was to keep moving. Because that sounded like a good idea to her, she quickly finished her soda and added the empty cup to the tray he had ready to carry to the waste can.

They left the pizza place together, stepping out into the crowded mall. In the center of the common area, a Santa's workshop had been set up. Beneath towering decorated trees, animated elves hammered and swiveled among piles of huge gift boxes and oversize animated toys. In the center of the display sat a jolly Santa on a big chair, while a line of children waited noisily and impatiently to sit on his lap. Catching the Santa Claus's eye, Rob lifted a hand in greeting, receiving a cheery nod in return.

"Professional courtesy," he murmured, resting a hand at the small of Leanne's back to guide her around a group of kids dashing toward the end of the line to see Santa. "Looks like his beard is real."

Glancing back over her shoulder, she nodded. "I think it is. It's not nearly as full as your fake one, but it's still pretty impressive."

His hand was warm through her sweater. There was nothing suggestive about his touch, and he dropped his hand as soon as they were clear of the obstacles, but the warmth lingered, along with a funny little tingly feeling that burrowed deeply inside her.

Watch yourself, Leanne, she warned silently, preceding him into an electronics store at one end of the mall. *Nothing has changed. Once Christmas is over, Rob will go back to his exciting, high-profile life, and you'll be just a single mom office manager again.*

Whatever Eileen was scheming, Leanne couldn't imagine that those two paths could ever merge successfully for more than this brief holiday adventure.

CHAPTER FIVE

BY THE TIME THEY WENT into the bookstore, they had only half an hour until closing time. Leanne assigned Rob the task of finding a couple of good books for Cruz, while she concentrated on making selections for Victor and Ana. Knowing she was determined to pay for the books herself, and figuring that she didn't have a lot of extra money at this time of year, he kept an eye on the prices of the selections he made.

It had been a while since he'd had to do that, he realized. He wondered if he'd started to get jaded about the money he'd accumulated through his high-profile career. He would hate to think that were true. His dad had always said that when a man forgot to be grateful for the blessings he received, those blessings were liable to slip away from him.

It had been hard to rein himself in when buying

gifts for the Osorio kids that evening. He tended to get overly enthusiastic, and money really wasn't an issue for him. Leanne had tactfully guided his selections, seeming to know just what was appropriate without going overboard.

She seemed to be adjusting well enough to finding out who'd been hiding beneath the Santa beard, he thought tentatively. He could tell that it had shaken her at first, and she still looked uncomfortable whenever someone recognized him and asked for an autograph or a photo. That was only natural; sometimes it still felt strange even to him that someone would get all excited about possessing his name scrawled on a napkin or a scrap of paper. But she was starting to act a bit more relaxed with him again, giving him hope that his minor deception hadn't put a permanent wedge between them.

They met at the registers with five minutes to spare. He'd chosen two behind-the-scenes books about racing by authors he recognized and respected; she'd chosen a couple of princess storybooks for Ana and two popular adventure books for Victor.

"I hope they don't have these," she fretted. "I chose very recent releases, so maybe they haven't gotten them yet."

"Same deal as the clothes," he reminded her. "If

they want, they can bring them back and swap them."

"That's true." She piled the books on the counter and pulled out her credit card, along with a card that gave her a bookstore discount. Biting his tongue to keep from offering to pay, he stood back out of the way.

They carried the remaining packages to his car, locked them inside, and then Rob walked Leanne to her car a few rows over in the emptying lot. "Thank you again for doing this with me," he said as she unlocked her car door. "You really made the whole process much easier than it would have been on my own."

"I enjoyed it," she said, and sounded as though she meant it. "We got a lot done in a relatively short time."

"Yes, thanks to you."

She opened her car door.

Not wanting to say good-night just yet, Rob detained her again. "So about the gifts. You think they should be wrapped or should I just take the stuff in the shopping bags?"

She frowned a bit, as if she was surprised he'd had to ask. "They should be wrapped, of course. Every child loves to pull off wrapping paper."

"Oh. Okay."

"Do you have someone to help you with the wrapping?"

"I'm sure I can find someone." He searched his mind for possibilities, but the guys he usually hung out with—primarily his crew chief and teammates—didn't seem like the gift-wrap party types. Mrs. Calhoun, the wife of his motor home driver, who often accompanied her husband on the road and took care of things like cleaning the RV and stocking the kitchen, would probably have helped, but the Calhouns were taking advantage of off-season to go on a long-awaited cruise.

After only a moment, Leanne shook her head. "I'll help. When do you want to get together again?"

"Really?" He grinned, hoping it wasn't too obvious that he'd been hoping she would volunteer. "That would be great."

"Uh-huh." Obviously, he hadn't fooled her for a moment. "Are you free tomorrow evening?"

"Yes." He mentally canceled a couple of indefinite plans he'd had for the next evening, none of which sounded as appealing as wrapping gifts with Leanne and Kylie. "My place or yours? I live on Lake Norman, about a half hour from your house.

You and Kylie would be welcome to join me for dinner tomorrow evening, followed by a wrapping party. Or I can bring the stuff to your place. Whichever is more convenient for you."

He waited patiently while she mentally debated. Their breath hung in the shadows between them, mingling in an intriguing way, and she was starting to shiver a little since she still wasn't wearing a coat, but she took her time making up her mind.

"I'll come to your place," she said finally. "It would be easier than schlepping the stuff back and forth. But you don't have to feed us."

"I have to eat, anyway," he answered with a nonchalant shrug, downplaying their plans as much as possible so as not to make her nervous. "I'll throw some burgers on the grill or something. You and Kylie like burgers, don't you?"

"Well, sure, but—"

"It's no harder to grill three than one," he added.

She sighed, releasing another cloud of steamy breath, and nodded. "Fine. I'll bring a salad."

"Sounds good. Get in the car, your lips are turning blue."

She slid behind the wheel and started the engine so the heater could start doing its job. Digging a notepad out of her purse, she wrote down the address and directions he gave her. "I'll see you about six, then," she said, replacing the pad in her purse.

"I'll look forward to it."

Only after she'd bade him good-night, closed her door and driven away did he realize that she hadn't said she was looking forward to it, too.

"DUMB. DUMB, DUMB, DUMB."

"What did you say, Mommy?" Kylie asked from the backseat.

Glancing into the rearview, Leanne forced a smile. "Nothing, sweetie. I was just, um, humming with the radio."

"Oh. It didn't sound like that song."

Since Leanne had never even heard the Christmas song currently streaming from the speakers, that was no surprise. "I guess I was off-key."

She was definitely off-key. She never should have agreed to come to Rob's house tonight. She had almost asked him to come to their house, instead, but that hadn't felt right, either. Frankly, she hadn't wanted to remember him there when Christmas was over and they were no longer spending time together. Silly, she supposed.

She still cringed when she remembered the conversation she'd had with Eileen earlier. Eileen had acted entirely innocent when Leanne accused her of deliberately concealing the fact that "Santa Claus" was her cousin Rob. She'd forgotten to mention it, she said unconvincingly. When Leanne had asked outright if Eileen was matchmaking, Eileen had rather too quickly changed the subject. Leanne had let her get away with that ploy, but had made sure to reiterate to her neighbor that she wasn't interested in getting involved with anyone. This was just a holiday charity collaboration, she had insisted. Nothing more.

Eileen had looked entirely too pleased with herself when she'd found out that Leanne and Kylie were dining with Rob that evening, even though Leanne had protested that they were merely meeting to wrap gifts.

"These sure are big houses," Kylie remarked, craning her neck to look out the side windows at the Lake Norman mansions decked out in Christmas lights. Trees and wreaths glittered in nearly every window, trees on perfectly landscaped lawns dripped with lights, animated Santa Clauses and manger scenes and deer and snow people festooned the grounds.

Leanne noted that, despite all the Christmas cheer, many of the estates were securely gated. As was Rob's. Following his instructions, she lowered her window and pressed a button on a box beside the drive. A moment later, the gate opened. She drove through, then glanced in her rearview mirror, watching as it slid closed again. She swallowed.

"Wow." Kylie craned her neck to study Rob's house. "This one's big, too."

It *was* big. Not as ostentatious as some they had passed, but it definitely made a statement, she decided, parking in the big circular driveway. She knew very little about architectural styles. Was it French? English? Made of stone and brick, it had lots of windows, several roof points, a couple of chimneys and a covered porch jutting out over the large, double doors with leaded glass panes. A Christmas tree gleamed in the big, arch-topped window to the left of the doors, and two fragrant balsam wreaths hung on red ribbons on the doors, but that was the extent of the decorating that she could see from outside.

"I want you to be on your best behavior," she warned Kylie. "And don't touch anything," she added.

"Okay, Mommy." Kylie climbed the two steps onto the small porch, almost bouncing with excitement. "Can I ring the doorbell?"

But the door had already opened. Rob stood

framed in the doorway, smiling at them. "You're welcome to ring the doorbell if you like, Kylie."

Giggling, she reached up to push the lighted button, then laughed again when a deep, regal-sounding chime echoed through the house behind him. "Cool."

Chuckling, Rob moved aside to allow them to enter. "Come in. I just took the burgers off the grill. I hope you both like them well-done."

"We do," Leanne assured him.

He reached for the covered dish she'd retrieved from the backseat of her car. "Let me take that so you can remove your coats."

Kylie was already shrugging out of her hooded red parka, revealing the red-and-white striped sweater and jeans she'd worn beneath. Leanne slipped out of her own warm coat, also casual in a black turtleneck and dark jeans with black boots. Rob was dressed in similar fashion in a black sweatshirt bearing the black-and-red logo of his sponsor, jeans and sneakers. His dark hair was a bit mussed and he smelled appealingly of barbecue smoke.

Kylie was staring up at Rob. Leanne realized that it was the first time her daughter had seen him without the Santa costume. Rob must have become aware of that fact at the same time. He grinned down at her. "Well? Do I look like you thought I would?"

"You look good," she assured him.

Leanne felt her lips twitch in response to what she considered a massive understatement.

"Thank you," Rob said gravely.

"Mommy said you're a race car driver and you're famous. She showed me your picture in a magazine."

"Did she?" He flicked a glance at Leanne, who shrugged lightly. She'd wanted Kylie to know who they'd be dining with that evening.

"I like your house," Kylie added. "Your Christmas tree is pretty."

"Thanks. I bought it predecorated," he admitted. "At a charity benefit last month. I haven't had a chance to buy many ornaments and decorations for myself yet. I just bought the house last year and I've been on the road so much since that I haven't had a chance to personalize it as much as I would like."

The tree was visible to the left of the open, two-story, marble-floored foyer. It sat in the bow window of a formal dining room with dark green walls, wood trim, green-and-gray mottled marble columns and a tray ceiling centered by a crystal and bronze chandelier. The dining room table, decorated with a massive Christmas centerpiece of greenery and poinsettias, was traditionally styled in a dark wood, with red, hunter-green and cream-striped seats on the eight lyre-back chairs. A matching sideboard held silver and topiaries and a china cabinet held a set of gold-edged cream china and sparkling crystal glassware.

Straight ahead of the entry was a den furnished in comfortable leather sofas and deep chairs grouped to make the most of a big stone fireplace. Again, she saw lots of dark wood and hunter green, apparently a color he liked, but numerous lamps and a crackling fire made the room look warm rather than dark. A staircase on her right led upstairs.

"Your home is very nice," she said.

He looked pleased by the compliment. "Thanks. If you'd like, I'll take you on a tour after dinner. The decorating is sort of minimal in places, but I had it professionally done, and I was very pleased with the way it all turned out."

He seemed genuinely proud of his home. She didn't blame him; it was lovely.

Saying that he thought they'd be more comfortable eating in the breakfast room than the formal dining room that evening, he led them through the den, still carrying the covered bowl Leanne had brought. A wall of glass windows looked out over a covered deck on which sat wrought iron tables and chairs and a big barbecue grill. The lake was visible only as glimmers of the reflection of landscape lighting, since there was no moon that night. Only then did she realize that there must be another floor beneath them, since the deck was well off the ground.

The breakfast room opened off a big kitchen done in a medium-dark wood and green-and-black quartz countertops. The appliances were top-of-the-line, stainless steel. She wondered how often he actually used them.

"I don't cook a lot," he admitted as if reading her thoughts. "Mostly I use the microwave and the grill. Hamburgers and steaks are my specialties, though I've been known to smoke some pretty decent ribs."

"I like hamburgers," Kylie announced.

He smiled. "I'm very relieved to hear that."

He'd set the burgers, buns and "fixings"—cheeses, onions, tomatoes, lettuce, pickles and condiments—on the roomy bar. He put Leanne's cold pasta salad on the bar along with a bowl of baked beans he admitted came from a can but smelled delicious, anyway.

As they assembled their burgers and filled their plates, Leanne noticed the room that lay diagonally off the breakfast room. Seeing her looking that way, Rob said his Realtor had called it a hearth room. It had a huge rock fireplace with built-in bookcases on each side, and two glass walls looking over the lake. The furniture was casual and inviting, and she thought it would be a nice place to read or relax and watch the activities on the lake. She could almost picture herself sitting in the deep, flowered armchair by the fireplace, sipping coffee and reading the Sunday paper.

Putting that image firmly out of her mind, since she doubted she'd even visit this house again, much less read a morning paper here, she concentrated on her meal. She didn't have to worry about awkwardness falling between them. Not with Kylie there to keep the conversation lively as she told them all about the party her class had held on the last day of school yesterday, about the sleepover she'd attended last night, and about how jealous all her friends were that she was getting to be an elf and help Santa Claus.

Rob listened intently to everything Kylie had to

say, making the appropriate comments when she gave him a chance to speak. Leanne made no effort to shush her daughter. It was too easy to let Kylie take the lead in keeping the conversation going.

"I have dessert," Rob announced when they'd all eaten as much as they could. "Do you want it now, or would you rather wait until after we've wrapped some gifts?"

"Dessert?" Intrigued, Kylie cocked her head. "What kind of dessert?"

"I picked up some cupcakes at my favorite bakery this afternoon. I figured everyone likes cupcakes."

"I lo-ove cupcakes." Kylie sighed, dragging out the word for emphasis. "But I'm a little full."

"We'll wait, then." He glanced at Leanne. "We'll have some decaf coffee with ours, maybe."

"Sounds good. Let me help you clear this stuff away and we'll start wrapping."

"I thought we were going to take a tour," Kylie protested, carrying her plate to the sink.

Leanne hadn't realized Kylie had picked up on that offer. "That's not necessary, Kylie."

"But I want to see Rob's house."

"I did offer," he reminded them.

Leanne nodded. Secretly, she wanted the tour, as well.

Beaming like the proud home owner he was, Rob showed them the mudroom that led from the kitchen to the laundry room and the three-car garage, then took them back through the den to the downstairs master bedroom suite. Having Kylie with them made that a little less awkward than it would have been, Leanne decided. As it was, she had a difficult time not looking at the huge bed that dominated the bedroom. The bath was almost obscenely luxurious, appointed in marble and bronze with a tub big enough for at least three and a stone-walled shower. The walk-in closet was the size of Kylie's bedroom at home.

"Very nice," she said, trying not to sound as if this were the biggest closet she'd ever seen. Which it was.

A half bath was tucked in beside the stairs that led up to the third floor, where he showed them three more bedrooms, two and a half more baths, a media room styled like a movie theater and an office. Like the main floor, this one had a full terrace all across the back looking over the lake. As he'd said, the rooms were decorated somewhat minimally, all very nice, but lacking true personality.

Kylie was particularly impressed with the media room with its stadium-style leather seating for a dozen people. "Do you watch movies here?" she asked, motioning toward the big screen.

"Not very often," he admitted. "I'm not here that much. I usually just watch TV downstairs."

Kylie looked wistfully over her shoulder as they left that room, and Leanne figured the child was envisioning one of her favorite animated movies playing on that screen with her friends filling the comfortable seats. She supposed it was going to be time for another "let's be grateful for what we have" speech during the drive home.

The lower level looked like a place where Rob would spend time with his friends. The finished basement level held a pool table, a couple of video game consoles with big-screen TVs, several comfy club chairs, a beautiful octagonal game table with invitingly cushioned chairs and a full wet bar complete with four stools, a fridge, dishwasher and microwave. There was another diagonally situated gathering room, which she could tell lay directly beneath the hearth room upstairs. This one was set up for conferences with a long table, a built-in computer screen and a dry-erase board. Team meetings? she hazarded, wondering if he sometimes held strategy meetings here with his crew chief and other key team members.

A wine cellar and a complete guest suite with a small sitting area and a private bath separate from the half bath that serviced the level completed their tour. Most of the back wall down here, too, was glass, opening onto a terrace that led out to a lawn that sloped down to the lake, where she would bet she would find a boathouse and a dock.

"You spend a lot of time down here," she said, looking around the main room. Here were the personal items that had been missing upstairs. Trophies and framed photographs displayed on glass shelves. More framed photos of Rob with several very famous faces on the walls.

"I do," he said with a nod. "This level is what sold me on the place, frankly. I could see myself hanging down here with my buddies during off-season and the occasional day off during the summers. I hardly ever go up to the top floor, which feels a little empty to me. And on the main level, I spend most of my time in the kitchen or my bedroom. This is where I come to just relax and entertain myself."

"Can we play pool?" Kylie asked, studying the cues hung on the wall.

"Not now, Kylie. We have gifts to wrap. That's why we're here, remember?" Leanne was reminding Rob as much as her daughter.

If he was trying to impress her with this tour, he had succeeded, but it hadn't changed her mind about going out with him. If anything, it had only reinforced her conviction that they had too little in common to even attempt dating. She wasn't the type to want to be with him because of his money or fame. She didn't really believe he was trying to win her over with either, but even if he had been, it wouldn't have worked.

Though Kylie looked a little disappointed, she didn't resist when they started back upstairs. She'd probably recognized Leanne's don't-argue-with-me tone.

"I figured we could do the wrapping on the breakfast room table," Rob said, taking them back toward the kitchen. "It's big enough to spread everything out. I put all the gifts and the paper and ribbons and stuff I bought today in the hearth room."

"I want to help," Kylie insisted.

"We definitely need your help," Rob assured her.

Together they dragged out all the wrapping supplies. Kylie examined all the gifts Leanne and Rob had bought the evening before and pronounced them satisfactory, to Rob's visible amusement.

They set up a wrapping assembly line with Rob doing the cutting, Leanne the wrapping and ribbon-tying and Kylie sticking on bows and gift tags. Rob kept them laughing during the process, carrying on with Kylie and teasing Leanne about her perfectionism in wrapping. The gifts piled up and the time slipped past, and Leanne was aware of a vague surprise at how easy and pleasant it was between them.

Rob's phone rang several times, but usually he just glanced at the caller ID and let the machine pick up. He took a call from his mother and one from his public relations representative. He carried the phone into another room to chat with his mother for a few minutes, so Leanne heard only his fond greeting, but he stayed in the kitchen for the business call. Though she tried not to eavesdrop, she got the impression he was setting up a photo shoot for the following week for an article about the upcoming racing season.

"It won't be long until you start the season again, will it?" she asked when he hung up.

He measured another sheet of wrapping paper in preparation for cutting. "The first race is in February at Daytona. Do you follow NASCAR?"

She made a face. "I know a little about it. Hard

to live in this area and not at least know something. But I have to admit I haven't followed it closely. I'm always busy with other things on weekends."

He glanced at Kylie. "I can understand that."

"Mommy said you were a champion," Kylie said to Rob, proving she was listening to their conversation.

He nodded. "Not this last season, but the one before that. I finished second in the season that just ended."

"Oh." The child thought about it for a moment, then gave him an encouraging smile. "That's okay, Rob. Second's still pretty good."

"Thank you, Kylie," he said, his lips twitching.

"I bet you'll win next year."

"I'm certainly going to try."

"You spend a lot of time on the road, don't you?" Leanne asked, carefully wrapping the box holding Ana's ballerina dress.

"A minimum of thirty-six weekends a year. I have a nice motor home I stay in at the tracks, but it's not like being here."

"Do you ever get tired of it? The traveling, I mean."

"Sure, sometimes," he replied with a shrug. "But

that's just part of my job. I love racing enough to put up with the downside."

"Have you ever had a wreck in your race car?" Kylie asked, leaning her elbows on the table to gaze up at Rob in fascination.

"Several," he replied with a wry smile. "That's part of the job, too. But the safety measures have come a long way in the past few years. I don't worry much about being hurt."

Leanne wondered if the people who loved him—his mother, perhaps—were as serene about the hazards of his chosen career.

"I'm tired of wrapping. Can I go watch TV?" Kylie asked.

"There's a TV in here, over the fireplace," Rob said, motioning toward the hearth room. "Come on in, and I'll help you find a show you like. Maybe you'd like your cupcake while you watch?"

Kylie looked hopefully at Leanne, who frowned. "I'm not sure you want her eating a cupcake in there."

He laughed. "Trust me, she won't hurt that room. My crew chief's kids have crashed in there in front of the TV with all kinds of snacks and drinks. I specifically made that room kid-friendly. C'mon, Kylie, I'll help you get set up."

Continuing the wrapping, Leanne watched sur-
reptitiously as Rob helped Kylie settle at a glass-
topped table with a Christmas-decorated cupcake,
a small glass of milk and a couple of paper napkins.
She sat on one of several leather-covered cubes in
the room, which he assured her were the favorite
seats of his crew chief's kids. He then turned on the
flat-screen TV above the fireplace and, at Kylie's
request, tuned in a kid's channel.

He was good with Kylie, as he had been with
all the children she'd seen him charm. It bothered
her a little that Kylie gazed up at him so adoringly—
as if he were Santa Claus and a superhero all
rolled into one.

Kylie didn't have a lot of male role models in
her life. Leanne's father wasn't really a part of their
lives, and was very awkward with them on the rare
occasions when they saw him. Leanne's stepfather
was another rather reserved man who didn't relate
well to children—her mother had been consistent
in the type of men she'd married, Leanne thought
glumly. Eileen's husband, Jack, was very fond of
Kylie, and he'd been teaching her to play chess.
Kylie enjoyed that, but Leanne was aware that there
was a daddy-shaped hole in her daughter's life.

As hard as she tried to be everything Kylie

needed, she could never make up for the fact that Kylie's father had wanted nothing to do with her. Leanne had gotten involved with someone again, when Kylie was almost four. That relationship had fallen apart partly because the man she'd been infatuated with had become impatient with her round-the-clock responsibilities to her child.

He'd tried, she would give him credit for that, but ultimately the bonds between them hadn't been strong enough to overcome the obstacles. Kylie had been so disappointed when Trent had suddenly disappeared from her life that Leanne had vowed never to do that to her again. She'd promised herself she wouldn't even attempt to date until Kylie was old enough to understand the intricacies and vagaries of adult relationships—whenever that might be.

Eileen had accused her of overreacting to a few setbacks. Of being a bit cowardly and paranoid. Leanne had candidly agreed that all of that was probably true—but she was afraid to change. For Kylie's sake.

Watching Kylie now, smiling up so trustingly and fondly at Rob, Leanne felt a new ripple of discomfort. It was bad enough that she, herself, was developing an inconvenient crush on Rob.

She should have left Kylie with Eileen that evening, she thought with a frown. It was just that she'd hated to spend two evenings in a row away from her daughter.

"She looks comfortable enough in there," Rob announced, returning to the breakfast room. "Would you like to take a break for a cupcake and some decaf?"

Still attacking the quickly dwindling pile of packages, she replied without looking up, "I'm still too full for a cupcake, but I'd take a cup of the coffee, if you're making some anyway."

"Yeah, I am. I'm going to force down a couple of those cupcakes, and I need something to wash them down. Besides," he added with a grin, "all this cutting and taping is mind-numbing. I need something to clear my head—I'll just pretend it isn't decaf."

Reaching for the next gift box, Leanne hoped that would work for her, too. She definitely needed a clear head, to get through the remainder of this evening without making any foolish mistakes.

"Do you take milk or sugar?" he asked, pulling a carton of milk from the fridge and a bag of sugar from a cabinet over the coffeemaker. He gave her a crooked smile. "I keep meaning to buy a sugar bowl and creamer, but I always forget. I just scoop sugar out of the bag."

"Just a little milk in mine, please."

Their hands brushed when he gave her the mug. She reacted much more dramatically than she should have to the casual touch, feeling her cheeks go warm. Turning her head away, she hoped he hadn't noticed.

She took one sip of the coffee, then set the cup aside and turned back to her wrapping. It was definitely time to finish this chore and make her escape, she thought. It was getting just a little too cozy for comfort here.

CHAPTER SIX

BACK IN COSTUMES, ROB, Leanne and Kylie met in the parking lot of a long-term care facility Saturday afternoon to attend a party for the residents. Rob had offered to pick them up on his way to this appearance; Leanne had courteously, but firmly declined.

Something had happened last night to make her withdraw from him. He didn't know what it was, couldn't even pinpoint exactly when it had happened. It had seemed as if one moment they were getting along great, all warm and cozy, and the next she'd drawn back, becoming distantly polite, her eyes shuttered so that he couldn't read her thoughts.

He wanted to think she'd panicked a little because she'd realized they were getting too close, which might have made her start questioning her no-dating policy. But that was a decidedly self-serving interpretation of her behavior. More likely, he'd just annoyed her in some way.

Too bad. He'd liked having her and Kylie in his home. There had been something that had just felt…well, comfortable about sitting at the breakfast table with them. Something very right.

Why was it that the first woman he'd really felt connected to in a very long time was so adamantly opposed to letting him into her life?

He was no masochist. He didn't enjoy rejection. Nor was he a stalker. If she wasn't interested, he wasn't going to pester her to change her mind. He'd given it his best shot; now he had to accept that he'd failed. They had two more appearances to make together—this one, and one the following afternoon—and then it would be over. Time to concentrate on the new season, the next race for the championship.

But he was going to miss seeing Leanne and Kylie when Christmas was over.

"Hi, Santa," Kylie said, giving him a big wink.

"Hey, little elf." He tugged at her ponytail, making her pointy ears wiggle amusingly.

Holding up her basket, she said, "These are sugar-free candies. Mommy said the senior people at this place would probably like that better than the regular peppermints."

"That's a very good idea," he acknowledged with a glance at the rainbow-colored hard candies in her basket. His big gift bag was filled with warm lap robes tied with colorful ribbons rather than the toys or stuffed animals he usually carried.

"I didn't know old people liked Santa Claus," Kylie mused, looking at the decorated colonial-style nursing home. A steady stream of visitors entered and exited; some spotted the "Santa Claus family" and pointed and waved.

"Everyone likes Santa Claus," Rob replied, returning the wave of a gruff-looking man in overalls and a thick flannel jacket who was just climbing into his pickup after leaving the building.

He looked at Leanne, unable to resist adding softly, "They know Santa Claus would never do anything to hurt them."

"Not intentionally, perhaps," she murmured, so low that only he could hear her.

He had a very un-Santa-like impulse to find the man who had hurt her, who had left her so wary and guarded. He would not have been cheerful and jolly to anyone who had broken Leanne's heart.

Thinking of the man who had fathered Kylie

and had then chosen not to have anything to do with her, he began to clench his fists. He deliberately relaxed his hands, reminding himself to stay in character. But what kind of a sorry excuse for a man would walk away from his own child? Any guy should be proud and grateful to have a little sweetheart like Kylie in his life.

Not to mention Kylie's intriguing, stubbornly independent and not-so-secretly softhearted mother.

He held out his arm to Leanne, and she took it with only a fractional hesitation. Kylie hurried after them, her belled shoes and hat playing a merry Christmas tune.

The party was taking place in the dining room, which had been decorated to the point of holiday saturation. The residents sat at tables, many of them in wheelchairs, others with walkers nearby. A middle-aged man sat at an upright piano in one corner, playing holiday tunes. Some of the guests listened with visible pleasure, others talked over him, but most seemed to be having a good time.

Just before they entered the room, Rob heard Leanne murmur a last reminder to Kylie about what to expect from some of the more confused seniors. From what he'd observed of Kylie so far, he doubted that she would be fazed.

He was right, of course. Kylie was the hit of the party. She flitted from person to person, dispensing candy and hugs with equal enthusiasm.

Rob enjoyed the smiles that greeted him, his heart twisting when the eyes that met his were too distant and unfocused to respond even to Santa Claus. He pressed gifts into trembling hands, and bent close to listen patiently to quavering reminiscences of Christmases past.

Leanne was also engaged in several lengthy conversations. Several of the women particularly admired her red velvet dress with its Victorian-styled bodice and long, full skirt edged in faux fur. He heard a couple of them tell her they'd worn similarly styled dresses in their youth. Some of the men flirted outrageously with her; she handled that with her usual serenity, teasing back while staying just out of range.

He couldn't stop watching her. He had to force himself to concentrate on his own role when what he really wanted to do was just stand there and admire how pretty Leanne looked in her curly white wig and rosy cheeks with multicolored Christmas lights haloing her face.

Somewhat wistfully, he wondered if anyone

ever asked Santa what *he* wanted for Christmas. Rob had an answer ready if he should be granted one Christmas wish.

LEANNE COULDN'T IMAGINE why it actually annoyed her a little that Rob was as amazing with senior citizens as he was with small children. She figured it had to be because everything she discovered about him only made him more fascinating to her. How was she supposed to continue to resist him when he just kept being so darned nice? Couldn't he do something…anything?…that would make him less attractive?

She even thought he was sexy in his Santa suit. Those warm brown eyes gleaming behind his little wire glasses. The quick glimpses of dimples behind the beard when he smiled. The rich music of his laugh. The gentle way his strong, gloved hands wrapped around frail, unsteady ones. Knowing how he looked beneath all the padding and fake whiskers wasn't doing a thing to keep her pulse rate regulated.

They spent an hour at the facility, mingling, chatting, singing holiday songs. Kylie played a Christmas carol on the piano, one she had memorized from her weekly lessons. The applause that followed pleased her; she grinned from ear to ear as she took her bow and then relinquished the piano to the man who had been playing earlier.

Leanne and Rob had stood together in an out-of-the-way corner to watch Kylie's performance. They clapped along with everyone else when she finished.

And then a woman sitting in a wheelchair nearby called out, "Lookie there! Mr. and Miz Santa are standing beneath the mistletoe."

Leanne glanced up automatically. Sure enough, someone had pinned a spray of plastic mistletoe on the ceiling just above where she and Rob stood. It had been almost hidden among the plastic snow-flakes and ornaments hanging from ribbons pinned to the ceiling.

"Mistletoe, mistletoe," someone else called out with a laugh. "Let's see a kiss."

"Oh, no, we—" Stammering, Leanne started to move quickly away from where she stood, but a wheelchair suddenly blocked her path.

"You have to kiss," the silver-haired woman in the chair chided. "It's Christmas tradition."

"Kiss her, kiss her," several others chimed in.

Kylie stood laughing nearby, obviously amused by her mother's predicament.

Rob placed a hand at the small of her back. "Looks as though we have no choice," he said when she looked up at him. "We *are* under the mistletoe."

She felt her cheeks warm, knowing her face must be almost as red as her dress. But because she didn't want to spoil the party, and because the guests seemed to be so amused by their new game, she decided she should play along.

She rose on tiptoe and pressed a quick kiss on Rob's cheek, just above the fake beard. His skin was warm and smooth beneath her lips, but she didn't linger long enough to savor.

The chaste peck did not satisfy their raucous audience. His eyes dancing with mischief as the onlookers encouraged him, Rob suddenly wrapped his arms around her waist, tilted her back and planted a big kiss directly on her mouth.

She was bombarded by sensations, almost too many to process at once. The feel of his lips against hers. The strength of his arms supporting her. The softness of the beard against her face. The sounds of applause and laughter just audible above the buzzing in her ears. His lips…

In reality, the kiss probably lasted only a few seconds, but it felt much longer to her. It was a good thing she didn't have to do anything but smile rather stupidly and stand there when he finished, because she wasn't really up to anything more. She wasn't sure she could have spoken coherently had she been required to try. At least they seemed to have entertained their audience, who were laughing and clapping. The pianist began to play a tune about kissing Santa Claus, and those in the room who knew the lyrics sang along.

Leanne decided that was as good a way as any to make their exit. Giving Rob a look, she motioned to Kylie to join them and they made their way to the door, waving and calling out, "Merry Christmas" as they left.

Leanne made sure Kylie was securely strapped into the backseat, then closed the door and turned to Rob. "Well," she said after clearing her throat, "that was…interesting."

He chuckled. "They were a rowdy bunch, weren't they?"

"They were incorrigible," she said with a shake of her head. "Worse than any of the children we've seen so far."

Laughing, he shrugged. "They were just having some fun. Can't blame them for wanting to do that when they get the chance."

She frowned at him. "You didn't have to indulge them quite so enthusiastically."

He stroked his beard, a gesture she suspected was intended to hide a grin. "It was only for the sake of the residents," he assured her. "It wasn't as if I wanted to kiss you. Or that I'd been thinking about doing so for a couple of weeks now. Or that I was just hoping for any little excuse to do it without getting my head knocked off."

"Rob." She planted her hands on her hips and frowned at him. "We've talked about this."

"Can't stop me from thinking about it." He reached for the handle of her car door and opened it for her. "It's getting colder. I'm freezing my jingle bells off."

He was certainly in a good mood. Because of the kiss? Or because of what he thought it had accomplished?

Had he somehow sensed how dramatically she had reacted to him? How hard she was having to work at that very moment not to remember every detail of the way his lips had felt against hers?

"I'm not going to date you, Rob," she said in a low voice.

He motioned toward the car, urging her to get in. Only when she was behind the wheel and fastening her seat belt did he lean in to murmur into her ear, "I'm not interested in dating you, Leanne. I'm interested in courting you."

He closed her door before she could stammer a response.

"SO, HOW ARE THE SANTA family appearances going? You have your last one this afternoon, don't you?"

Moving out of the path of the crowd leaving the church after services Sunday morning, Leanne made sure Kylie was occupied with a couple of her little friends before demanding of Eileen, "What were you thinking when you set me up with your cousin?"

"Set you up?" Eileen's eyes went round in an expression of total—and unbelievable—innocence. "I have no idea what you're talking about."

"Did you suggest that he ask me out?"

Her neighbor's face lit up. "Rob asked you out?"

"Yes."

"Please don't tell me you turned him down."

"Eileen, you know my policy about dating." Not to mention her policy about—she swallowed hard—courting. She didn't even want to think about what Rob might have meant by that; not that she'd thought of much else since she'd left him yesterday.

Shaking her head in disapproval, Eileen sighed. "Honestly, Leanne. Rob is a nice, successful and, might I add, a great-looking single man. He loves kids. He isn't a jerk and he's not a womanizer."

"I know, I know. He's darned near perfect," Leanne muttered. "That doesn't change anything."

"Why not?"

"We've had this discussion before. I won't risk having Kylie hurt if a relationship doesn't work out."

"I wonder if it's really Kylie you're protecting so fiercely—or yourself."

The pastor came up to greet them and chat for a few minutes, putting an end to that conversation. Eileen excused herself shortly afterward to join her impatient-looking husband. Taking Kylie's hand, Leanne led her daughter through the parking lot to their car, where she made sure Kylie was buckled in before climbing behind the wheel.

She thought of Eileen's words during the short drive home. Of course she was protecting Kylie. Everything she did was for Kylie's benefit.

Biting her lip, she glanced in the rearview mirror, catching a glimpse of her daughter who was looking out the side window and singing along softly to a pop song playing on the radio. Had Eileen suggested that Leanne was actually using her daughter as an excuse to keep from taking risks again? That was just absurd.

Wasn't it?

ROB HAD JUST SETTLED his white wig on his head when his cell phone rang Sunday afternoon. He glanced at the screen, then lifted it to his ear. "I can't talk long, Bill. I've got to leave in ten minutes."

"Another Santa gig?"

"Yeah. Last one," he replied regretfully.

"Where is it this time?"

"It's a Christmas party at a local fire station. For the families of the firefighters. We'll be posing for pictures and passing out candy, just a drop-in appearance, really."

"Sounds like a group of people who'd like to know who's really behind the Santa beard."

"No. I'm going for the kids, and the only celebrity they want to see this time of year is Santa Claus."

"You should at least let Maddie drop a few mentions of how you spent your Christmas vacation.

You know, after it's all over. You'd earn lots of PR points for having played Santa for all these charity events."

"No," he said again. "I told you, Bill, this isn't a stunt. I'm doing it strictly for my own purposes, and I don't want to publicize it. For one thing, I might want to do it again next year, and it would be hard to do so if people were watching for me."

"Okay, fine. So, today's your last day with the pretty Mrs. Claus, hmm?"

Rob was already walking toward the door. "Oh, I wouldn't say that."

"Yeah? Does that mean you've made progress in talking her into dating you?"

"I don't want to date Leanne, Bill."

"Oh? So you've changed *your* mind?"

"I wouldn't say that, either."

"Oh?" Bill sounded confused. "So what do you want?"

"I want to marry her."

He could hear Bill sputtering when he snapped the phone closed.

CHAPTER SEVEN

THE PARTY AT THE FIRE STATION was a big success. Very crowded, but everyone seemed to be having a good time. And as usual, the appearance of Mr. and Mrs. Santa Claus and their helper elf was a big hit.

Firefighters' children crowded around them, and Rob and Kylie handled the attention with their usual skill while Leanne did her best to keep up. She thought she'd done a pretty good job during their appearances that month, but she had to acknowledge that Rob and Kylie were much more comfortable in the spotlight than she. Rob, of course, was used to all the attention. Kylie was just born to it.

She watched as Rob visited with every child in attendance, giving them his usual patient attention. Kylie jingled around the room, passing out candy, being teased by the firefighters, cajoling herself a chance to sit in the ladder truck. Leanne snapped her picture doing just that, grinning hugely as she gripped the steering wheel, her elf ears hidden beneath an oversize fire helmet.

This would be their last engagement for the season. She knew Kylie would miss dressing up in her costume and being the "candy elf." As for herself, she had enjoyed the experience for the most part, but she would be somewhat relieved when it was all over. Working full-time during the week, appearing at one or two events on the weekends and trying to keep up with her housework and other responsibilities was a bit tiring. And then there was Rob....

She still hadn't decided if he'd been teasing when he'd said he wanted to "court" her. He was quite the joker. Maybe he'd just wanted to see her reaction, not expecting her to take him seriously in the least. Sort of like the mischief she'd seen in his eyes when he'd bent her back for that under-the-mistletoe kiss. He just liked seeing her flustered.

And yet there had been something in the tone of his voice....

No. He'd been teasing. Surely.

Maybe she would miss the teasing. A little. She

was pretty sure she would miss Rob more than a little. She thought it was pretty good, all in all, that this holiday fantasy between them was coming to an end.

"You know, that guy looks familiar to me, for some reason," she heard a burly firefighter nearby murmur to one of his coworkers. "It's something about his eyes. Just can't quite put my finger on it."

His friend punched his arm. "Well, of course he looks familiar, Mike. He's freaking Santa Claus."

Mike frowned and shook his head. "No, I meant the guy wearing the costume. I think maybe I've met him before."

"Yeah? Maybe you have. Why don't you ask him?"

"I tried. He just sort of laughed and started talking to one of the kids again."

"So it's probably someone you know. You'll find out later."

Mike nodded, still frowning toward Rob. "Yeah, I guess. There's just something about him...."

Leanne moved to Rob's side. "It's about time for us to take our bow and leave, isn't it?"

His fuzzy white eyebrows rose a bit. "Are you in a hurry?"

"Well, it is time. And I just overheard one of

the firefighters trying to figure out why you look so familiar."

Comprehension lit Rob's eyes. "I see. It does sound like it's time for us to go. Let's make our dramatic exit, shall we?"

She looked around quickly. "We won't be leaving under any mistletoe, will we?"

He laughed. "Not that I see. We could always pretend...."

"Behave yourself," she murmured from behind a bright smile for the benefit of their audience.

Signaling Kylie to join them, they began to make their way toward the door, doing their now-practiced waves and calling out, "Merry Christmas."

Mike, the firefighter Leanne had overheard a few moments earlier, started their way, but was detained by someone who engaged him in conversation. She hurried Kylie out the door, following quickly behind her. Rob closed the door behind them with a gusty exhale of relief, and then both of them laughed.

"What's going on?" Kylie asked curiously, looking up at them.

"Nothing," Leanne assured her. "Get in the car."

"How come you didn't kiss Mommy again today?" Kylie asked Rob impishly as she opened her car door. "Everyone liked it when you kissed her yesterday."

"That was just a joke yesterday," Leanne answered repressively. "Because of the mistletoe we were standing under."

"It was funny," Kylie said with a giggle.

Rob lightly chucked her chin. "You laughing at us, elf?"

She giggled again. "Maybe."

"Get in, Kylie. It's cold."

Kylie started to automatically obey her mother's instruction, but then suddenly stopped. She turned to Rob with big, distressed eyes. "Oh."

Frowning, he went down to one knee. "Kylie? What's wrong?"

"This is the last one, isn't it?"

She didn't have to clarify. Rob exchanged a quick glance with Leanne before saying gently, "It's our last Christmas appearance. You were a great elf, Kylie. You should be very elf-satisfied with your performance."

She tried to smile at his pun, but her lower lip was quivering. "I'm going to see you again, aren't I? I don't want to say goodbye."

Leanne twisted her hands in front of her.

Wasn't this exactly the sort of thing she'd been trying to avoid?

"Of course we'll see each other again," Rob assured her. "We're friends, right?"

Biting her lip, Leanne wished he'd been a bit more vague. Maybe a noncommittal, "We'll see." Something that hadn't sounded so much like a promise. But Kylie's face brightened, and her eyes cleared, and she threw her arms around Rob's neck, visibly reassured. "We're friends," she agreed. "I'll see you, Rob."

Rob hugged the child warmly. "See you, Kylie."

He helped her into the car, made sure her seat belt was fastened, then closed the door and turned to Leanne. "I don't want to say goodbye, either," he murmured.

"Rob."

"Just think about it, okay? You have my number if you decide you'd like to give us a chance."

"I'll think about it."

He seemed to take some encouragement from that, since it wasn't an outright rejection. "Great. I won't bother you about it. Just let me know if you'd like to have dinner or something and we'll see where it goes from there, okay?"

She nodded.

"In the meantime," he said, his tone changing,

"I'm delivering the gifts to the Osorio kids on Christmas Eve. I made arrangements with their mother to drop by at about four that afternoon."

"Did you?" She thought wistfully of how much fun it would be to see Ana's face when she saw her stack of gifts. "Are you going as Santa or as yourself?"

He shrugged. "I thought I'd go as Santa. Mrs. Osorio thought they'd get a kick out of that, even though she knows who I am really."

She cleared her throat. "Um—maybe they'd enjoy seeing Mrs. Claus, too?"

He grinned, reaching out to squeeze her hand. "I was hoping you'd offer. Why don't I pick you up this time? It would be a lot easier than trying to meet at the Osorio's apartment."

He wasn't giving her a chance to change her mind. "Okay, fine. But, Rob—this is just about Christmas, okay? It doesn't mean you and I are... Well, you know."

He gave her fingers another little squeeze, then released her and stepped back, lifting his hands. "I understand. I'll see you Thursday, okay? Three o'clock."

Picturing the Osorio children again, she nodded. "All right. Thursday."

She noted that Santa looked almost smug— elf-satisfied, he would probably say—as he moved toward his car.

ROB WONDERED IF IT WAS a little strange that he no longer felt at all odd going out and about in his Santa costume. Maybe it would be a good thing when the holidays were over and he donned his racing uniform again, he thought with a wry smile as he parked in front of Leanne's house on Christmas Eve.

Leanne must have been watching for him; she came out of the house almost before he'd turned off the engine. Dressed in her costume that looked as natural to him now as his own, she moved down the steps and toward his car as he climbed out to welcome her.

"Where's Kylie?"

"She's at Eileen's house, watching Christmas shows with Eileen's granddaughter, Lucy. They had several, so they'll be occupied for a while. Eileen was serving them hot cocoa and Christmas cookies when I left, so Kylie's pretty much in holiday heaven over there."

Rob had met his cousin's granddaughter at a family reunion last summer during an off week from racing. From what he recalled, Lucy was a little younger than Kylie, a dark-haired, dark-eyed charmer.

"Eileen almost begged me to let Kylie come over this afternoon," Leanne added with a slight laugh. "Being the only child in the house, Lucy was getting restless and much too impatient for the day to be over so Santa would bring her gifts. I thought it was better for Kylie to play with Lucy rather than accompany us. That way the Osorio children don't have to share 'Santa's' attention."

Rob opened the passenger door of his car for her. "I remember how slowly Christmas Eve passed when I was a boy. My sister and I used to drive my mom crazy asking her what time it was. How much longer till Santa comes? She used to try to come up with all sorts of activities to keep us occupied until bedtime. It was probably the only day of the year we didn't argue about taking our baths and going to bed."

"Will you see your family tomorrow?" Leanne asked when he slid into his own seat and closed his door.

He nodded as he reached for his seat belt. "We're meeting at Mom's condo tomorrow after-noon to open gifts and then have our big Christmas dinner. My sister will have lunch with her husband's family, then join us at Mom's."

"Does your sister have children?"

He started the engine. "No, she's only been married for a year. Mom can't wait to have kids in the family."

"Mmm." Leanne fidgeted with the faux-fur trim of her sleeve.

"Will you be seeing your mother tomorrow?"

She shook her head. "Kylie and I are driving to Charleston, West Virginia—where my mother and her husband live—Saturday. We're leaving early that morning and coming home Sunday. It's about a four-and-a-half-hour drive, so we'll be there by lunch on Saturday."

"So you're going the day after Christmas."

"Yes. My mother and stepfather are spending Christmas day with his son's family in Winfield."

"What about your dad?"

"He's in Belize. He'll be there another few weeks, I think. He brought our Christmas gifts by before he left last month. I put them under the tree to open tomorrow."

She really wasn't very close to her family. How many times had she been rejected in her life? Was it any wonder she was so self-protective against being hurt again? Yet he could tell that it was against her nature to be so guarded. She'd been so caring, so giving with everyone they had visited as Mr. and Mrs. Claus. It had been her idea to help him provide Christmas gifts for the Osorio children. She was teaching her daughter about charity and generosity and compassion. And she had a smile that lit up her face, and a musical laugh that all but begged to be released more often.

"Tell me about your Christmas with Kylie. What will you do after we deliver these gifts?"

As he had expected, her eyes lit up when she thought of her daughter. "There's a candlelight service at our church this evening at seven. Afterward, Kylie and I will return home and I'll read 'The Night Before Christmas' before tucking her into bed. When she's asleep, I'll set out her gifts from Santa. She'll be up at a ridiculously early hour in the morning. Tomorrow we'll play with her gifts and have a nice lunch we'll make together. I bought a DVD for us to watch in the afternoon. I'll make popcorn and…"

She stopped suddenly, as if she were afraid she was talking too much. "You know. That sort of thing."

He glanced away from the road ahead to smile at her. "It sounds ideal."

He was absolutely sincere. It did sound like a perfect, quiet Christmas. How he would have loved to share that time with them.

"IT'S SANTA! MAMA, CRUZ, Victor, look! It's Santa!"

Ana's announcement was made at an earsplitting volume, the squeal that followed so high that Leanne almost winced. Had there been a dog nearby, she figured it would be howling in pain, but she couldn't help smiling in response to the child's excitement.

Rob was Ho, Ho, Hoing for all he was worth as he carried the big bag filled with gifts into the bare-bones apartment. Leanne followed, her arms filled with a few packages that hadn't fit into the bag. She smiled at Esther Osorio, who had opened the door to them.

Somewhere in her early forties, Esther seemed reserved, but pleasant. While there was visible embarrassment about receiving charity, she seemed grateful for the gifts for her children. She offered them coffee. Rob declined, murmuring that he couldn't drink while wearing the beard, but Leanne accepted.

The apartment was very small, with a sparsely furnished living room, dining room and kitchen combination and a hallway leading to what Leanne suspected were only two bedrooms. Her guess would be that Esther and Ana shared one room while the boys shared another. It must be so difficult for Esther to support three children since her husband had died and she'd been laid off from her job.

"This coffee is delicious," she said after taking a sip of the fragrant beverage lightened with a little cream. "Do I taste cinnamon?"

Esther nodded a bit shyly. "I like to add a little cinnamon to the coffee."

"It's really good."

"I made polvorones. Would you like one?"

"Yes, please."

Rob joined them at the small table while the children ripped into their gifts. He was unable to resist trying one of the little almond sugar cookies. They all laughed when crumbs sprinkled into his beard, but he assured Esther it was well worth the mess. "These are great."

Esther looked pleased. "Thank you. I enjoy cooking."

Another high-pitched squeal from Ana told them she'd opened her ballerina dress. She twirled around the room, knocking into the little Christmas tree sitting in one corner of the room, strung with popcorn and paper chains. There were only a few gifts beneath that tree, showing how little Esther had been able to afford for extra purchases.

"Ana," Esther murmured in a tone Leanne recognized from one mother to another.

She looked then at Rob and Leanne. "This is the nicest thing anyone has ever done for us," she said, her dark eyes moist. "I don't know how to thank you."

"Thank you for letting us do this for them," Rob replied gently. "You've made this a very special Christmas for us, too."

Cruz approached the table then, clutching his MP3 player as if it were embellished with priceless jewels. "This was too much," he told Rob, his head high. "You said you were only going to bring things for Victor and Ana."

"Your mother told me how much help you are to her," Rob replied. "You deserve a few rewards for being such a good son and brother."

"Thank you," Cruz said with the innate dignity Leanne associated with the teen.

"You're welcome."

"Cruz, come see my doll. She looks like me," Ana called out, drawing him back across the room.

Victor was on the tattered couch, his gifts piled around him as he concentrated on the handheld video game. His face was creased with concentration, his dark eyes alight with pleasure.

Wanting to show off her gifts to someone else, Ana motioned for Leanne to come admire them. Leanne did so with a smile, enjoying the child's appreciation. While she and Ana chatted, Leanne noted that Rob and Esther had fallen into what appeared to be a serious conversation. She couldn't tell what they were saying, but Esther looked first surprised, then hopeful, and then cautiously excited.

She wondered if Rob was telling Esther that he'd found her a job. She knew that had been one of his goals.

A few minutes later, Rob stood, obviously in preparation to leave. "I'll see you next week," he said to Esther, who smiled tremulously and nodded.

Rob accepted a big hug from Ana and grateful handshakes from Victor and Cruz. "I'll see you again," he assured them all.

Both Rob and Leanne bade the family Merry Christmas again, and then left them to their holiday.

"That felt good, didn't it?" Rob asked as he drove toward her house again.

"It did. What a nice family."

"They are, aren't they? You can tell Esther runs a tight ship, despite having to be gone so much."

"With Cruz as her first mate," she said with a smile.

He chuckled. "Yeah."

She wasn't sure it was any of her business, but she simply had to ask, "Did you find Esther a job?"

"I did. If she decides to accept it. She's interviewing next Tuesday."

"Is it a good position? Will it give her more time with her kids?"

He reached up to pull off his hat, wig and beard, revealing tousled dark hair and a big grin. "I think it's a pretty good position. I hope she agrees. I want to hire her as my housekeeper."

"Your housekeeper?" Leanne wasn't entirely surprised.

Keeping one hand on the wheel, he pulled off the fuzzy eyebrows with his other hand as he answered casually, "Yeah. I've had people come in once a week to clean, but the place gets kind of musty when I'm gone so much during the season. Esther would be responsible for cleaning and laundry and shopping and cooking during the two or three nights a week I'm home. Basically running the household, you know?"

And well compensated for her efforts, Leanne suspected. "That sounds ideal. It's a long commute for her, though."

He shook his head. "You didn't notice the guesthouse?"

"Guesthouse?" She frowned, trying to picture his property.

"It's sort of nestled in that stand of trees off to the west side of the house. The lights weren't on the night you were there, and we never went outside, so I guess you didn't see it. Anyway, it's a little three-bedroom cottage with a nice kitchen and living room. The former owner employed a couple to take care of the house and grounds, and they lived in the guesthouse. I'm going to offer it to Esther and the kids."

"You barely know her." She couldn't help pointing it out. "What if it doesn't work out? Do you really want three kids running around your place all the time?"

He shrugged. "I've always thought there would be kids running around my house someday. And I suppose I know Esther as well as anyone else I could interview and hire for the position. There's always a chance it won't work out, isn't there? I can't let that stop me from trying, when it could turn out to be perfect for all of us."

There were so many messages embedded in those words that she wasn't sure which to focus on first. She decided to go with the safest. "You don't think the kids will mind moving? They'll have to go to new schools. Make new friends."

"Esther didn't seem to think they'd mind so much. They only started attending these schools after her husband died and she had to move last year."

"You certainly talked a lot while I was entertaining Ana."

"We'd already discussed some of this on the phone, when I called her to set up the time for today."

Leanne turned in her seat to stare at him. "You offered her the job before you even met her?"

"I told her I was looking for someone," he corrected. "I described the job and asked if she would be interested in interviewing. She was very interested. All we did today was set up a time for her to come to the house for the interview. Next Tuesday. If she likes what she sees and wants the job, it's hers. I just have a good feeling about all this."

"You make up your mind very quickly."

He shrugged. "I know what I want when I see it. I always have."

She thought about that as he parked in front of her house.

She didn't immediately reach for her door handle. "I suppose you have plans for this evening."

"No. All my holiday plans are for tomorrow."

She moistened her lips, feeling a surge of cowardice go through her, almost convincing her to swallow the words she wanted to say. And then she thought about what he'd said about not letting the fear of failure hold him back from trying.

"I mentioned that Kylie and I will be attending a candlelight service at seven."

He seemed to go very still before he nodded, his gaze locked on her face.

"Maybe…would you like to go with us?"

He let out a long breath, making her realize that he'd been holding it as he'd waited for her to ask. "I'd like that very much."

They looked at each other without moving for several long moments, both aware of what a huge step she had just taken.

"I'll go home and change," he said, glancing wryly down at his red velvet suit. "What time should I pick you up?"

"The church is only a five-minute drive from here, but we should probably be a little early to get a seat."

"I'll be back just after six-thirty, then."

"That sounds about right." She reached for the door handle then.

Rob stopped her with a hand on her arm. "Leanne…"

She turned her head to look at him.

Moving slowly enough to give her a chance to back away, he leaned toward her. "I don't have any mistletoe on me…."

She rested a hand on his chest. "We don't need any," she murmured, lifting her mouth to his.

The last kiss had shaken her to her toes, even though they'd had an audience and they'd been playing the roles that had brought them together. This one, with no one to see them, no reason to pretend to be anyone but themselves, was life-changing.

She lifted her hand to his cheek, feeling the lean, strong planes of his face without the thick, fake beard. His lips were warm and firm against hers, then so soft when he angled his head to take the embrace deeper. His arms felt so right around her, as if she had found a place for which she'd been searching for a very long time. She felt another quick rush of panic, but she fought it down.

It was time for her to stop being such a coward. To stop hiding behind excuses and start living her life again. Maybe she would get hurt again…but maybe she wouldn't, she thought as he drew back, smiling at her in a way that brought a lump to her throat.

"I'll see you in a couple of hours," he said, brushing his lips across her forehead.

"Um—" She cleared her throat and resolutely opened her door. "I'll be ready."

At least, she hoped she was ready for this.

CHAPTER EIGHT

LEANNE WAS AWARE of the curious looks when she and Kylie walked into the church with Rob. It was the first time she'd ever brought a male guest with her—and for that guest to be R. J. Sanger had to be even more of a surprise for everyone. She could see the recognition dawning on several faces around them.

Festive in a dress with a green velvet bodice and a green-and-red-plaid taffeta skirt, Kylie clung to Rob's hand. She was delighted to have him with them that evening, and she preened a little when her friends saw them all together.

"Rob!" Eileen approached them with a bright smile, her husband, son, daughter-in-law and granddaughter trailing behind them. "Isn't this a nice surprise?"

Rob greeted his mother's cousin and her extended family warmly. He patted little Lucy's head, though she hid behind her mother shyly, having no memory of meeting him six months earlier.

Eileen looked at Leanne with an approving smile. Feeling her cheeks warm a bit, Leanne touched Rob's arm. "We'd better take our seats."

Kylie wanted to sit between them, and Rob didn't seem to mind. Leanne tried to concentrate on the service—the familiar scriptures, the well-known carols, the stirring performance by the handbell choir. Candlelight flickered in the darkened church as they sang the last hymn, lighting the nativity scene at the altar and, as always, she felt a lump in her throat. She loved these services, loved sharing them with her daughter. Glancing out of the corner of her eye, she thought of how right it felt to have Rob there with them.

They didn't linger after the service. Kylie bounced excitedly in the backseat during the ride home, singing Christmas carols. Rob teased her by pointing out stars and airplane lights, asking each time if she thought it was Santa.

"Can Rob come in and hear 'The Night Before Christmas?'" Kylie asked Leanne when they arrived at home.

"No, that's okay, Kylie. I don't want to intrude on your family traditions," Rob assured her.

"You wouldn't be 'truding. Would he, Mommy?"

"Not at all," she assured him.

"Really," she added quietly when he looked at her doubtfully. "We'd love to have you join us."

So what if he wasn't around next Christmas? She and Kylie would still have their Christmas routines.

They drank cocoa while Leanne read the poem. She was a little self-conscious with Rob there, but he sat quietly, listening as attentively as Kylie. Kylie almost quivered with impatience to say the last words with her. "Merry Christmas to all, and to all a good night," they recited together, making Rob laugh.

Closing the book, Leanne said, "Okay, munchkin, go get ready for bed. Santa can't come until you're snugly tucked in."

"Okay, Mommy." For once, Kylie was eager to go put on her pajamas.

Sitting on the couch beside Leanne, Rob asked, "Did you ever find out what it was she particularly wanted for Christmas?"

She sighed. "No. She told me not to worry about it, that Santa would take care of it. I hope she isn't too disappointed when she doesn't get whatever it is."

"I'm sure you've provided a very nice Christmas for her."

"I tried to get a few things I knew she would like.

Some of them are wrapped under the tree. The others I'll put out after she falls asleep."

She glanced at the tree and frowned when she saw a couple of gifts that had not been there earlier. "What are those?"

Looking innocent, Rob said, "What?"

"You put some presents under our tree, didn't you? When?"

He chuckled. "When you were making the hot chocolate. I swore Kylie to secrecy. You can open them tomorrow."

"But, Rob, I—"

"I just wanted to get you both something. You've given me so much tonight."

"I haven't given you anything."

Touching her cheek, he smiled gently. "Oh, yes. You have."

"Actually, there is one other thing." She stood and walked to the tree, where she lifted a wrapped box. Somewhat nervously, she turned back to him. "I got this for you, but I wasn't sure I would have the nerve to give it to you."

He looked surprised that she'd gotten him anything. "You didn't have to—"

"It was an impulse," she said, all but shoving the box at him. "I was shopping, and— Oh, just take it, okay?"

With a laugh, he did so. "I'm not waiting until tomorrow to open it."

He peeled off the paper. "Hey," he said a moment later, "this is great."

Twisting her hands nervously in front of her, she felt the warmth of her blush on her cheeks. "It seems like sort of a silly gift to get a man who can buy anything he wants. But I know you don't have a set."

He seemed genuinely pleased by the stainless-steel sugar bowl and creamer set. She'd seen them on sale while she'd been shopping for last-minute gifts, and she'd thought of how nice they would look in Rob's kitchen. She'd bought the set on a whim, though she'd wondered even then if she would ever give it to him. She'd had a vague idea that maybe she would send it to him after Christmas with a prim little note thanking him for the dinner he'd cooked for her and Kylie.

"It's the perfect gift," he assured her with a smile that made her knees weaken. "Something you chose because you knew I needed it, and you know I like things for my house. Thank you."

Dressed in a long red nightgown with white piping, Kylie came back into the room to say good-night. "Rob got to open a present?" she asked, zeroing in on the wrapping paper scattered around him.

Laughing, he suggested that they open the gifts he'd brought them. He didn't have to twist Kylie's arm. She pounced on her gift, while Leanne opened hers more cautiously, hoping he hadn't overdone it.

He'd bought them matching gold bangle bracelets. Kylie was thrilled as she slipped the small circlet on her wrist and admired the way it gleamed in the light. "Look, Mommy, it's just like yours. Aren't they pretty?"

"They're beautiful," Leanne murmured, smiling mistily at Rob. So maybe he had spent too much, but Kylie was so delighted to have a bracelet just like her mother's that Leanne couldn't protest.

Rob knew her weaknesses a bit too well, she thought—but she was finding it more difficult all the time to worry about that.

ROB MADE HIMSELF LEAVE an hour later. Kylie was snugly tucked into her bed and he and Leanne had shared a very pleasant interlude on her couch. What had begun as a few kisses had escalated to heated embraces that had left him aching, but optimistic that she was finally letting down her guard with him.

"I think we should slow down a bit," she warned him as she saw him out. "We've only known each other for three weeks, and I still worry about disrupting Kylie's life."

She looked so pretty standing in the glow of her Christmas lights with her red hair tousled by his hands, her cheeks flushed, her lips still damp from his kisses, her clothes a bit disheveled. Slow down? He was almost shaking with impatience to carry their relationship to the next level. He didn't care that it had been only three weeks; he had fallen for Leanne the first time he'd laid eyes on her. He'd fallen almost as hard for her adorable daughter.

Still, he made himself say, "We'll take it at whatever speed you like. I'm in this for the duration."

Shaking her head, she studied him in bemusement. "You sound so sure."

"I am sure." He knew that was all she was ready to hear, so he contented himself with brushing one last kiss against her lips. "Good night, Leanne. I'll call you tomorrow."

"Good night, Rob. Merry Christmas."

"It's the best Christmas ever," he assured her, knowing he was grinning like an idiot.

EPILOGUE

THE DINING ROOM WAS AGLOW with Christmas lights, fragrant with balsam and cinnamon. The long table almost sagged beneath the weight of a Christmas feast prepared by Esther, with assistance from Leanne, Kylie and Ana.

Sitting at the head of the table, Rob took a satisfied inventory. Leanne sat at his left, listening intently to something Kylie was telling her from the next chair. Rob's mother sat at his right, beaming at Kylie with proud, grandmotherly affection. Ana, Victor and Cruz were on their best behavior as they filled their plates under their mother's watchful eye. Esther had finally been persuaded to stop fussing with the meal and sit down to join them.

So much had changed in the past year. He and Leanne had been married for almost a month now, since the weekend after the season had ended. It had ended particularly well for Rob, who could now claim two NASCAR Sprint Cup Series championships. Yet even that accomplishment took second place to his family, he thought, proudly eyeing his wife and daughter.

It hadn't all been easy. There had been a lot of adjustments for all of them during the season. He'd wanted Leanne and Kylie with him as much as possible; Leanne had been determined to maintain as normal a life as she could for Kylie's sake. It had required compromises on both their parts—and Rob wasn't accustomed to making compromises. He'd forced himself to learn how.

They had rung in the New Year together, appearing in public as a couple for the first time. By Valentine's Day, Leanne had finally admitted that she loved him. He'd proposed on July 4. They'd married the day after Thanksgiving. Every holiday was special to him now because he shared them with her.

Things were working out well with the Osorio family. Esther ran his household like a well-oiled machine. Leanne would be free to concentrate on Kylie, and the other children they hoped to have soon. She and Kylie would travel with him as much as possible during the upcoming season, though they would make sure Kylie's education did not suffer for it. Leanne had already talked to several of the other racing wives for pointers and advice.

Rob had helped Cruz get a part-time job in the shop, sweeping floors and running errands. Cruz thrived in the racing setting, and Rob suspected his young friend and protégé had a bright future in the sport. Victor and Ana also seemed quite happy living on the estate and were doing well in school, enjoying the extra time they could spend with their mother. They maintained their separate family routines, but Rob had insisted they share a Christmas meal together. He liked having everyone gathered around for the holiday.

This was what he'd wanted when he'd bought his big house—to fill it with family and friends.

Everyone was stuffed to the groaning point by the time the meal ended. Leanne and Rob's mother insisted on helping Esther clean up, while Rob helped Kylie assemble a toy she'd gotten for Christmas. Cruz, Victor and Ana had returned to the guesthouse to enjoy their own gifts.

Kylie studied the newly assembled dollhouse in satisfaction. "That looks good. Thank you, Daddy."

She'd been calling him that for a couple of months now, her own idea. Every time he heard it, he melted a little. Leanne insisted it was all she could do to keep Rob from spoiling Kylie rotten. "You're welcome."

She wrapped her arms around his neck, leaning comfortably against him. "I had fun being the candy elf again this year."

"I had fun being Santa again," he assured her. It was a tradition he hoped to continue for a long time.

Suddenly struck by something he hadn't thought about for a long time, he pulled back a little to study her face. "Kylie, remember last year? When you said there was something in particular you wanted for Christmas, but you wouldn't tell us what it was?"

Smiling, she nodded. "I remember."

"What was it, anyway? Did you get it?"

Her laugh was as musical as any Christmas carol. "I got it."

"Well?"

"I asked for a Daddy," she told him, patting his cheek. "And now I have one. I think you might be the real Santa Claus, after all."

Sensing movement in the doorway, Rob looked up to find Leanne smiling at them with moist-looking eyes. He reached out a hand to her. She laid hers in it and lowered herself to sit beside them on the floor.

Wrapping one arm around Leanne and the other around Kylie, Rob shook his head, his voice a little rough when he said, "I'm not the real Santa, Kylie. But I believe in the guy. He gave me everything I wanted for Christmas, too."

Kylie laughed happily as Rob leaned down to brush a kiss on his wife's smiling mouth.

HQN™

We *are* romance™

"Win a date with a NASCAR champion!"

From acclaimed author

PAMELA BRITTON

AND THE WINNER IS…

Dana Johnson? *What?* Turns out Dana's friend secretly entered her in the contest to win a dinner date with NASCAR driver Braden James. Burned by her former fiancé, Dana tells Braden he's off the hook, but he says they're on. His sponsor—a matchmaking Web site—is counting on him. But when the last flashbulb pops, will their slow burn ignite into a very real romance?

Slow Burn

Available now wherever books are sold!

www.HQNBooks.com

PHPB400

HQN™

We *are* romance™

**From the acclaimed authors of *RISKING HER HEART*
comes a fantastic new NASCAR®-licensed book!**

LIZ ALLISON &
WENDY ETHERINGTON

**Sometimes the road to love
takes some unexpected turns....**

When a highway accident destroyed his dreams of defending his championship title, NASCAR driver Bryan "Steel" Garrison had to give up racing. Now president of Garrison Racing, he still feels winning is everything. He doesn't have time for beautiful physical therapist Darcy Butler...until she helps Bryan realize that the only way to win it all is to heal his body...and his heart.

Winning It All

Available now!

NASCAR® and NASCAR Library Collection are registered trademarks of the National Association for Stock Car Auto Racing, Inc., used under license.

www.HQNBooks.com

PHLAWE402R

HARLEQUIN

NASCAR

Maggie Price
BANKING ON HOPE

Ever since the explosive scandal that ended his high-flying NASCAR career, all charter pilot Brent Sanford wants is to clear his name. Hope Hunt, Sanford Racing's new team-building consultant, is the last thing he needs in his life right now. Hope wants to believe in Brent's innocence; he insists he was set up. But is she ready to put her heart on the line?

**Available December 2009
wherever books are sold.**

www.GetYourHeartRacing.com

NASCAR18530

HQN™

We *are* romance™

New York Times and **USA TODAY**
Bestselling Author

LINDA LAEL MILLER

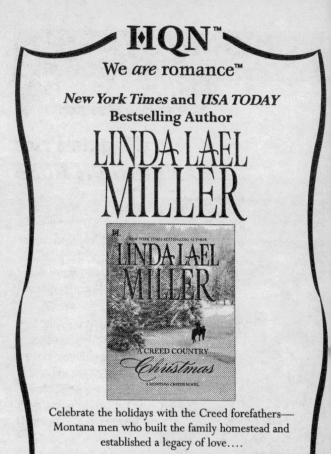

Celebrate the holidays with the Creed forefathers—
Montana men who built the family homestead and
established a legacy of love....

A Creed Country Christmas
A Montana Creeds Novel

Available now!

"Linda Lael Miller creates vibrant characters and stories I defy you to
forget."—#1 *New York Times* bestselling author Debbie Macomber

www.HQNBooks.com

PHLLM405

REQUEST YOUR
FREE BOOKS!

2 FREE NOVELS
FROM THE ROMANCE/SUSPENSE
COLLECTION PLUS 2 FREE GIFTS!

YES! Please send me 2 FREE novels from the Romance/Suspense Collection and my 2 FREE gifts (gifts are worth about $10). After receiving them, if I don't wish to receive any more books, I can return the shipping statement marked "cancel." If I don't cancel, I will receive 4 brand-new novels every month and be billed just $5.74 per book in the U.S. or $6.24 per book in Canada. That's a savings of at least 28% off the cover price. It's quite a bargain! Shipping and handling is just 50¢ per book.* I understand that accepting the 2 free books and gifts places me under no obligation to buy anything. I can always return a shipment and cancel at any time. Even if I never buy another book from the Reader Service, the two free books and gifts are mine to keep forever.

185 MDN EYNQ   385 MDN EYN2

Name	(PLEASE PRINT)	
Address		Apt. #
City	State/Prov.	Zip/Postal Code

Signature (if under 18, a parent or guardian must sign)

Mail to **The Reader Service:**
IN U.S.A.: P.O. Box 1867, Buffalo, NY 14240-1867
IN CANADA: P.O. Box 609, Fort Erie, Ontario L2A 5X3

Not valid to current subscribers of the Romance Collection,
the Suspense Collection or the Romance/Suspense Collection.

Want to try two free books from another line?
Call 1-800-873-8635 or visit www.morefreebooks.com.

* Terms and prices subject to change without notice. Prices do not include applicable taxes. Sales tax applicable in N.Y. Canadian residents will be charged applicable provincial taxes and GST. Offer not valid in Quebec. This offer is limited to one order per household. All orders subject to approval. Credit or debit balances in a customer's account(s) may be offset by any other outstanding balance owed by or to the customer. Please allow 4 to 6 weeks for delivery. Offer available while quantities last.

Your Privacy: Harlequin is committed to protecting your privacy. Our Privacy Policy is available online at www.eHarlequin.com or upon request from the Reader Service. From time to time we make our lists of customers available to reputable third parties who may have a product or service of interest to you. If you would prefer we not share your name and address, please check here. ☐

BOB09

Buckle up...and hold on tight
with three fast-paced stories by
New York Times bestselling author
Vicki Lewis Thompson,
USA TODAY bestselling author
Nancy Warren
and award-winning author
Dorien Kelly!

Racing Hearts

They're in
for the ride
of their lives!

New York Times Bestselling Author
Vicki Lewis Thompson
Nancy Warren • Dorien Kelly

*Be sure to catch this heart-racing anthology
in stores February 2010!*

HARLEQUIN®

www.eHarlequin.com

PHNATH740